For Better for Worse

By

Jenni Roussell

Dedication

To my amazing Grandchildren
Liam, Leo, Nathan and Delta
May you each be the best version of yourself.
All my love forever - JR

Chapter One:

The Gallery opening had been a huge success. Looking at her watch Raya felt bushed. Melissa O'Connor, her friend and business partner, ushered the last of their guests out of the door and locked it behind them before the pair sat in their office to go over the evening's events.

'How many works did we sell?' Raya wondered aloud as she kicked off her four-inch heels and accepted the glass of bubbly Melissa offered.

'We had fifty on display and I counted twenty-nine red stickers, and the receipt book agrees.' Melissa took a swig of her drink. 'However, some of those we are selling on behalf of the artist. I'm starved, canapes just don't do it for me. Why don't we lock up here and get some food? One of our guests gave me his card suggesting we meet him here,' she said, tapping the card as she sipped her wine. 'The Olive Branch,' what do you say?'

'I've heard about the Olive Branch, have you been there before?' Raya asked. Her friend shook her head.

'The guy who gave me his card, Tony Romano, owns the restaurant. He looks pretty smooth,' Melissa winked.

'I don't need smooth, in fact smooth scares me to death. I just wish Paul could have been here.' Raya missed her boyfriend Paul Martin, a resident doctor studying to become a paediatrician.

'I couldn't hang around waiting for the little time you two have together. Be warned Raya, it will be no better when he's a consultant,' Melissa told her. Raya felt too excited about their opening to dwell on the downside of loving a hardworking doctor. Although she knew in her heart, he didn't really love her, not the way her parents had loved each other, she thought him a good man. Thinking about it, she felt hungry too. Neither she nor Mel had eaten anything much all day they were just too excited. Their special event ran from six pm till eight and it had gone almost eight thirty. Their gallery had been open for six weeks but tonight they enjoyed their formal grand opening.

'I guess we can clean up in the morning. The caterers have done most of it already. They were gone by five past eight. Is your friend waiting for you?' Raya pointed to a stretch limo with darkened windows.

'I don't think so, it's the stretch limo from the hotel over the road. He did say to phone him so he can save us a table.' Melissa got busy on her cell phone as Raya touched up her makeup and brushed her thick honey coloured hair and twisted it up into an elegant updo.

'Guess what? Tony is sending his car to pick us up. I told you he's smooth, he must have known we would want to eat at his restaurant.' Raya pulled a face, amused yet dismissive. Melissa, her old school friend now business partner, a tall red-haired woman, with a stunningly curvy figure and the palest fair skin, wanted to go out and party. The two young women had met as thirteen-year-olds at an exclusive convent school for girls in Sydney, the Saint Germaine Boscardi Academy. Although only a small school most of the students went on to some tertiary study. Melissa, whose father, a Senator of many years service, had three older brothers. A real handful, as her father had described her. Melissa's love of fine art saved her. She and Raya both graduated from the University of Queensland with a degree in fine arts.

Soraya Farrington was an only child; her mother Sophia Farrington had been RH negative and suffered a string of miscarriages. She died in a car crash before Soraya turned eleven. Soraya or Raya to her friend Mel, had been raised by her loving father with the help of a loyal housekeeper. Mark Farrington, a property developer, had died of a massive heart attack barely six months earlier. At seventy, and with a known heart condition his doctors were not surprised but Raya had been heart broken. At the time she had been at the university of the Holy Sacred Arts in the Metropolitan City of Florence, Italy, just two months away from completing a master's in fine art. The course had a strong classical and religious art component which complemented her love of art history, especially iconography. On his death bed Mark Farrington made it clear Soraya must return to Florence and complete her studies, then he had someone he wanted her to meet with a view to marriage. Before she could even return to her studies her father suffered another, and this time fatal, heart attack. After his funeral, still grieving and heart broken, she returned to Florence as her father had directed. As soon as she completed the course she came home to Australia. Three months later she and Mel opened Gallery Euphemius in downtown Brisbane.

'Mel, there's a guy knocking on the door,' she called to her friend who checked the rear doors were locked and barred.

'Back's all secure,' Mel called. 'Gee I'm ravenous.' After punching in the alarm code, the pair left via the front door of the gallery.'

'Mr Romano is waiting for you ma'am,' the driver said as he opened the door of the Mercedes.

'Oh, I think I'll just get a cab home. I'm really tired. I won't be any fun,' Raya said, suddenly feeling drained.

'Oh no you don't,' Mel grabbed Raya's arm and pushed her into the vehicle ahead of her. 'You can't bail on me tonight girlfriend. Look I'll give you a late pass tomorrow morning,' she said, grinning. The gallery didn't open until ten which could hardly be called early, but then it didn't close until six on weekdays.

Their driver steered them across the city to a fashionable area past Eagle Street, near the pier, where The Olive Tree restaurant overlooked the Brisbane River. Once under the portico the women stepped out of the vehicle and the concierge ushered them to the reception desk where Tony Romano waited to escort them to a table. The table he had reserved for them stood out over the illuminated river. Dressed in a dark suit with an equally dark shirt, he looked the epitome of elegance, a little too polished and suave for Raya's liking. He reminded her of the kind of men her father had always done business with, and he had insisted she kept her distance from them, as though they were not quite his choice of men for her. Tony sensed her hesitation and went out of his way to ensure she felt welcome. Offering his strong hand, he complimented her on the gallery.

'You must be very proud of the opening tonight.' His dark eyes studied her face, mesmerised by her green-blue eyes framed by strong, straight dark brows. The eyes themselves were shielded by dark lashes highlighting their jewel-like colour. Against her amazingly symmetrical bone structure and tanned olive skin, those eyes were captivating.

'Yes, we are, thank you,' she said, with a sweep of her lashes as she withdrew her hand.

'Nice place you have here,' Melissa commented looking around, unaware of Raya's guarded response and Tony's fascination with her.

'We think so,' he mused absently, signalling a waiter. 'You ladies are my guests tonight.' Immediately Raya frowned she did not want to be beholden to this man for anything. Seeing her expression he said, 'I insist, think of it as my welcome to the city.' Before she could comment, Melissa thanked him graciously. Mel had learned the art of making the most of a situation like this from her politician father, whereas Raya's father had taught her there was no such thing as a free lunch.

Melissa, an effervescent woman, would be a delight at any table. Her vibrant mass of riotously curly red hair was an attraction on its own. Her colouring screamed Irish ancestry. Her father, Senator Seamus O'Connor was considered a man of integrity. Catholic, conservative and commanding, he was headed for leadership in the senate.

The waiter brought a bottle of Champagne to their table, along with an ice bucket and three glasses, then proceeded to pour their drinks. He offered them each a menu and left them for a few minutes.

After a quick scan of the menu Raya decided on mushroom risotto with truffle cream. While Tony and Melissa discussed the menu, Raya scanned the room. At a table nearby a man in his thirties sat dining alone. There seemed something about him, something indefinable. Well dressed in a dark suit and dark shirt with a silver tie, his long legs protruded from the table proffering elegant well shod feet, the type of smart looking footwear often seen in Italy, Raya remembered. It struck her he had the look of a Mafiosi don, albeit a very handsome one. The thought evoked a shiver and then a smile. Tony, with his thick head of coiffed dark hair fitted the same descriptive. In fact, there were several men in the restaurant who appeared to have the same look. If the city were Florence, where she had studied, the scene would not have been out of place. This eatery had the look of an authentic trattoria with the best Italian food. However, she would never have gone to meet a stranger in a restaurant in Florence, her driver would have been an older man whom the nuns trusted to drive her from the university to the convent where she lived. Sadly, sexual assaults on young women were common. The nuns did everything in their power to protect the women in their care and her father paid them handsomely to do so.

'Raya, what would you like to eat?' Tony's voice jolted her back to the present. Looking up she saw the waiter poised to take her order. Apologising she told him her choice and added quietly,

'and some Pellegrino water please, unopened.' Slightly distracted, she excused herself to go to the powder room. She walked towards the entrance foyer where the powder rooms were indicated, immediately noticed the lone diner looking at her she averted her eyes as she passed his table. In the powder room she splashed her face with cold water, the hot evening felt sultry, and Raya felt a headache coming on. After drinking a large glass of water for the headache, she smoothed the wispy tendrils of hair that escaped away from her face, after washing her hands, she checked her general appearance in the huge mirrors. The shot silk sheath dress she wore displayed the hallmarks of classic design. The deep blue green colour looked stunning against her skin. The diamond studs in her ears were her only jewellery.

Back at the table Tony asked Melissa, 'tell me is your friend unwell?' His concern touched her, and she enjoyed telling him about her enigmatic friend.

'I'm not surprised it seems so, especially tonight. Her father died a few months ago and he had been her only family. The money to open the gallery came from him, not from his estate, it hasn't passed probate yet. Today she had a call from her father's lawyer, he needed to see her urgently. It seems she has an older brother, she met him today for the first time.' Tony's eyes widened as Melissa who had enjoyed several glasses of wine at the gallery had allowed the alcohol to loosen her tongue. She regaled him with the curious details.

'It seems her father changed his name by deed poll and moved interstate from Melbourne when he married her mother. Apparently, her father had a son whom he provided for. We don't know the story, except we believed Raya's father to be a devout Catholic. You said you came from Melbourne, right?' she asked, not waiting for a reply. Did you ever hear of a Marco Ferrantino? Well, that name belonged to her father, except he changed it to Mark Farrington.'

'I knew a Vince Ferrantino; we were at school together,' Tony said blandly.

'He must be her brother. How old are you? I'm sure she said this brother was forty-two.'

'The man I know is a property developer, who owns a few clubs,' Tony said skirting around the age thing. He didn't want the young woman to see him as old.

He knew Vince Ferrantino was a powerful businessman. What could he possibly want with a half sister he had never known? Then it occurred to him. 'How old is Raya?' his intense stare made Melissa uncomfortable.

'Twenty-eight the same as me, but her father kept her on a pretty tight leash.'

When Raya returned to her table the lone diner stared straight at her. Looking beyond him to her table she realised the man could not be Italian, too tall. Italian men were not typically tall. His features were more Arabic. He looked swarthy and particularly handsome. With his dark hair and olive complexion he looked like her mother, a Sicilian of middle eastern decent, who had an eastern bloc, grandmother in the mix too. They fascinated her, people from the Byzantine Empire whose history, like their art, was centuries old and she loved it. As soon as she sat back at the table Tony appeared overtly interested in her. Raya could tell from the way he eyed her. She feigned a bad headache,

'I'm sorry, I don't feel well. I should go home it's been a tiring day, I'll just get an Uber Angel,' she took out her phone. Uber Angels were female taxi drivers.

'Of course,' Tony said courteously, 'at least let me get you something for your headache, a paracetamol perhaps?' She thanked him. He stood and went to the reception desk then came back with a familiar foil card of paracetamol. Opening it with his thumb he took a capsule 'one or two?' she held up two fingers and he smiled as Melissa poured her a glass of water. A few minutes later the waiter arrived with their food.

'Don't let your food get cold Melissa, I will put Raya into her cab and come back to join you.' Tony took Raya's elbow and guiding her towards the reception area. 'Your car hasn't arrived yet,' he said frowning. Not wanting to cause a fuss she suggested he went back and ate, 'your food will get cold.' she insisted.

'No, I'm not leaving you like this when you're not well, I'll wait with you.' He sounded annoyed. 'If your vehicle doesn't arrive soon, I'll have my driver take you home.' His voice sounded distorted, distant, her head felt worse, and her legs turned to jelly. Tony grasped her arm, saving her from falling down the steps. The fresh night air hit her, and she heard him saying something to the concierge. A car arrived and he helped her into it, saying something she couldn't hear to the driver.

Chapter Two

Back at his table Tony sat down.

'Is Raya alright?' Melissa asked, hungrily forking up her spaghetti. 'I had the waiter take your food to keep it hot.' Tony smiled at her, a knowing, almost cunning smile.

'Yes, I had my driver take her home. Her car didn't arrive, and she didn't seem at all well.' The waiter set down his hot scallopini.

'Does she live by herself?' he asked absently, as he poured Melissa another glass of wine.

'Yes, although Paul asks her to move in with him, she refuses.' Tony raised an enquiring brow at her remarks. 'Paul Martin, her boyfriend, he's a doctor. He's got two more years of his residency then he'll be a paediatric consultant. Those guys work horrendous hours and I think she doesn't move in with him because already he takes her for granted and she knows it.' Melissa's lip curled in disgust.

'The man's a fool,' Tony's words came quickly.

'I agree, especially after she met her brother. I don't know what transpired between them, but I'll tell you this for what it's worth, I bet it's all about money. Her father had it and she had been his only heir until Vince arrived on the scene.' Melissa was mouthy. Although quite stunning she could not hold a candle to Raya, Tony thought as he let her babble on while he finished his meal. Then the Maître de caught his eye.

'Mr. Romano, I've had a call from the Buon Appetito, they have a situation needing your attention,'

he said quietly but loud enough for Melissa to hear.

'Why didn't they call me?' Tony asked as the Maître de studied Melissa and smiled.

'They didn't want to disturb you sir,' he said still smiling. Melissa felt important bring with Tony, whom everyone deferred to.

'Oh of course, thank you,' he excused himself and taking out his phone he called the restaurant Manager. He turned his back he walked away from the table. In thirty seconds, he came back. 'I'm sorry, can we do this again sometime soon. I must attend to this.' He waved his cell phone.

'Thank you, I will look forward to it,' she said feeling their dinner had been doomed from the start. 'I must go too; it's been a long day.' He offered to give her a ride home which she accepted. Tony had gone out of his way as the Buon Appetito she understood was in the opposite direction to her apartment.

Raya could see she had been driven into an underground carpark, but it could not be her underground carpark because hers only allowed for residents, and you needed a code to enter it. Besides this one looked far too big. Now she felt completely groggy as though the worse for drink. But she had finished neither of the two glasses of wine she had been offered. Strong arms held her upright, they belonged to a man in a smart suit. Unable to focus and struggling to stand she held on to the walls of the lift. It seemed to be going up and up, her building only had a basement and three floors. This ride went on forever. She protested desperately trying to garner her thoughts and focus her eyes. The man said nothing as the lift doors opened into a large foyer and from there into a huge sumptuously decorated apartment. This place did not look like her apartment. She fought to get away from the strong man but collapsed. Picking her up in his arms he dropped her heavily onto a huge almost circular bed. The décor looked unfamiliar, definitely not her room. Desperate to get away yet totally unable to do anything let alone move, she lay face down on the bed. Every single fibre of her being said, 'fight.' The zip of her dress slid open, she froze, gripped by sheer panic. Mustering every ounce of her strength she turned over and screamed. A large hand struck her face, hot, hard and stinging, knocking her back into total inertia. She felt her dress being torn from her body she passed out.

A gentle rocking and daylight stirred Raya. She sighed, stretching her arms. Conscious of her familiar lemon tee shirt nightie with "sweet dreams" emblazoned on the front she closed her eyes resting in the comfort. The room rocked; she opened her eyes in a blink. This bed looked totally foreign not her bed. Her nightie yes, but the room looked like a large cabin on a boat. Ah, the boat is what gently rocked. She cast a panicked glance around the room. A man sat comfortably in a huge built-in wingback chair, nonchalantly reading a book. Dressed more casually than the previous evening he still looked suave. The man, the one from the restaurant, the tall lean powerful looking, possibly middle eastern man.

'Who in God's name are you?' her tone and words surprised even her. 'Where am I?' she demanded. Just then she heard a knock at the door. A man entered carrying a tray and set it down on the bedside table. It looked like a continental breakfast, orange juice, fresh berries, yoghurt, tea and milk. Exactly what she normally had for breakfast. Suspicious, she said nothing until the tray carrier left them.

'You kidnapped me,' she accused, then watched as the corners of his mouth twitched.

'I didn't kidnap you. Actually, I rescued you.' his voice sounded deep definitely not Australian; however, she couldn't detect any accent. A little haughty but no indication of where he came from. 'You're on board my yacht.' he added, watching her eyes move around the room. 'My name is Bart Lombardi. I'm the man to whom you were promised.'

'What? Can you hear yourself? You're a thug, you kidnapped me. This is the twenty first century, you will be caught. There are cameras everywhere.' Her voice almost at concert pitch, still it had little effect on this man.

He let out an audible sigh and spoke almost in a whisper.

'Calm down, you need to replace your fluids. Have your breakfast, relax, take a shower, your clothes are in the wardrobe. When you're calm, we can talk.' Standing, he moved towards the door. 'We're almost in international waters in case you were thinking of jumping overboard.' As soon as he left the room with one sweeping motion, she cleared the nightstand of the tray which crashed to the floor. Its contents strewn across the carpeted room. She wanted to cry but would not give him the satisfaction of thinking he had brow beaten her into submission.

In the huge bed feeling scared and sorry for herself she tried to remember the previous evening and what exactly had happened. 'I arrived at The Olive Branch restaurant with a bit of a headache, I remember being poured a glass of bubbles, but I didn't drink it. I felt sick and went to the bathroom where I cooled my face. Then I went back to the table and phoned an Uber Angel to go home. Tony Romano offered me some paracetamol. I took two with a glass of Pellegrino which I watched Melissa open.' Thinking about it she had watched him pierce the blister pack containing the paracetamol. he had asked her if she wanted one or two. When she held up two fingers Tony smiled, then escorted her to her ride. Because their food had arrived, he told Melissa to start without him. Things became fuzzy after they drove off. She had a vague memory of an underground carpark, an apartment and a man slapping her. She couldn't remember anything else.

Right at this moment she had a terrible thirst, her mouth felt gritty, and she desperately wanted to clean her teeth. As she lifted her head from the pillow it throbbed. It felt like a hangover, not a common feeling for Raya but she had experienced one or two in her early university days. Perhaps she shouldn't have swiped away the breakfast tray. The orange juice and tea had looked inviting. She licked her dry lips and forced herself to get up. Seeing the contents of the tray on the lush thick carpet she felt guilty, just as well nothing had broken. She gripped the bathroom door handle and desperately looked for something else to support her. The vessel they travelled in seemed to be making good speed. His yacht. he said. Her 'hangover' made her feel fragile, she took a glass from the holder and filled it with water from the cold tap. It tasted so good, downing it quickly she took another then another, pushing her thick mane away from her face as she bent over the basin. In the mirror she could see her face looked slightly swollen on one side. It hurt when she touched it.

A quick look around the bedroom revealed built in drawers and the wardrobe he referred to. What did he say his name was? Bart Lombardi the man to whom you were promised. She knew her father had been old fashioned, but this sounded ridiculous. Surely, she would have known about a betrothal. Something irritated at the edges of her memory. As he lay dying her father mentioned a man, an old friend she should talk to, for the life of her she couldn't remember the man's name. Her father spoke about giving her hand in marriage to... She couldn't remember. She thought her father had been confused due to his illness. He always talked about her making a good match, whatever did he mean?

'Wow,' she said aloud as she opened the wardrobe door. It appeared to be full of her clothes from her wardrobe, from her own apartment. Quickly she opened the drawers, her underwear, her swimmers. In the bathroom she saw her hair dryer, makeup, and perfume. When she opened the curtains, the window could not be called a little porthole it looked huge, bigger than her bedroom window at home. Quickly she drew the curtains closed again, but then very slowly reopened them. She realised, she couldn't see a balcony nobody could see in, and she had an uninterrupted view of the ocean. A set of electronic binoculars lay on the second nightstand, she picking them up and looked out to sea. Sure, now she could see land, she didn't believe they were in international waters. They were travelling northeast she could see because the sun shone on her right but also it stood high in the sky. A glorious day she felt comforted by the fact she had her own clothes and things around her. She remembered having something for a headache in her makeup bag. Getting it out, she took one then looked at it carefully. The way the blister pack already had a crack where the capsules popped out, made her freeze. What if Tony Romano had swapped her paracetamol for something else? Knowing she, herself, had been responsible for the crack in the wrapping this time, she wondered about the previous night?

Ten minutes later, showered and dressed in faded denim cut-offs and sneakers with a white tee shirt she sat busy drying her hair when the cabin door opened.

'Don't you bother to knock?' she asked, irritated, as she sat on the bed. He stepped inside the room and took up residence in the huge wingback leather chair, ignoring her question.

'Breakfast not to your liking?' he asked sardonically, surveying the floor. Furious at the whole situation she threw her hairbrush at him, he caught it. 'I'm not the enemy here Raya,' his voice terse.

'Well, you broke into my apartment,' she feebly replied.

'No, I had one of my people do it and they didn't break in. They used your key.' Looking at his watch he suggested calmly. 'Dry your hair then I'll explain. You deserve to know.'

'You bet I do. Kidnapping is a very serious offence.' Ruffling her hair, she wanted it to dry quickly.

'In Australia maybe, but not in Sicily,' his glib reply. 'Have you ever heard of Fuitina?' Immediately she put down her hairbrush and turning off the dryer she sat on the end of the bed.

'Possibly, well vaguely, I have memories of the nuns in Italy talking about it in hushed tones, its like the English going over the border to Scotland to marry at Gretna Green, isn't it?'

'Well, the only similarity is they end up married, but no, it's not what you think. It is the practice of kidnapping young single women with the intention of having sex with them.' Hearing his words, she gasped and covered her mouth, blinking back tears she pointed at him. Pursing his lips, he shook his head, his face grim.

'Sometimes the sex is consensual, but it matters not because the women are then obliged to marry the kidnapper for the sake of honour.' His voice, something about it struck her, the hint of an accent, She heard it again but couldn't place it.

'Well, I'm Australian and protected by Australian law.' Sticking out her chin she mimicked his pursed lips. The sight of her lips made him swallow hard; luscious, and delicious he closed his eyes to avoid thinking about how they might taste.

'You are Italian too. Your parents took you there and registered your birth in Sicily,' he said firmly. 'But not as Farrington. You are registered as Soraya Minu Ferrantino, daughter of Marco Francis Ferrantino and Sophia Minu Madani Ferrantino.' He stood now with his arms folded as though he were standing guard, his biceps straining at the bands of his tee shirt.

'Bullshit, my birth certificate says Farrington,' Raya's voice rose an octave higher showing her annoyance. Then she remembered her brother, the one who only appeared yesterday, Vince Ferrantino, the one who told her their father had changed his name by deed poll years ago when he married Raya's mother. This same brother who claimed he would be running her father's companies and whom she knew nothing about, until yesterday. Raya fell silent then she looked up to see Bart studying her intently.

'Now I think about it, I have vague memories the nuns in Florence said years ago one particular woman refused to marry her rapist or coercer and so there is case law they quote when saying matrimonio riparatore is not legal. It cannot be enforced. There are punishments.' she said weakly knowing some strange customs still existed in parts of Italy, particularly in the south and Sicily.

'True, but now young people use fuitina for more modern uses. Like running away and marrying without their families' blessing, or to have sex before marriage.' Now he stood in the doorway, intimidating; his broad chest, the size of him, his bark facial scruff he had been clean shaven in the restaurant she felt sure.

'So why am I here? This fuitina business is bullshit.' She watched as he shook his head.

'Tsk-tsk, language, easy to see you went to university in Australia.' He grabbed her hand and pulled her to her feet. 'Come on I will tell you the truth and you can check for yourself. Then if you want my protection, well I'm here. In any case you need me, but we have a situation,' he said curtly. Bart led her by the firmly gripped hand to the vessel's state room where windows opening on to a deck. The décor looked simple, modern and very elegant. High quality furnishings were deployed to best advantage and comfort. The colour pallet although neutral was far from bland. Navy and ecru fabrics, blonde wood panelling, tan leather and gold trimmings. A young man delivered a tea tray with morning tea and coffee. The pastries smelt divine and made Raya hungry.

If Bart had decided to rape her, he would have done it by now she told herself. She leaned over him as he sat on the couch next to her and picked up a warm pastry filled with custard crème and lightly dusted in icing sugar. he smiled. Unbeknown to her she had icing sugar on her nose as she hungrily devoured the pastry. Bart poured her a cup of tea with milk.

'Let me tell you the story so far,' he set down her teacup and saucer. 'Until yesterday you believed Chad Murphy would be running your father's companies for two years at least, in accordance with your father's will. However, Vince Ferrantino your older brother, made a claim on the estate as he is allowed to do under Australian law.' After sipping his tea for a few minutes, he leaned over and wetted his finger then wiped the tip of her nose. Seeing her shocked expression, he said, 'sugar, you had icing sugar on your' he waved a hand in front of his face.

'Well, what you probably didn't know is your father kept in touch with Vince and had provided for him and his mother, your father's first wife whom he divorced. In the eyes of the catholic church, he could divorce because technically they were not married in the eyes of God. When Vince grew up his father, er your father and he had businesses in common. In fact, he provided for Vince from his estate, and he had no need to contest the will. Vince is greedy, he owes money to Tony Romano for a commercial development in Melbourne that went sour. Tony thought Vince had been an only child. My sources tell me Tony Romano wangled an invite to your gallery opening in order to meet you. Vince had told him about his beautiful little sister who is now wealthy in her own right. He promised if Tony got you alone in a compromising situation, he would give his blessing to a marriage. They planned to let you think getting tipsy and ending up in Tony's bed had been all your own idea. They would let your doctor boyfriend know you spent the night in Tony's apartment. Your behaviour would take the lustre off your crown for his conservative catholic family and Tony would mop up the mess suggesting he make an honest woman of you.' Bart raised his eyebrows as if to say, what do you think?

'Paul's not stupid. Your idea would never fly. I bet if I had a blood test, they would find traces of a date rape drug in my system.' The idea, although entirely possible, appalled her.

'Ah so you do believe Tony slipped you something last night,' he said, pleased she at least heard what he had to say.

'Is Tony's bedroom decorated in purple and gold?' she asked with a curl of her lip.

'I don't know, I've never been to his bedroom.' Thinking for a moment he pulled out his mobile phone and scrolling through the text messages he pulled up a photo of her. She appeared sprawled out and face down on a bed wearing only a black bra and knickers. Handing her the phone she read the message before zooming in on the bed. 'Boss, is this her?' She could see the bedspread fabric they had wrapped her in looked gold.

'Where's the bedspread you wrapped me in?' she asked.

'I don't know. Well, it may be here somewhere. I'll need to ask my people.' Doesn't he do anything for himself she mused? Bart stood and paced the salon. Raya stood wanting to know the time.

'I need to talk to my business partner. She will be freaking out if she can't locate me.'

'It's not eleven yet, you can phone her shortly, but I need to know you won't turn feral on me. First hear my side of this story.' Sitting down again he began. 'As a young man your father behaved just like Vince. His extravagant lifestyle meant he overexposed himself financially and nearly went broke a couple of times. My father bailed him out. They were good friends. My mother died when I was a small child, she drowned. After my father mourned her, he met a beautiful young woman while visiting his family in Palermo, Sicily. Your father had divorced, and he and my father were in Palermo together. My father fell madly in love with this woman and planned to marry her. He believed she loved him too. Only your father compromised her, and she felt obliged to marry him. I speak of your mother.' Raya flew at him, wildly pounding his chest with her fists.

'I don't believe you. You're a liar. My parents loved one another. My father, he doted on my mother.'

Bart held her roughly and bent as if to kiss her. When his lips were millimetres from hers, he stopped still. His warm breath touched her lips, but he pulled back, and his expression changed, turning from annoyance to anger.

'I don't doubt you for one moment. But for her it didn't start out being love. Before you were born your father turned over a new leaf, no gambling, not even in his own clubs. After changing his name, he became the dedicated father, husband and businessman. He moved to Brisbane from Melbourne. It looked as though his past life of wine, women and song had been left far behind him. My father never forgave him. But something passed between your mother and my father, and she convinced him she loved Marco Ferrantino and your father wanted forgiveness from mine. So, they agreed you, Soraya, were promised to me as my bride.' His eyes narrowed and he inhaled deeply as he turned away from her. She realised he didn't actually want to be betrothed to her. 'You were two years old and I only twelve. All my life my father told me what a prize I would have. Only like you, I wanted to choose my own life partner.' The look he gave her appeared to be barely disguised repulsion.

'Well then, it's simple you go your way and I'll go mine,' she replied glibly. Her remarks served only to infuriate him further.

'I'll be damned if I'll let another Ferrantino ruin my life.' The words dripped venom, his nostrils flared, and his fists clenched and unclenched. Determined not to show fear she said with hauteur.

'And I'll be damned if I accept blame for this.' With his voice barely a whisper he surprised her.

'No, you're not to blame so I decided to help you.'

'How very magnanimous of you. What's in it for you?' she re-joined. He smiled at her words, a cruel smile.

'About the time your father died, mine too became ill. Terminal cancer.' To his surprise he expressed sorrow. 'He began tidying up his affairs. On my thirty eighth birthday he told me I had to find you and marry, or he would pass succession of his not insubstantial empire to his brother, my uncle. The man is a half wit, no business acumen and he has some expensive habits.' He sniffed tapping each nostril, indicating cocaine. 'I located you through the television interview you gave about the gallery and the arcade where it's located, Gallery Euphemius. I think you like puzzles and history,' he looked her in the eye softening his expression a little. 'Yes, you could say euphemistically you own the building, but actually my father holds the title deed in a convoluted holding company where our fathers were in a partnership. If my father doesn't get what he wants, then he exercises his rights as the majority shareholder.'

Raya sank back in her seat. She honestly believed her father owned the building freehold and he had left it to her. Only the rents from the other tenants would keep her gallery afloat until it became financially viable. Three years she had budgeted. Yes, she considered it hers, her gallery. She had sold Melissa a twenty five percent share of the Gallery business for one dollar. That way Melissa her best friend would have a vested interest in ensuring its success. Raya still owned the building and had underwritten the business for three years knowing she had the assets to cover any shortfall. This happened before Vince showed up.

'This can't be happening. I need to talk to Melissa and Paul,' she said anxiously.

Chapter Three

Bart took her to his onboard office and gave her back her mobile phone, fully charged.

Phone messages and texts lit up the screen with urgency.

From Paul.

'Hun where are you? what's going on and who the hell is this Vince guy who claims he's your brother. I'm busy from this afternoon another forty-eight-hour shift, then exams again. call me please. P oxox'

Then Melissa,

'Hey Partner, how are you, you did not look well last night after we closed the gallery. Phone's been going mad, Paul's worried but not as worried as me. call me xoxo.'

Then Vince,

'Hey little sister, Tony Romano has been telling tales I didn't even know you knew him he's like a brother to me. Have you been a naughty girl? Do I have to kill him now? only joking, does Paul know? you call me.'

Then Tony Romano,

'Mio Caro, you never mentioned your brother is Vince Ferrantino my good friend, I worried about you I had you taken home, I didn't mean to frighten you. I should have been there when you woke up. forgive me Caro. Call me please.'

Lastly Chad Murphy.

'Raya, your half brother has formally contested your father's will, everything will be in abeyance for months now, please call me.

The only upsetting message came from the creep Tony Romano, calling her his darling indeed. Now she really did believe Bart had saved her from him. Pressing Melissa's number, she waited for her to pick up.

'Mel, look I'm fine, the thing is it hit me last night. I'm really still in shock over Vince turning up months after Dad's death. It's quite complicated. Don't trust Vince he's contesting the will formally, my lawyer advised. Did you know he and Tony Romano are friends? This is serious Melissa, do not tell anyone particularly Vince or Tony anything at all about my business or my family affairs. Can you manage without me for a while, get Wendy the weekend girl to work extra if you need to. I'm going away for a bit.' Looking up she could see Bart scribbling on his desk pad. Seeing *for one month at least* scribbled down she shook her head furiously. He shot her his death stare. Her throat constricted with his imagined fingers around it and her lip trembled as he put his large hand around hers gripping the phone.

'I don't know how long; it might be a month at least.' Bart softened his grip on her hand. 'I'll be buying artwork while I'm away, and you buy the kind you like too, just the amount we agreed though, till I get back. Love you.' she sniffed and killed the call.

Had she done the right thing? Feeling anxious she asked him where they were going.

'To Nicodemus, I usually fly but I wanted to get to know you, and have you understand the gravity of your situation,' he said as a matter of fact.

'Wait, wait, where is Nicodemus and what is the gravity of my situation?' she sounded panicked.

'Nicodemus is fifty nautical miles northeast of Great Keppel Island. As for the gravity of your situation, well I didn't hear what your business partner actually said to you, but you haven't spoken to your doctor friend yet and from his message to you, I don't think he has time for any shenanigans. What will he say after your brother and

Tony get back in touch with him?' Bart smirked and she wanted to slap him.

'Right then I'll ring right now, is your time correct?' she asked looking at the brass clock on the wall. 'Good his shift doesn't start for another couple of hours.' Picking her cell phone up she pressed his number and Bart leaned over and put him on speaker holding her fingers so she couldn't fiddle with her phone while she spoke.

'Paul, it's Raya.'

'Oh hun, are you all, right? Mel said you weren't well, then you had a minor meltdown and decided to get away somewhere for a month.' He sounded breathless as though he were taking the stairs with a heavy load.

'What did Vince say to you? How come you spoke to him?' She cut to the chase, so much ground needed covering.

'Mel told me he is your brother and he's contesting your father's will.' Trust Mel to spill her innards, straight after I asked her not too. 'Vince said, as the head of the family, I needed to defer to him. I thought your father came out of the ark. Cripes Raya, this guy is cosa nostra and I can say that because my mother's Italian. He wanted to know my intentions for God's sake. When I said I wanted you to move in with me his voice went strange, and he said, "over my dead body".' Paul chuckled a little before adding, 'I wanted to say it can be arranged, trust me I'm a doctor, but I thought better of it. I've never met the guy. Hang on a minute hun I have a call waiting; I'll call you back.' He killed the call.

'Is he for real? Do you feel loved and protected by him?' Bart's tone was derisive 'he sounds more like a stand-up comedian than a medical specialist.' Folding his arms across his chest he leaned back in his ergonomic chair. 'Will he even bother to call you back or will he get side-tracked?' Hardly had he finished the sentence when her phone rang. This time Bart swiped it open as Raya said 'Paul?'

'Who the hell is Tony Romano and where the hell are you Raya?'
Paul's tone sounded demanding.

'Tony's a guy who came to our Gallery opening last night and I'm
on my way to...' she considered her words carefully, 'I'm on my way
to Great Keppel Island.' she said quietly.

'Well, your new...' he too looked for the right word before
deciding on 'this aging lothario had the temerity to say you spent
the night with him and he could prove it. Then he mistakenly sent
a photo of you to Doctor Peter Martin, you can imagine how well
that went down with my old man. Fortunately, I persuaded Dad it
had to be some scammer; it couldn't be you. You were buck naked
sprawled out on this bed face down. But I'd recognise your arse
anywhere. It was definitely you. What the hell is going on Raya?' He
sounded irritated then he said. 'I shouldn't have pushed you to move
in with me. When you said no, I became furious. I put it down to
Catholic guilt. Especially after I talked to your brother's gorilla, Tony
Romano. I know I'm never there for you but just two more years
then I'll be through.'

Raya turned away from the phone, Paul always had some excuse.
thinking about it she felt he did have more time than he led her to
believe. The doctors were legally obliged to have a twenty-four-hour
break after a long haul of forty-eight hours on duty and days on call.
She didn't ask, feeling sure he had kept something from her. Raya
had learned to be super sensitive to the nuances of his speech now.
Sadly, Melissa's right sadly, he's selfish and he's played the overworked
doctor card so well.

'I'll call you tomorrow,' she told him and killed the call.

'Do you trust him?' Bart asked.

Does this man know something he's not telling me? she
wondered.

'Of course, I do, without trust we have nothing' she said weakly.
he picked up her mobile phone from his desk and slid it across to her.

'Phone your brother and ask him what's going on?' he said dryly. Numbed by all the goings on she called her brother.

'Vince, it's Raya.' A deep throaty voice rumbled out of Vince, a man so like her father as a young man she found it hard to hate him.

'Do you always behave like a tart? First your doctor friend says he wants you to move in with him. Then my old friend Tony calls me, embarrassed, believe me it takes a bit to embarrass Tony. He didn't know you were my sister when you willingly went back to his apartment with him. He sent me a picture of you my little sister lying naked on his bed. When I asked him the name of his latest squeeze and he said Raya Farrington, I became furious and embarrassed. His latest squeeze is my little sister. He swore and begged my forgiveness, he knew me as an only child.' Vince sounded cold and calculating as though enumerating the points in a tennis match. Six-love. 'Tony will do the right thing, but listen to me sister, you disrespected him. Is this how our father brought you up. I don't think so.' sucking in a breath Raya launched forth in a diatribe.

'No, you listen to me you creep; this is an orchestrated litany of lies. You have an agenda, and I won't stand by and let you ruin me.' looking up she caught sight of Bart's face as he tried desperately to control the involuntary quirking of his lips. Still in full flight with her rant she never stopped for breath. 'Don't think I will roll over and let a selfish man with your dubious intent ruin my life. I have options and marrying Tony Romano so you can settle an old debt is not one of them. I will drag every skeleton you ever had haunting your cupboards into full view of the gutter press and enjoy chewing you up and spitting you out.'

She heard a clapping noise at the other end of the phone.

'Bring it on little sister because you will be doing it in poverty as Vince Ferrantino doesn't play to lose. I play dirty and I play to win. Wherever you're hiding out I'll find you and you won't get an offer better than Tony Romano.' For a moment he never spoke, then in a considered voice he asked.

'Did you read about a body washing up in the Hinchinbrook Channel in today's Courier Mail? There are always ways Soraya.' Then she heard a click. Vince had disconnected her call. Frightened by his words she dropped her head to avoid eye contact with Bart. A warm hand covered hers and he suggested lunch.

The day looked beautiful on the Pacific ocean and the cool sea breeze made eating outside a delight although it played havoc with her wild hair all spiralling into curls. Bart whispered something to the man who served the food and minutes later he returned with a hair tie. Embarrassed, she thanked him, but it didn't matter, her appetite had gone. All she had eaten in the last twenty-four hours had been a breakfast pastry her stomach roiled in turmoil.

'May I?' she asked taking her cell phone from her pocket.

'Just this once, I don't approve of devices at the table but this time you may go on.' he said. Could the man read her mind? She googled the Courier Mail. *The dismembered torso of a man has been found set in concrete and floating in a black plastic rubbish bin in the Hinchinbrook Channel today. The Police suspect foul play.* What an understatement.

Bart insisted she ate something, the food looked beautiful. She took some fruit and poured a cup of tea.

'I have decided your idea had merit; we'll stop at Great Keppel island on our way to Nicodemus. We can get married there.' At her gasp he looked up. 'Hear me out before you complain. Your brother has given you few options. What I propose is we marry, then go and see my father and tell him together. Then we can return to our normal lives and after a few months we can apply for a divorce. I will give you a generous settlement and even help you fight your brother's claim to your inheritance. There will be rules of course. I will expect your full discretion, you tell no one this is a sham marriage, not Paul, not Melissa and definitely not your brother or Tony.

For the benefit of the story, we met in Florence. I go there for business sometimes and as the nuns kept you cloistered away until after your graduation, we kept a low profile until we were back here in Australia. It has only been four months, but we love one another.' He could have been rattling off the ingredients for a stew of lamb's tripe for all the passion in his voice. 'This way we both get what we want. Vince won't mess with me, and I will keep you safe. In return my father will be pleased I have settled down at last with my betrothed and you will charm him as I know you can. So, I will stay number one in the family business.' Raya turned her face away from him. This was not what she had planned for her life, nor did she want it.

'Go and have an afternoon nap. We will arrive at Great Keppel around five today. I have arranged everything.' The arrogance of the man he had already organised it and yet she had not even thought it through properly. Standing up to leave he reached for her hip, she froze. Taking her cell phone from her pocket he promised to give it back later. She needed to rest now.

To her surprise her cabin had been cleaned and tidied. Lying on the comfy bed she processed the morning's revelations. Sheer disappointment filled her when she thought of Paul. Never once did he say he loved her, trusted her or he would be there for her. A quite self-sufficient woman she didn't need constant declarations of love. Her father told her regularly he loved her, saying she looked beautiful and bright. She expected all fathers told their daughters such things. Still, he had been her constant and he treated her well. There had always been an expectation she would work hard, following his example. He had pointed out to her what traits a woman would be wise to look for in a husband. Paul had many of them and his family appeared important to him. Raya didn't have family except for her father and now his dreaded replacement. Paul and Raya were both Roman Catholic and although neither were as rigid about the practice of it as their families, it had always been important, and one needed to marry in the Church. It occurred to her if she married Bart on the resort at Great Keppel it would be a civil ceremony with a celebrant and so not deemed legal by the Catholic Church as they were both Catholic. Bart must know what is required of Catholics, but then he didn't love her or want to marry her, and divorce would be impossible if you married in the Catholic Church. So perhaps he had thought it through. She would be ever grateful to him for saving her from the disgusting creep Tony. The man's abhorrent behaviour scared her, and he would be her only option if it were left up to Vince, or even her, without Bart's influence. Paul would not be the type to make any hasty decisions. It would be at least three years before he would be marriageable according to his grand plan. Then he hadn't actually spelt out all the details of his grand plan, so she had no guarantees she even featured in it.

A knock at her cabin door woke her, this time a woman in her fifties wearing a uniform like the male stewards, came into her room with a tea tray. Raya smiled at the woman whom she noted wore a gold wedding band.

'If you need anything ma'am phone me,' she pointed to the telephone on the nightstand. 'My name is Kerryn. My number's on the card under the phone.' Raya thanked her and sat up noting the bedside clock said four thirty, she had slept for a couple of hours. On the tray along with the tea she noted a cucumber sandwich and a warm pastry plus some fruit. After devouring the lot, she got up, knowing in her heart she would marry this man in the civil ceremony, and now she had to find something to wear.

The wardrobe although huge seemed half empty. Raya did not own hundreds of garments. What items she had were classics with dozens of accessories. Rifling through her wardrobe she found the silver sparkly ball gown she had purchased in Florence for her graduation ball. She loved it. Her father disapproved of a little too much flesh showing, he insisted the designer make a matching bolero, so she completely covered up. He never got to see her wear it, because he died, and she graduated in absentia. It would be ideal for a bride. She could take off the bolero later in the evening. Then she noticed a white gown still in it's cotton cover by the designer 'Rashaan.' Bart had supplied a gown, in her size too. No way would she wear it. She would look the part and she would do it under her own steam, but no way would she wear a white gown to a sham wedding. Before she could commit to this arrangement, she needed to talk to Paul one more time. Picking up the bedside phone she called Kerryn.

'Will you please get my mobile phone from Mr Lombardi. I need to make a call.' Two minutes later Bart arrived and handed her cell phone to her. His dark eyes narrowed. She ignored him. As she swiped open the phone, she could see a message from weekend Wendy as she called her. Wendy a fine arts student in her final year, worked the gallery in the weekends and she never phoned Raya. Opening the message, she noted an attached photo, with shaking hands she enlarged it. Paul in scrubs passionately kissing a woman about his age, also in scrubs, with a stethoscope around her neck. Wendy had taken a little video. They were seated in the back booth of the Chocolate Frog, a café opposite the hospital. Raya and Paul often chose a back booth, it afforded privacy. As the video played, she watched Paul and this woman and immediately knew they were intimates. The way he looked at her, the way she smiled at him as he gently took her face in his hands and his kiss, open mouthed and urgent. Never had Paul put so much energy into kissing her. The acrid taste of bile filled her mouth, she didn't even read what Wendy had written. A picture is worth a thousand words. Sinking down on the bed she dropped the phone. Bart didn't bother to look at it, he already knew the man cheated on Raya.

'I'm sorry,' Bart's only words before leaving the room. Paul's cheating behaviour became the decider that she would marry Bart. It's simply a business arrangement she told herself. So why did she spend this length of time getting ready? From the windows in her cabin, she watched as the super yacht pulled along side the wharf.

What they were doing here at Great Keppel Island she had no idea. The island, closed after it had been flattened by a cyclone then sold to developers who closed permanently. Now whatever remained on the island had been vandalised. It dawned on her part of the island had once been a national park. Regardless, under the law it was Australian soil and for the marriage to be legal they needed a celebrant to perform the service on Australian soil. A ship's captain can't marry them in international waters, it's not legal in Australia. So here they were on a sad derelict island all so he could tick the boxes and say they were married. Raya looked in the mirror one last time. She had twisted and rolled her beautiful hair in an elegant updo, her makeup worthy of a vogue front cover. Her silver sandals complemented her gown. A knock sounded on her door.

'Are you ready? My people have set up on the beach.' It sounded like Bart's voice.

'Yes', why did she feel so coy? Raya Farrington, the confident businesswoman. He opened the door, and they stood staring at each other. Him in a tropical white dinner jacket, white shirt, white tie, and cummerbund with his long legs in black trousers. His scruff trimmed to designer stubble. Standing stunned he appraised her in the silver gown and jacket, her hair up with tiny soft wisps of curls escaping and softening the look. When she looked at him, he took in her jewel like eye colouring. They were so soft and translucent, not

quite blue and not quite green, her lids drooping burdened by the
weight of a thousand long dark lashes.

'You look beautiful,' he said honestly and taking her arm he
guided her to the white sandy beach, walking slowly along the wharf
pointing out features along the way. She kicked off her sandals as
soon as they were on the sand. A canvas gazebo had been set up to
shield them from the hot afternoon sun. It had been decorated like
a wedding marquee with chairs and one long table. A smaller table
with two chairs had been placed nearby. Bart could smell the delicate
fragrance of her perfume. For the first time since they had met, she
took the time to carefully study his face, noting his curly dark hair
and thick straight brows. At first, she had been struck by his angular
jaw and chiselled features, but for a long lean sinewy kind of man
with height and strong musculature, his features looked so strong.
What did it matter so long as he didn't beat her? Suddenly she had
a memory of the previous evening. Touching Bart's hand she said, 'I
remember now. Last night somebody hit me hard, a man slapped my
face,' she touched the spot 'it still feels sore.' His hand gently stroked
her face.

'It's not swollen anymore, thank the Lord. It looked a little
puffy when I first saw you on board' his finger felt gentle,
and his face expressed concern.

A welcome party from Bart's yacht surprised Raya.
Recognising Kerryn she felt relieved at seeing a familiar
face. Bart introduced 'his people' as he referred to them.
Kerryn's husband, the yacht's Captain Theo Cooper. Their
chef a young man in his mid-twenties. Dion Lamb
appeared self-conscious when introduced. Blossoming
like a flower he grew another several inches when Raya
asked him if he made the delicious pastries and he
confirmed he did. Next a young woman, called Rosa,

wearing a pretty lemon floaty dress said she helped Kerryn. Lastly a balding man of slight build his dapper silver suit a little loose his expression harried. 'This is Carl my right hand,' Bart said.

'Oh, poor you,' Raya said and both men cracked a tiny smile.

Two burly blokes about Bart's age stood sentinel at the end of the line. Both in light weight dark suits, Joe Kelly and Bob Costa, they looked ex-military each man wore an ear bud like a security detail, discreet but their appearance looked more minder than cousin as Bart had introduced them. Were they expecting pirates on the island? Joe Kelly's scrutiny disturbed her. She got vibes that he did not like her.

'They all multitask, they have to, it is the nature of the work.'

It occurred to her she had no idea as to the nature of his work. The Captain Theo Cooper explained he also worked as an authorised wedding celebrant. Flowers sat on the white cloth covered table, the gazebo had been draped in white tulle.

Raya complimented Kerryn on her red silk evening dress as she wondered what 'his people' thought of this affair. Do they know the whole affair is a charade or did they think it the sudden whim of a wealthy man, to marry in haste like this or had he planned it for some time?

'Ladies and gentlemen,' Captain Cooper called, 'Mr Lombardi, Miss Farrington.' Bart stepped across the sand in long strides, his feet now bare. He took Raya's elbow guiding her to the small table set up for the purpose. In a well-practiced manner, the Captain made a short speech about the sanctity of marriage, the value of family and the power invested in him by the state and in front of these witnesses etc before handing each of them a card from which they read their vows. Bart's voice sounded strong and deep. When it came to Raya's turn, she found her normally confident voice had evaporated and her nervousness became apparent. Putting out his hands Bart took both of Raya's and Rosa stepped forward to hold out the card for Raya to read her vows. He held her hands in his strong grip, and she wondered if he might be afraid, she would bolt. But where could she possibly run to? Feeling numb because the man she thought she loved cheated on her and left with no option she committed to this stranger. With faltering voice, she finished her vows and when Bart let go of her hands they trembled. The Captain declared them husband and wife. Then in the time-honoured tradition gave the groom permission to kiss his bride. Like a startled gazelle Raya stood frozen as Bart covered her mouth with his. The little gasp she emitted allowed him room to plunder her mouth as he enveloped her in his arms. She remembered instantly seeing Paul on video passionately kissing some unknown woman in this fashion. It ignited a fire of rage within her, and she responded with equal passion to this man, whomever he may be. She would play the game to be free from them all, Paul, Vince, and Tony. A whoop reverberated around the tented gazebo as breathless and amazed Bart stood back. Raya simply gave him a sweeping glance through her lashes as she too moved back. Bart watched her little pink tongue darting over her luscious lips in an incitement fit to lure a saint.

After signing the paperwork, the formalities were complete. Music played on someone's mobile phone. Kerryn and Rosa served drinks and canapes. Kerryn had plucked some waxy orange blossom from a deserted garden near the wharf and used it in the floral arrangement. Cutting it into two-inch sprigs she artistically pushed them into Raya's abundant hair. Then she proceeded to take photographs. Bart slouching in a directors chair lazily watching seemed fascinated by the effect. Clearing his throat, he beckoned to Kerryn and whispered something in her ear. The woman smiled and agreed. 'Yes sir, I'll have them ready by tomorrow morning.' Them being the dozens of photos she enthusiastically snapped with a very flash looking camera. After a few more drinks the party went back to the yacht for dinner, a beautifully presented feast of Pacific rim cuisine.

Dinner over, Bart suggested a dance during which he never spoke a word. So, Raya took his lead and remained silent. With the ordeal over she relaxed and made an effort to get around their small group. Normally easy going she found it enjoyable to talk to people and put them at ease, finding points of common interest or humour.

Bart came over to her and taking her hand he pulled her to her feet and whispered in her ear they would leave now. Leave for where? Without a word to their guests, they snuck below.

'Much as you were enjoying yourself you could at least pretend to be interested in your husband.' He scolded directly into her face as they stood at the foot of the stairs. Furious, she said nothing. Picking up Raya's shoes behind her Bart called to her. Ignoring him she let her cabin door slam closed in his face. Annoyed, he called again opening the door to her cabin.

'Don't' he managed to say as he stood motionless, realising she stood there in the throws of stepping out of her gown. 'Tonight, I sleep in here, on the island we have separate rooms.' Standing in her bra and knickers she turned from him.

'I don't remember that in the agreement I signed?' she sighed, sounding tired. Actually, thinking about the agreement, it had been very thin on detail except for the eyewatering settlement she would be granted on their divorce. He didn't answer, instead unbeknown to her he studied her backside. Turning to see why he had not answered, she noted he tilted his head to one side with an expression of bewildered enjoyment. His expression appeared similar to those she had seen at galleries when men ogled interesting paintings of women in various stages of undress. Naively she wondered what they thought about. This time he sighed and then commented, 'he's right, I think I too could recognise your backside anywhere now.' Remembering Paul's comment to her upon seeing her naked on Tony Romano's bed she picked up a shoe from the floor and threw it at him. He ducked and it hit the wall. 'Of course, I'd actually have to see it naked to be sure,' he continued, grinning.

'There's your pillow, you're on the floor,' she threw a pillow at him.

'I'm not sleeping on any floor, don't look at me like I'm a sexual predator, I won't touch you.'

When she returned from the bathroom in a tee shirt nightie, she couldn't see him. However, a trail of strewn clothing could be seen before she caught sight of him on top of the huge bed on the opposite side to her covered only by a cotton bed throw, with his feet protruding. Ignoring him, she climbed into bed turned off the light and went to sleep.

Chapter Four

Raya stirred to consciousness by all her senses, first smelled strong hot coffee and sweet pastries, with the daylight begging to be acknowledged but she refused to open her eyes, aware it felt like a warm sunny day. Then she heard whispers and felt warm fingers stroking her arm and down her back. The special sense of nearness to another made her reach out. As soon as her fingers became entangled in downy hair atop hard muscle, she blinked open her eyes. Kerryn busied herself setting down a breakfast tray on the nightstand. Next, she opened the curtains. Bart lay beside Raya looking smug and sex, very sexy, and very close and oh god, is he naked? Sitting up with a start, she covered herself she too lay there buck naked. The cabin looked like a bomb had gone off, clothes everywhere and an empty champagne bottle with two flutes, smudged, used flutes one still half full, his of course.

Raya groaned audibly and a little laugh escaped Kerryn who excused herself. For a long moment Raya froze. 'What happened here?' she croaked in a whisper once they were alone.

'Nothing happened, still they believe it did,' he gestured to the door.

'Then why are we naked together in bed and don't you dare tell me *your people*?'

He grinned, 'no this is all down to me. We're newly weds remember.'

'I hate breakfast in bed, a cup of tea when I'm sick and nothing else.' Sitting on the bed edge she pulled at the sheet. It didn't move, he wouldn't let go of it. Suddenly he stood up minus any sheet and stretched his long lean lithe body. Confident in his nakedness like

Michelangelo's David, he didn't flinch from her gaze. Whereas she nearly fell onto the floor when he relinquished the sheet. Finally, wrapped like a sheeted mummy, she found her robe.

I need a shower,' she said grabbing clean underwear from her draw. Ignoring her, as though purposefully wanting to intimidate her he walked around her taking the breakfast tray from the nightstand. He placed it down on the café table in front of the window, brushing her with his bare buttocks on his way back.

'Oh, for heaven's sake cover yourself I've seen more male nudes than you ever came across in any roman bath.' She sniffed, pulling her robe around her tighter.

'Ah yes, but at the University of the Holy Sacred Arts they were probably all marble or gay.' Scoffing, he gave her his look the one where she felt his long fingers constricting around her throat. The shower in her ensuite looked reminiscent of a Roman bath house, except for the enormous shower heads at either end of the enclosed area the size of a huge bath. Wearing a baggy shower cap to keep her mass of hair dry she lathered up and turning under the feel of the heavy fresh water she noticed his legs then him all of him at the other end using the other shower head staring at her, she had no privacy lock on the bathroom door. His expression went from smug to self reproach as he watched her wilt, defeated, under his relentless exhibitionism.

He hadn't touched her; he had adhered to their agreement, apart from pushing the envelope as far as he could. He enjoyed doing it. It's a power thing Raya told herself. So, the balance of power will shift and when it does, I will grab it with both hands. Drying off quickly in the bedroom she studied her hands. The wedding band a circle of diamonds looked stunning. A row of baguette cut diamonds going around in a complete circle set in platinum. Never would she have chosen such a flashy wedding band. When she jokingly commented she couldn't work in such a ring he had quipped his wife wouldn't be working. She ignored his remark. She liked working and had a business to run. When he emerged from the shower wrapped only in a skimpy towel, he surprised her by opening her wardrobe, sorting through it he took out a smart sundress suitable for a party or the races and handed it to her.

'Wear this dress today, not those,' he said curtly, his lip curled as he pointed to her white palazzo pants, 'not those, show some respect. Today, you meet my father.' Instantly she understood his father must be as draconian as her own father had been. Although she did wear trousers, she never wore them to any 'occasion' or even to work, if she knew her father might turn up. Now he had gone she thought she could please herself. Not so, it seemed.

Raya sat in the wheelhouse calmly admiring the view. Hair hanging freely down her back in amber waves with sun kissed strands, feet bare with toes punctuated by shiny red nails. Her floral sundress gathered off her shoulders in a little ruffle. It fitted snugly over her bosom and then gathered in underneath before billowing out in metres of soft floral cotton, flattering and feminine. The Dior sunglasses matched her perfume. On the seat beside her sat a huge straw sunhat. Large gold hoops enhanced her ears and encircling her wrist a gold bracelet, her mother's favourite gold link bracelet, each link elaborately patterned.

Captain Cooper in his white uniform stood at the helm. Sitting opposite Raya, Bart looked relaxed, his long legs apart he sat slouching something she noted he did often. Today he wore white trousers and a black shirt open at the neck. His gold wedding band complemented his gold bracelet and his sensual tanned skin. The man appeared uber confident and vain. had he chosen his own wedding band she wondered, or did he have 'his people' do it? Turning away from him she took in the view. Watching in awe, Raya could see the island Nicodemus coming closer to her. It appeared huge and atoll like in places where it rose from the sea like a giant stone monolith. Small white beaches visible around every second corner. It looked green and lush with palm trees waving in the gentle Pacific breeze.

'Oh, this is breath taking,' she whispered amazed, the men glanced at each other knowingly.

'There are more than a dozen beaches, where lovers can go skinny dipping,' mischief filled Captain Theo Cooper's face as he watched Raya's eyes widen. 'No one will ever see you,' he grinned openly now.

'But we have rules for safety,' Bart's deep voice rumbled sternly. Raya nodded, remembering he'd said his mother had drowned.

A long jetty came into view and through her binoculars she saw two vehicles waiting for them, a small bus and an open jeep parked there with a driver. A tar sealed road appeared to wind its way through a gap in the hills and she noticed boat sheds, buildings and cottages.

'After lunch I'll take you on a sight seeing tour.' A plane flew overhead and circled the island before disappearing. 'It's the supply plane from Rockhampton, it comes in once a week. Although technically we're self-sufficient, there is always something we want.'

'Nicodemus is home,' Theo Cooper sighed. 'We love it here.' A wistful tone reinforced his words.

'Home to how many exactly?' she asked.

'Exactly I can't tell you, but its near one hundred and it's a moveable feast depending on what's happening,' Bart elaborated. 'We do have an exclusive resort on the island catering for sixty guests. It offers employment for some of our people. There was an old resort on the island when my father bought the place. We refurbished it completely. Now the resort basically covers our living expenses. The family estate is secluded and fenced off as private property.'

'Wow, I've never heard of the island or the resort,' Raya said amazed.

'We don't advertise it; word of mouth keeps it booked in advance like a private club,' he sounded bored.

It took an hour before they reached Bella Vista, only because Bart seemed to be taking his time as though putting off the dreaded moment when he would introduce her to his father.

Alone now in the open jeep which he drove, leaving it's driver to return with the others, she sat in silence. The huge villa could be seen long before they arrived. It surprised but it also disappointed. It surprised because it looked like a slice of Italy in the middle of the Pacific ocean. It disappointed because even though the best Australian sandstone, had been shipped at great expense to build the elegant new villa and had slavishly reproduced the traditional features something seemed to be missing. For Raya, a Master of Fine Arts from the University of the Holy Sacred Arts in Florence it looked like a poor imitation. New and pristine, it lacked the patina of decaying elegance she thought of as "her Italy". An Italy whose intrinsic history of thousands of years and thousands of lives did not show here. How could it be here? This is the new world order and it held it's own majesty it's own beauty if she could but find it. Bart turned as she sighed; he could see from her face something seemed amiss. Mistaking her sadness for apprehension he reminded her their marriage had been a serious formal arrangement with mutual benefits, but it would be finite. Then he turned away from her, annoyed. It looked to her as though it had been all about him.

'You have more or less described any marriage, with one exception,' she whispered. Smiling he agreed. He had of course assumed incorrectly the one difference being other marriages were until death. Whereas Raya held a different view, for her life is finite, and what their marriage lacked is love. Love, the superglue keeping relationships together through whatever life held. Thinking of Paul made her sadness almost palpable. Taking out her mobile phone she returned to the video clip and the message sent by Wendy. The message she had never read until now.

I'm sorry I had to tell you because it's not the first time I've seen them together. Raya emitted a sad little gasp. Bart took the phone from her and after reading the message he squeezed her hand.

'Did you really love him?' his deep voice kindly. She looked up into his concerned face, as he watched her eyes well up and magnify like changing ocean currents. Raya hesitated for moment because although she felt fond of Paul and trusted him, he had never been the love of her life. Bart, almost pained, wiped away a single tear running down her cheek and sighed, she wondered at the dichotomy of his actions. Had he been hurt too?

This time when she got out of the vehicle no one came to greet them in a fanfare of smiling faces, only a lone dog sleeping in the open doorway. Large, black and rather fat, the Labrador looked quite grey around the muzzle, it barely lifted its head in greeting.

'He's Enzo's dog Luigi, he's too old and fat to walk far so Papa must be out walking.' Bart announced. A plump woman of indeterminable years appeared wearing a cotton dress and apron, her dark silver hair pulled back in an old-fashioned bun.

'Welcome home my dear boy, Enzo will be so happy to see you. He's sleeping,' she wrinkled her nose and gave a little shake of her head. 'He's not good, sleeps a lot but he'll be down for lunch.' They hugged and then her eyes alighted on Raya, and she gripped her in a hug. 'Bella signora, so like your mother' then quickly she turned. 'You found her then?' she said to Bart, did everyone know about them except her?

'And I married her,' his triumphant reply. Tears filled the old woman's eyes, and she kissed Raya on each cheek exclaiming her thanks to the Lord. As if remembering his manners Bart introduced the woman as his aunt, Teresa Kelly, his father's sister.

'And Joe's mother?' Raya said joining the dots remembering the military looking bloke with an earphone who appeared not to like her. His people, quite literally.

'Yes, Joe's my boy, he and his family live here on the island. You go and freshen up. Enzo will be down for lunch soon.'

Bart took Raya's hand and guided her down a long corridor to his suite.

'This is the master suite where you will stay.' It had been decorated boutique hotel style, luxurious but unremarkable.

'The bathroom is through there.' He opened the door to a large bathroom, separate toilet complete with bidet, two handbasins, a ginormous marble tiled shower with two shower heads equally enormous, they must have endless water she thought. Then she spied the most incongruous thing, a large French bathtub. Well, perhaps not so incongruous she had seen them in Italy after all. In stark white it clashed with the rest of the warm gold coloured marble. Then he opened the door at the other end of the bathroom. 'This is the dogbox where I guess I'll be sleeping for the duration,' he said sardonically.

Shrugging, she didn't buy into the discussion. It looked like a full-size double bedroom when all said and done. Both rooms had magnificent harbour views.

'Which ocean is out there?' she asked, having completely lost her sense of direction.

'We are surrounded by the Pacific Ocean but you're looking at the sea between Yeppoon, Australia and us,' he said. For a moment she felt completely lost in the warm tranquillity of it all. 'Come along, we have to meet Papa.'

'What is his name?' she asked realising she knew nothing about the man.

'Enzo Salvatore Lombardi, seventy-six years old and a pain in the...' she frowned at his remark.

'Bart,' he liked it when she used his name albeit in a rebuke. Enzo Salvatore Lombardi he's the man her father tried to talk about before he died, she felt sure of it.

Taking her hand, he whispered sincerely.

'This is the hard part, please do your duty, it is not solely for me. Many people's livelihoods are at stake here.' Before she could ask him to elaborate, the black Labrador, Luigi, suddenly came to life fairly bounding past their open door towards the sound of his master's voice.

'Where is he Teresa?' the strong male voice called. Grabbing Raya's hand Bart pulled her out into the hallway and down towards the voice.

'Papa,' the two men hugged, Enzo old and frail his voice seemed his strongest feature. 'Papa, meet my bride.' Raya embarrassed, at her part in this enormous deception stood back slightly, her head bowed in contrition...

'Oh, come here and let me look at you, my dear.' Coyly she stepped forward and he hugged her. Then tilting her face up towards his she watched as his old lips trembled and he sniffed back tears he couldn't control. 'Soraya, you are beautiful just like your mother. Sophia looked like a traditional Italian beauty.' The old man whose accent had grown thicker as he aged, became emotional and Raya helped him into a chair in the living room.

Just then Teresa's voice could be heard berating her oldest son, Joe.

'Teresa, what's going on out there?' Enzo called and Bart bolted from his chair to investigate. Male voices were heard and a moment later the three of them came into the living room, Bart stood smiling a large manila envelope in his hands. Opening it he pulled out a bunch of wedding photos, handing one bundle to his father and the other to Joe. Teresa scrambled to remove her apron which she promptly placed under the cushion on her chair so she too could enjoy the photographs. Bart handed Raya the latest edition of the Courier Mail. He indicated an update of the story of the dismembered body found in the Hinchinbrook Channel.

'What a handsome couple you make,' Old Enzo said honestly. In a complete turn of face, he said to his nephew Joe Kelly, 'did you know about them before the surprise wedding?' his tone accusatory.

'Of course, uncle,' he laughed. 'You know Bart and I have been confidants since boyhood. It doesn't mean I tell my Mumma,' laughing again he added, 'I value my wedding tackle too much to betray his confidence,' he pointed to Bart in jest.

'Excuse me sir,' Raya said deferentially, 'Are you not happy with this marriage?' Surely, I didn't go through this farce for nothing. 'I mean I know it's sudden but it's what we wanted and we're both consenting adults.' Bart moved, sitting down on the arm of her chair, he put his arm around her.

'Father, I never wanted anything so much in all my life. At my age you were a widower with two kids. As soon as I saw Soraya, I knew she was for me.' Don't trowel it on too thick you're not being nominated for an Oscar, Raya thought. Sitting in his grandfather chair Enzo Lombardi had the gaunt appearance of a man wasting away, his jaw set as implacably as if rigor mortis had grasped it. Long seconds went by before Teresa announced,

'I know what disturbs my brother because it disturbs me too Bart. You didn't get married in the Church.' Raya sucked in a staccato breath and Bart squeezed her shoulder. 'I know you and even Joe don't go to Holy Mass every Sunday, but at least he and Maria got married in the Church.' The old woman all but wrung her hands. Then Enzo spoke after sucking in a huge breath-taking great effort.

'I can understand your hurry to make Soraya your wife. But what troubles me the most is not just your immortal souls but the overt lack of real commitment to the sacrament. God does not permit divorce, unlike the state. Even your beautiful mother' he looked at

Raya 'had the decency to commit before God.' His old voice rose with every sentence until Bart stepped in.

'Papa, we didn't do this to hurt you. I guess we were simply selfishly thinking about how much we wanted each other. Please let Soraya and I talk about this, this afternoon. Believe me we are committed to one another.' Bart gave his father the look, the one forcing her to touch her throat to ensure it felt free from his strong hands squeezing the life out of her.

'Remember who controls this company. We cannot have someone who sets the wrong example,' Enzo said in a threat.

Raya rendered speechless at the prospect of a loveless marriage looming before her said nothing. In fact, she sat unusually quiet for the entire lunch. The men talked business and although she answered Teresa's questions the older woman spoke to the younger woman who served the meal with more enthusiasm.

When the meal ended Teresa excused herself, Joe and Bart said they needed to attend to some business and went to the home office. Only Enzo and Raya remained, and she wanted to be anywhere but here. The old man tenderly lifted her right hand, admiring the bracelet.

'Your mother's favourite piece of jewellery. I gave it to her you know, so now it has come full circle back into the family.' Raya had absolutely no knowledge of the history of her bracelet but then she had been a child when her mother died.

'I'm sorry nobody told me,' a feeling of total inadequacy pervaded her spirit. What could she say?

'I loved her very much, we should have married, but these things are not always simple. Families,' he offered by way of explanation. Wanting her to tell him first-hand the real story he sat quietly.

'My father loved her very dearly too. He never married again after her death he had been heartbroken.' Her comments seemed like excuses for what, she felt unsure. Did he tell her the truth? Did her father only tell her how he felt after his wife had died?

'She wrote to me you know,' Enzo said softly.

'When, before or after she married my father?' the thought seemed improper somehow.

'No, afterwards when you were a baby.' he smiled. 'Her words gave me the strength to go on. Who said, "Tis better to have loved and lost than never to have loved at all."

'The Englishman Lord Alfred Tennyson.' Raya smiled, 'I love Leo Buscaglia best. "Love is always bestowed as a gift -freely, willingly and without expectation. We don't love to be loved; we love to love."

'Are you trying to tell me something my dear?' he studied her face, now animated with joy and instantly he loved her too. But was it simply a fantasy about a woman he knew years before? 'I'm not as well educated as you or Bart. I do like to read, and we have a huge library here. I don't know Leo Buscaglia, but he sounds knowledgeable.' Wanting to bring the conversation back to her mother she wondered about this man.

'I wish I had letters from my mother to give me strength. I only recently learned I have a half brother and I don't like him at all. I've only met him once, but I don't like him,' she said honestly.

'Did you like Bart when you first met him?' the old man wanted to know.

'No, I did not, he came across as arrogant and overconfident.' She said automatically as Enzo smirked.

'And now?' he asked cautiously. Laughing, she refused to lie to this man who seemed to be growing on her.

'Now I see how thoughtful and considerate he is, he cares.' It felt honest and easy to come by.

'What about passion?' he asked, looking across at her through thin hooded eyelids as dry and fragile as crepe paper. Thinking for a moment she remembered, her wedding kiss and blushed scarlet feeling the heat rising from her bosom and covering her cheeks. It didn't go unnoticed.

'I think your son surprises even himself at times, and I'm not talking his passion for his work which is easier for others to see.' Her luscious lips quirked and from the look of understanding on his old face she had acquitted herself well with the answer.

Chapter Five

Voices in the hallway indicated the men had finished their business. Bart stood in the open doorway suggesting they take a look around the island.

'Get some comfortable shoes,' he commanded. In their bedroom suite she found suitcases of her clothes had been delivered from the yacht and rummaging she found some sports shoes.

As they drove along the tar sealed road past houses and buildings, he headed towards a gap in the hillside. After parking the vehicle, they walked up a small path towards the rocky outcrop which formed a natural lookout. A strong manmade iron fence acted as a safety barrier and back from it, a concrete bench seat. They both enjoyed the breathtaking view, neither mentioning the obvious issue between them. He pointed out, the large water tanks beside each house. Then in the distance he pointed to where a natural spring bubbled fresh water. Along the coastline he indicated to a desalination plant only used during droughts but tested annually.

'We've never run out of water yet,' he said confidently. He handed her some binoculars and pointed out banks of Solar panels on the roofs of the houses and other buildings. 'The piste de resistance is the windmills, you cannot see them from here, but they generate most of our electricity.' He looked to her for approval.

'It's all very magnificent, but I think we need to talk,' she told him firmly. He agreed and taking her hand he guided her down a zigzag path to a small beach. To the right of it a large wide arch could be seen in the rocks which led through to yet another beach. Finding a shady tree, he sat down, pulling her down with him.

'I'm sorry, I honestly didn't expect my father and my aunt to be so...'

'Catholic?' she offered, and he shrugged.

'Well, it's the way we were brought up I guess, but what I didn't tell you before is if my father does not nominate me as the heir to his empire then my uncle will kick all the family off the island as soon as he is in control. He has other plans for this island. They are not legal. My cousin, Joe Kelly, used to be an inspector in the Federal Police before he came to work for me. We headhunted Bob Costa, also ex Federal Police drugs squad then serious fraud office. Joe and Bob don't know what hold my uncle Sammy has over Enzo, but the family are concerned. We run legitimate businesses, but people can be bought, and money doesn't grow on trees.'

'So, you want me to sacrifice myself for your family?' she sniffed haughtily.

'Hear me out Raya, I don't want to do this anymore than you do. I planned another life for myself, it included every male she ever had anything to do with, even her beloved father lied to her by omission, failing to tell her he had been divorced and she had a half brother and he had changed his name. There appeared to be no point in drawing attention to her situation, Bart had other considerations and she would simply be collateral damage.

'I graduated with a law degree,' he went on, 'and business led me to other things. Running hotels and holiday resorts had never been on my horizon.' Looking out across the sea, he said on a sigh.

'The problem began after I graduated university my father's companies were not looking good. He had bought this island years before with the dream of family living here in idyllic self-sufficient splendour. However, he was in over his head, borrowing to pay down debt. It all went wrong.

At the time, I had the only university degree in the company apart from my brother-in-law, who is our accountant. Together we kind of took over. To my own surprise I have a talent for making a dollar turn into five and I became a corporate raider. I bought rundown resorts and other businesses, for the sole purpose of stripping the assets and selling them on. I hate to admit it, but I became very good at it, and I became hardnosed and horrible.'

Wow what an admission Raya thought.

'Ten years ago, I started giving back. I enjoy philanthropy, we set up a research institute, Lombardi Intellectual Investments. The research is medical and social, and now it is almost financially self supporting. I say almost, the trouble is it has grown so much. We do have other financial supporters out there but its an ongoing commitment, another thing Sammy doesn't want to be burdened with, he tells my father. He's a slimy little weasel playboy on the fringes of society. There are some men in Australia who form its underbelly and see him as a kind of Don. He appeals to my father's vanity, and he claims a broken heart prevented him from finding true love. So, he beds and never weds every available woman, and some who are not actually available.'

'I take it Uncle Sammy is on the board of the Lombardi Enterprises. Does he do anything else?' Raya wanted to know; grateful he had at least been talking business to her; many men of that ilk think the "little woman" shouldn't involve herself in business.

'Yes, the problem is he's a loose cannon and only brings his dealings to the board when he needs money or forgiveness. Both Bob and Joe believe Vince Ferrantino and Sammy are in cahoots.'

'Oh God, I'm so sorry,' she whispered, scared by the thought.

'It's not your fault or your problem. The Feds are all over them. It is just a matter of time,' he said.

'Speaking of time, your father doesn't look well. How much time does he have, do you know?'

'Only God knows the answer. But here's the thing Raya, he is of sound mind and the silly old fool has this romantic notion Sophia's daughter - you - are the only person who can help him save face, as the Chinese say, and give him back his dignity and make the family complete.' The whole concept infuriated Bart.

'No pressure,' she snapped. 'You must have known about this so-called arranged marriage years ago, you're how old?'

'Thirty-eight,' he spoke as if he had all the time in the world to choose to marry. They both knew he hadn't wanted to marry, until it had been forced upon him. 'Enzo only became terminal around the time your father died, and so we agreed to let you mourn. But then your brother and Tony appeared on the scene and things changed. About this catholic wedding, you would have run a mile if I had suggested it first. God knows you go to church very little, about as often as me, high days and holidays, hatching, matching, and dispatching. I'm sure we can get an annulment if we enter into the covenant of holy matrimony. Especially, if it's with the sole intention of ensuring my father doesn't allow his lunatic brother to destroy thirty plus families and hundreds of lives. I'm sure we could get an annulment because of this preexisting condition.'

'You're as bad as Paul with his line, "trust me I'm a doctor."' She shook her head, 'we both know he can't be trusted.' It occurred to her Bart may not be trustworthy either, he could be hiding something.

'If you weren't required to go through with this charade,' she waved her hand. 'What would you want to be doing? I mean it occurs to me you might be in a relationship.'

His expression changed as rapidly as a door slams and he developed a small tick in his jaw muscle as he clenched his teeth. Now, she could all but feel those fingers around her throat. She looked at his hands to check the feeling had only been her vivid imagination. His fists were clenched too, she had struck a nerve.

'I noticed in our first agreement; I'm forbidden to form any relationships until our divorce is final. If I proceed with this marriage of convenience, then the same rule should apply to you.' The hauteur had returned to her voice. Silence stretched out between them for moments before he spoke.

'I'll have it amended,' he said coldly. It did not take a mental giant to see she annoyed the hell out of him, his body language screamed it. 'But there is a problem,' he said, startling her. 'There are no copies of our agreement because it is strictly between you and me everybody believes the marriage is real.'

'What do you mean? I signed it before we married. I have a copy in my things,' disbelief caused her voice to rise a few decibels short of screaming pitch.

'No, what you signed is a prenup, designed to cover what you would get in the event of divorce.' Thinking, he explained, 'I switched the papers. I didn't care if anyone saw the prenup, but I had no intention of allowing anyone to suspect this is not a regular marriage. I destroyed our original agreement.' The casual shrug of his shoulder gave her the urge to slap him, instead she covered her face with her hands.

'I can't believe this is happening to me. In less than a week, I gained an unwanted, undesirable brother who wants my inheritance and threatened my life. His lecherous friend drugged me for god knows what debaucheries, my best friend and business partner told the world and his wife my personal business after I expressly asked her not to. The man I loved whom I thought loved me, has been caught cheating more than once. Then I learn the man who tricked, coerced, whatever me, into a sham marriage for his own purposes also lied,' feeling better now she had got it out there. 'Who could have seen this coming?' she said sarcastically.

'I have never lied to you. I just failed to spell the details out clearly,' he said looking out to sea. On standing up he called excitedly pointing out to the ocean, 'look there's a huge pod of pilot whales.' The pair stood fascinated as they watched the spectacle. The beautiful creatures rose and dived as they swam together, some emitting melodic noises. 'I counted forty something in the pod,' he still felt amazed every time he saw them. 'Thank God they didn't come in too close. If one beaches, they all beach.'

'I have never seen anything so spectacular,' emotion caused her to turn her face from him. 'They are so lucky I could never imagine being a part of a huge family.' The words were out before she could censor them. Bart's family were *his* family, he realised she had no one. They stayed watching the huge pod of whales until the creatures were out of sight.

'We're truly blessed here; not only do we have our family around us most of the time, but we also get to see other spectacular families.' His love of family and this island exuded from every fibre of his being.

At dinner Maria and Joe joined them, and before Enzo appeared, Teresa told Bart and Raya firmly, 'Father O'Malley from Yeppoon is flying in tomorrow to see Enzo. I told him about you two and he has agreed to grant you the sacrament of matrimony. I explained the situation, he will talk with you both and hear your confessions and then bless your union in church.' The woman spoke as if it were all a simple oversite, easily put right.

Raya felt uncomfortable up she had been brought up catholic in a strict environment, with rituals and procedures. Melissa used to say Catholicism is a culture and it is ingrained into you. Sometimes it felt more like a cult. Aunt Teresa sounded like so many of the older nuns, they had this way of scaring you into submission with stories of hell fire and damnation. Remembering the stories, Raya felt ill, excused herself and left the room. Bart followed his bride to their suite.

He closed their bedroom door, and seeing Raya looked miserable he asked what he could do?

'Let me go home, I'm intimidated by this whole business. A civil ceremony is one thing, but a catholic wedding... I can't.' Her jewel-coloured eyes pleaded with him he almost felt sorry for her. Almost, but not enough to let her get away. He had way too much at stake for qualms as this point in the proceedings. 'Does all your family know we were betrothed as children?' watching his awkwardness and embarrassment she believed they did.

'Is it not usual under these circumstances for the couple to get to know one another before the nuptials?' she said sitting down on her bed and staring out across the bay. Bart sat down beside her, relaxing a little.

'Yes, but Tony Romano's actions meant I had to act fast. I planned to get to know you first, and I hoped you would like me and maybe we could make this work.' His voice softened showing none of his earlier arrogance. He looked into her face and gently touched her hair. 'Would you like to talk to Melissa?' he asked.

'Yes, but she would call the police if I told her what has happened. It's against Australian law to force or coerce anyone into getting married. It applies to all marriages,' she insisted.

'No, not quite true. There is an amendment to existing law being discussed, however here we are June 2012, and no such amendment has been passed. An arranged marriage, where both people freely consent to get married, is different from a forced marriage. Arranged marriages will always be legal in Australia. You clearly agreed to this marriage and even signed a secular prenup. You're an educated woman. I think you knew exactly what you were getting into,' Bart said decisively.

'I didn't have any choice,' she told him.

'We all have free will Raya, you simply accepted my offer.' His words were the final straw, what choice did she really have? Standing up she gazed out of the huge picture window, feeling trapped, coerced for the sake of honour. She had no way of getting away from him. He stood beside her in seconds.

'You claim you are not a liar, you intended to get to know me first,' she gave a sardonic laugh, 'I can tell you this, for what it is worth, you would have never bothered with me, because I am not compliant. I'm no door mat and I see I annoy you beyond the point of frustration. I have a mind of my own.' As she spoke, he smiled.

'Very true, probably the reason our parents arrange these things. I would be forced to put up with your behaviour while getting to know you,' he said as they stood staring out of the window watching the sun slowly sink towards the horizon.

'I would have told my father I'm not interested after the first meeting,' she replied, watching his facial muscles twitch with annoyance. 'You display an unbelievable arrogance for a twenty first century male.'

'I'm not arrogant enough to believe I could get away with snogging a woman in public, then claim to be in a committed relationship with another, and not expect it to be all over social media. Doctor Paul Martin is arrogant and stupid.' Raya couldn't argue, sadly, she felt stupid. 'We need to join the others for dinner, but before we go, I insist you call Melissa. You will feel better after you have spoken with her. You two have been friends more than half your lives,' he said firmly, not needing to be told twice she took her mobile phone from the nightstand and called her.

'Hi Mel, I wanted to talk to you, hear the sound of your voice,' she put the call on speaker. 'I've met someone.' Bart spun around to focus on Raya's face, almost giving himself whiplash doing it. She looked serenely calm. As though not totally focused on Raya's words Melissa burst out,

'your brother's been to see me. I think he threatened me, well he sounded polite and smarmy, but something about him is scary.'

'What did he say?' Raya asked.

'He wanted to know where you were. At first, he didn't believe me when I said I didn't know. He sounded pretty mad. Raya, I don't know what to make of this. He claimed you met up with Tony Romano after we left his restaurant. I said you were ill and went home. He claimed the whole thing had been a ruse, you ended up at Tony's apartment.' Melissa repeated herself as Raya's pleading eyes scanned Bart's face.

'You don't believe him, do you? It's not entirely true. Melissa, I'm Bart Lombardi, a long-time family friend of Soraya's she's with me. I intercepted her trip to Tony's apartment because I happened to be in the restaurant the night this happened, and I could see Raya did not willingly leave with Tony.' Bart's deep, resonant voice surprised Melissa.

'What?' she sounded incredulous.

'It's true Mel, I think Tony slipped me something other than a paracetamol. Bart saved me. Stay away from Tony he's not to be trusted,' Raya said as calmly as she could.

'Do the police know? Where are you?'

'I'm safe I'm here with Bart's family and yes, the police are aware of the situation. Look, we're just about to have dinner I wanted to make sure you're okay because I'm fine.' Just as she was about to end the call Melissa called out to her,

'Can I tell Paul; he's been driving me bonkers?'

'No, tell him he can go to hell,' Bart's voice rumbled.

Chapter Six

Father O'Malley, complete with his overnight bag arrived by air the next day. His name may have been Irish, but he looked and sounded like a true blue Australian, from the top of his balding sandy head with weather beaten face down to his size twelve boots. Hailing from Sydney, he grew up in Blackburn, one of the city's poorest and roughest areas. He enjoyed these trips to Nicodemus; they were an opportunity he would not have otherwise had. The island paradise seemed far removed from his normal boring duties in the diocesan office in Rockhampton. Enzo had always been very generous to the church using Father Frank O'Malley as his instrument of power. Only Bart had the guts to tell the old man he couldn't buy his way to heaven. Believing his son to be cynical where church and God were concerned, Enzo ignored him and lived according to his own self justified, often archaic, beliefs and customs.

The fact Father O'Malley, a streetwise and sharp man understood more than he let on meant hopefully he could see through Enzo's ridiculous powerplays, pitting Sammy and Bart against one another. Better still he would advise the foolish old man, who appeared to be going soft in his old age, that Sammy was a liability to the Lombardi Empire. One could live in hope, Bart thought, as he greeted the priest.

'Meet Soraya, Frank. Soraya meet Father Frank O'Malley.' Raya blushed, extending her hand as though the man could see into her soul.

'I've seen pictures of your mother; you look just like her,' he raised his tussocky brows in surprise.

'You know about her?' Raya said, surprised.

'Everybody knows about her or you, depending on which view of the story you're looking at.' The priest, a man in his fifties smiled at Bart whose expression softened and he nodded, agreeing. The three of them walked towards the open jeep.

'Well, I didn't know about him,' she pointed with an open hand at Bart. 'Looking back, I think my father tried to tell me on his deathbed,' she shrugged.

'When did you find out about him then?' Alarm was evident in the priest's voice.

'Oh, you know, when he whipped me away on his big white charger and I was dressed only in a bedspread. I felt obliged to marry him,' her voice sounded deadpan. Bart, at first stunned, burst out laughing and before long Father O'Malley started laughing too. When Raya never cracked a smile, the Priest remembered Teresa Kelly telling him about these two and composed himself as he climbed into the open jeep.

'Holy Matrimony is a serious business. It's not to be undertaken lightly; it is to sanctify the love of husband and wife and give them the grace to bear each other's weaknesses for life. Then there's the children they need to bring up, in the fear and love of God.' Frank O'Malley sounded as if he had learned the words by rote.

'I'm sorry father, but I will not bring up my children to live in fear of God who loves them.' Raya protested. Bart smirked at her challenge.

'Ah, I don't think I worded that well,' Father O'Malley sighed.

'Perhaps not, but it's exactly how the older nuns explained things to me. I don't think hell fire and brimstone work well in the twenty first century, and definitely not with young children.'

'I know you were brought up catholic so why would you undertake a civil marriage?' The priest countered sounding kindly but frustrated.

'I'll tell you with the protection of the confessional.' The hauteur came back in her voice, and she caught a glimpse of Bart half closing his eyes as if shutting them would dispel the truth.

'Right, I'll hear your confession as soon as I've seen Enzo,' he said.

Teresa welcomed the priest and offered him refreshments, saying she would bring a tray to him and Enzo, 'he's lying down,' she advised.

'Coffee?' Bart asked his aunt, and she directed the younger woman, Rosa to get it for him. Raya asked what his last slave died of under her breath and Rosa burst into peels of laughter.

'Insubordination,' he growled. The look he shot her had Raya covering her throat. 'I never asked her to make it. I merely inquired if there is any, there is always coffee on the go around here,' he relaxed his expression at the young woman's giggles. Making herself at home, Raya found the tea and made a cup of the gumboot variety. Bart followed her outside to a stone table under the large pergola his coffee in hand.

'Before you change your mind about this marriage, ask the priest about my family and this island, and any other damned thing you can think of. He is after all an independent source of information.' His coffee mug clunked on the stone table.

'I bet he's not, I bet he's in your father's pocket,' she said convinced of her truth.

'Your cynicism is extraordinary for someone so naïve,' he said softly. Ignoring his remark, she asked agitatedly, 'Give me one good reason aside from your family why I should marry you in church?'

'Because I'll treat you better than Paul ever would,' he said quickly, without thought, as though it came as a natural honest answer.

'What do you know about how Paul would treat me?' This time her voice held more curiosity than cynicism.

'Well, if his behaviour is anything to go by, he's not set the bar very high,' Bart said casually. His cell phone rang and seeing it was a business colleague he excused himself to take the call in the office. Enjoying the sunshine Raya closed her eyes, revelling in the glorious day, when she heard a male voice.

'How are you settling in?' She turned to see Joe Kelly; a solid man tall but not as tall as his cousin Bart. Joe held a coffee mug and sat down on a seat opposite her. Raya wondered at his attention because she felt sure he didn't like her.

'Why hasn't Bart married until now?' her question at first stunning him, it also amused. Cheeky wench, he thought, liking her spirit.

'Obviously, he hasn't told you. The love of his life went to work overseas for six months and came back married.' Firmly he held her gaze.

'Oh, did she hurt him badly?' she returned his look.

'Very badly, he didn't expect it at all, totally unexpected, well for him.' He sipped his coffee. 'After her, no one met his expectations, so he decided to humour his father and get to know you. Then Tony Romano ...' he shrugged. Raya blushed, remembering the photos the bedspread and the whole embarrassing incident.

'Is it you I need to thank? If it is, thank you most sincerely,' her face flushed scarlet. 'I hate to think what might have happened had you not come along when you did.'

'Well, I did and it's confidential no one need know about it unless they're involved. Tony Romano is a thug, and the police are watching him very closely now.' Hardly had he finished his words when Father O'Malley stood in the doorway looking out into the vine covered pergola.

'Soraya,' he called and immediately she stood and gathering her teacup and saucer she walked towards him, saying to Joe, 'confession time,' as she went.

'I'll just take this to the kitchen then we should go for a walk,' Raya advised.

The pair strolled through the garden, which terraced by another zigzag path led to a flat area with a huge specimen beech tree underneath which, stood a garden seat. They sat there looking out to the Pacific ocean.

'Right, shall we begin?' The priest took out a small purple stole about four inches wide and placed it around his neck, making the sign of the cross as he did so. The purple stole appeared to be just short of waist length with a gold cross embroidered at each end and trimmed with a gold fringe. Then making the sign of the cross over Raya he asked, 'how long is it since your last confession?'

Raya went through a list of trivial sins all catholics trot out when they can't think of what to say, not having committed anything cardinal. 'Bless me father for I have sinned, as I said it's six months since my last confession. I haven't been to Mass much since my father died. I've taken a little holiday from God. I've been uncharitable to my friend and business partner. I had impure thoughts when I saw Brad Pitt on TV, how many times? Oh, at least three.' She blushed and so it went on, until she said she was finished. Father O'Malley, who had been prompting her after every sin in a serious but slightly bored patriarchal tone, sounded frustrated to have to spell it out.

'What about Bart? have you not committed a sin with him?'

Shocked she blurted, 'no father, we never consummated our civil union.' He watched her jewel like eyes well up as she spoke.

'Why not? He asked amazed knowing there must be more to this. Immediately she felt embarrassed.

'Because it wouldn't be right. The thing is father, Bart saved me from a terrible situation. Well actually, he had Joe Kelly do it.' Pouring out all the sordid details of the night, she added, 'on his death bed my father tried to tell me he had arranged for me to marry Bart. But he kept saying "see Enzo Lombardi." I didn't understand.

Bart wanted to get to know me first, but after the Tony business which the police are looking into, we discussed it and decided to marry in a civil service.' All her words came jumbling out as honestly as she could formulate them. However, in his effort to spare her further trauma he had misinterpreted what she tried to tell him.

'Do you want children who you will bring up to know the light of God?' he asked solemnly.

'Yes father,' she sniffed.

'And what about Bart's weaknesses, can you live with those?' he asked. Raya felt so relieved to have shared this sordid affair with someone else, someone trustworthy.

Relieved of her secret she said, 'Oh I understand he has been hurt very badly; his heart broken and so he puts up this arrogant front, but he's kind and loving.' She remembered him with his aunt Teresa hugging her, teasing her. Sadly, she completely forgot the cold looks he gave her and his formidable glare. 'I wanted to tell you this in confession because I don't want anyone to know what happened with Tony Romano.'

Father O'Malley offered her absolution and never mentioned the Sacrament of Holy Matrimony again.

When he dismissed her with her penance of ten Hail Mary's, he asked her to send Bart out to him. Taking out his prayer book he began his Devine Office for the day.

When she located Bart, he sat in his office with Joe and both men noted her reddened eyes were a little too moist. They exchanged glances, aware that throughout her ordeal with Tony and his goon, and later with them, never once had she resorted to tears.

'Father O'Malley is ready for you in the garden under the beech tree where the garden seat is.' She went to her room to freshen up.

The priest sat deep in prayer when Bart arrived and sat down beside him. Not waiting to be invited he said, 'bless me father for I have sinned. It is two months since my last confession, right here under this tree from memory, and apart from some lustful thoughts which I squashed and didn't act on, there's my normal high-handed manner. However, I've genuinely tried to be a good person. Pride is a sin I'm guilty of,' he exhaled audibly a tad annoyed because he had no idea what Raya had told the priest. 'You know father I take my religion seriously, but I won't die in a ditch if I can't attend Mass every Sunday.' The priest believed a young family and a routine would focus his beliefs.

'What about this civil union? It is not a marriage; did you not commit a sin there?' The priest could not reveal what Raya had told him; he merely asked the question.

'No father, I wanted to get to know Raya before we committed before God. Events conspired against us, and I needed to protect her. We didn't commit any sin I'm aware of,' Bart believed what he said.

'It's true to say she had little choice but given time I'm sure she will see it as the right way. Soraya is a feisty little hellion so considering her weaknesses, I'm sure she can cope with mine. To be frank her stepbrother is a man of interest to the Federal Police and a real threat to Raya. She had no idea of his existence before her father's death. For both our sakes, she is safer under my protection.' The priest simply listened; the more Bart talked the better. Any questions might give rise to speculation or worse he might guess what Raya had told him under the protective seal of the confessional. 'Father, Raya is an educated, pragmatic woman. She knows what is expected of her within the sacrament of holy matrimony. We have both experienced disappointment from our own choices, so we agreed, perhaps our parents are wiser than we think. This won't happen overnight, but we have the rest of our lives.'

The priest gave Bart absolution and his penance then as a parting shot offered, 'tomorrow, I will join you and Soraya in Holy Matrimony. But you cannot sleep in your room tonight, move out to a guest suite.'

Chapter Seven

The house buzzed with people coming and going for business plus the priest and Enzo's nurse, who lived in a cottage at the back of Bella Vista. Soraya busied herself online sourcing artwork from international dealers as well as private sellers. After checking her website and loading new pieces she felt good. It felt good to be working. Unbeknown to her Bart sat on her bed watching her work.

'We're all expected in the living room in half an hour, get changed,' he said his voice even.

'Don't you ever knock or ask how you are? How did your confession go?' she bit her lip, watching him move in his shorts, those legs, thigh muscles. She shook her head to shed those thoughts, she had just been to confession after all. He stood now, holding up a dress a bright multi-coloured party dress with handkerchief hemline.

'No, not suitable for dinner,' she took it from him. He stood staring at her while he held the hanger.

'You choose,' he said after clearing his throat. 'Father O'Malley said he'd marry us to morrow. Uncle Sammy's on the island. He'll be joining us for dinner, so is Bob Costa and his wife Marian, they live on the island too, so ten of us for dinner. I just want you to know this is important.' Raya pulled the hanger from his grip.

'Okay what about this dress?' she held up a white dupion silk sheath, 'I'll do my best I promise.' The thought of meeting Sammy sounded daunting but at least she had been forewarned.

When Raya knocked on the adjoining bedroom Bart used, she gasped, he looked so powerful in dark trousers and a black and silver shirt. His aftershave wafted through to her. Standing tall, his long legs slightly apart his stern expression unreadable, he surveyed her.

The dress hugged her soft feminine curves, highlighting her tiny waist. He half closed his eyes not wanting to acknowledge the affect she had on him. Her honey-coloured mane had been folded softly in an elegant updo and already little strands had artistically escaped. Her makeup, reminiscent of a French cosmetic house, understated yet effective.

'We should go,' he said. Looking at him now she wondered about this woman who had broken his heart. Bart must have really loved her. After all she had managed to toss Paul off like an old raincoat the dog had claimed, and she had believed she loved him. Perhaps hurt hardens the heart?

As Bart introduced her around the room, he became aware of reactions towards her, particularly Sammy's.

'Wipe your chin uncle,' Bart feigned humour.

'Uncle? we're practically brothers, I was only a child when you were born,' he said, mooning into Raya's magnetic eyes as he held her hand.

'Fourteen, you were fourteen when I was born Uncle Samuel,' Bart reminded him.

'Exactly we're just like brothers.' Finally, Raya pulled her hand away from him with the sudden urge to wash it again. Maria Kelly and Marion Carta both in their thirties got along well. Both were teachers and now they had their children, they taught school on the island. Like good friends they bounced ideas off one another and gave their husbands cheek. What fascinated Raya as she watched them all had been the way they deferred to Bart and of course old Enzo. It became clear however Enzo sometimes went off on some tangent. While the family humoured him, he no longer appeared omnipotent. Still his succession plan did not appear as clear as it should.

Aunt Teresa took Raya by the hand on the pretext of showing her the rose garden.

'You can see what Bart is up against, Enzo's only with us for a limited time and Sammy is dangerous. Be honest with me, can you learn to love Bart?' her open face almost pleading. Fortunately, the dinner gong saved Raya as Maria called them from the shelter of the loggia. Relieved, Raya began to think about Teresa's words as Father O'Malley said grace. As soon as he had finished various family members began to question Raya. However, she deflected them in favour of asking Sammy a question, making him wince.

'Uncle Sammy, may I ask you a personal question?'

'Its just Sammy, Soraya and ask away, I'm transparent,' his smile reminiscent of a gorilla about to assert it's self in the social order.

'Why have you never married?' Bart stiffened beside her, and the room fell silent. Instead of giving her his hackneyed excuses Sammy simply said, 'to be honest I have never met a woman I could love until death do us part. I've not been as fortunate as Bart.' Smug self satisfaction claimed his features.

'Then you don't understand real love. It's not some youthful flight of fancy. It is something you consciously choose to do each day with the person to whom you are committed. I know this is hardly the right forum to discuss my parents. The truth is they loved each other very much. My father told me every day they were together my mother made the conscious decision to love him and he loved her for it. He said it made him a better person.'

Father O'Malley began nodding, or more like rocking, his head back and forth in agreement. Enzo's crepey reptilian eyes moved around the faces at the table. Now he understood Sophia had consciously decided to love this man who had compromised her and forced her to marry him. Oh God how he had mourned the loss of her love and that of his closest friend, Marco Ferrantino.

Even before the meal had ended Bart obligingly escorted old Enzo to his bed. Slowly the pair walked up the hallway to Enzo's suite.

'Tomorrow you and Sophia will marry in church,' Enzo confused mother and daughter.

'Soraya, Papa, it is Soraya I will marry in church.' the old man seemed to be losing his grip.

'Promise me you will choose to love her everyday of your lives together,' he begged his son. Thinking of the words literally, Bart agreed.

'I promise you everyday Soraya and I live our lives together I will choose to love her,' as far as he could see there would be no lie in this. But secretly he understood it would not be for very long.

Enzo could no longer put himself to bed without his nurse's help. His dinner had become soup, he couldn't comfortably sit long enough to watch the others eat their main course. How much longer would he live? He had morphine administered through a driver when he suffered a painful attack. Often, he refused it wanting instead to keep his wits about him. When he died Raya would be free to go her way, to choose her own life.

Back in the dining room Bart made reference to the monthly board meeting due next week, suggesting it should be held on the island because of Enzo's failing health.

After dinner, Raya complained of the heat and Bart suggested a walk in the cool night air. First, she ran off to change her footwear, returning in ballet flats.

'So, you've got me,' she said, resigned. 'This life is like a fishbowl how do you put up with it?'

'I have hideaways,' he said pragmatically. 'I do enjoy family when we get together. I want to thank you by the way, you impressed Enzo with what you said to Sammy at dinner.'

'It is the truth, not logical, but the truth just the same.' Stopping, she looked out to sea, gazing at the full moon in childlike wonder. Looking down at her he could see she lacked the height of faithless Rachel, who stood tall and with a strong athletic figure. Rachel

Rando enjoyed a determined yet fun loving personality, with classical good looks. Not a striking beauty like Raya, but then she didn't annoy him the way Raya did. With Rachel he had no need for arrogance. However, the woman became demanding and unyielding, her work ethic seemed over the top, totally inflexible commitment. Raya seemed to work around the edges, unstructured. Bringing himself back to the present he expelled a long breath, he would not be committing in holy matrimony to Rachel. She didn't even want him. Raya didn't want him either, he understood why. This would be a true marriage of convenience. It occurred to him the man Raya did end up committing to would be a very lucky man indeed, because when she committed it would be deep and meaningful. This charade had only one purpose, to get Enzo to confirm him as his sole heir, so he could be CEO and chairman of the board. Plain and simple, if only it were a straightforward matter.

'A penny for them?' Bart, who had been miles away, frowned. 'Your thoughts, what were you thinking?' Raya asked.

'Ah well, I had been thinking how glad I am I rescued you.'

'Why? I haven't committed to you before God yet,' she quipped reminding him in her own way she still had a little bit of power, although it seemed like bravado. Overall, she felt powerless.

'But you will,' he said shooting her his Basilisk like stare. Her hand flew to her throat in protection. They stood staring out over the ocean. It reflected the blue light of the full moon. 'It's a blue moon, they are the second full moon of the lunar month and occur only rarely, hence the expression, "once in a blue moon,"' Bart told her, watching her face with pleasure.

'It's beautiful, is it a good omen?' she asked.

'You know Catholics are not superstitious,' he berated her. 'Come on you need to get to bed, big day tomorrow.'

Chapter Eight

Tossing and turning, Raya couldn't sleep. Tonight, she had slept with the curtains open to allow the gentle sea breeze to cool her. Instead, it made the curtains wave ominously and tinted the whole room with an eerie blue tinge. Standing at the open doors, staring at the Pacific ocean she felt drawn to a haunting sound. In the light of the full moon, she could see a lone whale diving, calling in a low deep sound so majestic. She pulled on her light dressing gown and slipping into her ballet flats decided to watch and listen. Hurrying along the zigzag path down to the small beach Raya, full of emotion, listened transfixed. She heard something so troubling about this beautiful creature. Breathless yet excited, she sat in the stillness of the night. With no idea of the time or how long she watched, wondering why the whale swam alone, it's song, like nothing she had ever heard before. Beautiful and melancholy as if the creature swims around crying out to a mate who never comes. The song persisted as the whale leapt and dived across the vast ocean in search of a companion.

Back at the house Bart woke at the sound of a loud crash and then another. It came from the bedroom across the hall, his bedroom, the one where Raya slept. Quickly untangling himself from the sheets and pulling on his sleeping shorts he tiptoed across the hall and listened at the door. He heard nothing, he called out her name in a loud whisper. He didn't want to wake the whole household, so he opened the door. The bright moonlight illuminated the room tinging everything with a faint blue hue. Alarmed, as the doors and curtains were open, he flicked the light switch as he closed the bedroom door behind him. The bed lay empty. It looked like Raya left in a hurry. The island was safe but because half of it was a resort and he wasn't privy to the personal history of every guest, he quickly checked the bathroom and adjoining bedroom. Going back to his room, he grabbed his cell phone to call his cousin Joe, who took charge of security on the Island.

'Bart,' Joe answered immediately. 'What are you doing up?'

'I could ask you the same thing, it's three in the morning.' Bart said alarmed.

'Couldn't sleep so I did a spot check on the night security staff to keep them on their toes. I know Bob did it earlier but... Why are you calling?'

'Raya's missing, I heard two distinct crashing sounds coming from her room, went to look, the doors are open, and she's gone,' Bart told him. Then Joe who lived in a separate house on the island told Bart to go back and check the room again, thoroughly. He would be on his way.

'Don't touch anything,' his parting salvo. This time he noticed a glass of water from the nightstand had smashed on the tiled floor. Also, a heavy silver-framed photograph of the family in happier times had also smashed on the floor. It had been on a small table beside a large comfy chair near the window. Soon Joe arrived and the two men surveyed one another. Joe, dressed in old army camouflage work clothes he must have owned for years, Bart in boat shoes and sleeping shorts.

'You check the house I'll check the grounds,' Joe instructed 'and don't read the riot act if you find her, she's not staff and she's probably nervous. There is no turning back after tomorrow and you two haven't had a lot of time.' Joe had to be the only person who could speak with such honesty to Bart. the two were like brothers.

'Do you think something ...' Bart hesitated not wanting to mention the elephant in the room.

'I don't believe she's been kidnapped, so don't worry.' Joe gave Bart a brotherly arm pat. 'Maria reckons she's nervous, "scared spitless," were her exact words.' Giving Bart the thumbs up he left via the open doors. After a quick reconnoitre of the gardens he heard the familiar plaintive call, he recognised the whale and it's haunting sound. Always it filled Joe with awe and a feeling of being closer to God. Immediately he ran down the zigzag path to the little beach and as he approached it, he noticed Raya sitting listening to the whale. Out of earshot he phoned Bart saying he would bring her back. Not wanting to frighten Raya he stood almost beside her before he spoke.

'It's beautiful, isn't it?' he said softly. Raya turned her head as he spoke and the moonlight on her face made her look so vulnerable. But she said nothing. Joe sat down beside her.

'They say it's the loneliest whale on the earth. The sound is fifty-two Hertz, it's not just unusual, but outright unique. It's why we can hear it so clearly, because it carries underwater. But out in the middle of the Pacific ocean its like singing a love song no one can hear.'

'It's so sad, but I understand how the poor creature feels,' Raya said softly. Joe couldn't see her face, covered by a thick curtain of wavy hair. 'I feel totally lost.' the little voice inside her whispered aloud.

'Don't be afraid of Bart. All his life he's had an enormous presence, it surrounds him like an aura.' Joe relaxed and let out a small laugh, 'when we were kids and played dressing up, Bart always played the Cardinal or the king, nobody ever challenged him. He behaved like he was born to it. But now, it weighs on him heavily. You will be good for him.' He pressed a button on his tactical timepiece and the dial illuminated.

'Come on, let me take you back, soon it will be dawn and your friend's gone now.' With the whale no longer in sight he held out his open hand to help her up. The steep walk up the path felt like hard work.

'You shouldn't walk about alone at night; we have guests in the resort, and some have yachts. We close the resort for a month from Christmas week, the only time we have the whole place to ourselves,' Joe said, taking large strides as he spoke, his voice not even laboured.

When they finally arrived back at Bella Vista, the ceiling light illuminated her room and the door had been shut. Joe opened it, noticing the mess had been cleaned up. He quickly checked the other rooms having sent Bart back to the guest room earlier.

'You better get some shut eye. Mass is ten am, we only take tea and feed the children before Mass, breakfast afterwards.' Of course, they did, she knew what to expect.

Next morning young Rosa brought in a tea tray for Raya who could be heard in the shower. Leaving it on her nightstand Rosa went about setting out the wedding dress still covered in a soft cotton bag on Raya's bed. As she opened the bag it felt like unwrapping a gift within a gift. A shoe bag hung from the hook of the hanger; it contained white satin pumps with little kitten heels. Rosa put them beside the gown and turned to greet Raya who came out of the bathroom dressed in her bra and knickers.

'Morning Miss, this is a beautiful gown,' Rosa commented.

'You can have it if you like,' Raya said bleakly 'I don't think I will wear it.' Rosa laughed.

'You are too late. I don't need it I'm already married; I have two children,' Rosa announced proudly, then laughed. 'Ah, I had you fooled there for a moment, but you did meet the love of my life.' Her nonchalant expression stunned Raya. 'He's Dion Lamb, Mr Lombardi's chef. Horrified, Raya asked her age.

'I'm twenty-four and Dion is twenty-six,' she offered.

When Raya had first met them, she thought Dion a boy definitely not a twenty-six-year-old.

'Where do you live when you're not on the yacht?' Raya asked surprised.

'On the island here with my parents. They both work at the resort. We have everything here; we all love it.' Rosa pointed to the tray. 'Better drink it before its stewed and wear the dress Miss, it's expected.' Raya blushed, feeling like a spoilt princess. 'I'm a qualified hairdresser, I can do your hair if you like. I bought some of the waxy orange blossom, it blooms madly here in the subtropical weather. It looked good the way Kerryn used it on Great Keppel.' On the dressing table sat a large bunch of orange blossom fashioned into a crown like the Polynesian women use to decorate their hair.

'Do you have streaks in your hair? It's a very unusual colour,' Rosa asked, fascinated.

'No, the roots are warm brown, the sun lightens it in streaks like a tabby cat,' Raya laughed.

When Rosa had finished, her hair looked nothing like the urbane elegant updo she wore for the civil ceremony. Instead, brushed and beautiful it curled down her back and gently covered her shoulders. The crown of white waxy orange blossom looked perfect. It gave her an ethereal look.

Rosa had instructed her to stay in her room until she came to get her. Without question she did as she Rosa suggested. By ten past ten she began to feel anxious, but Rosa finally came and helped her into the silver Mercedes sedan, adjusting her abundant skirt of white silk. The bodice was an extravagant French lace over white silk, with lacey full-length sleeves. None of it looked like Raya's understated elegant taste, still it looked beautiful. 'Princess bloody meringue,' she could hear Mel saying, she bit her lip. She had no Mel with her irreverent remarks, warm hugs and flaming red hair. No Mel to be her bridesmaid as they had always planned had this been a real wedding.

The tiny church, Saint Nicodemus Chapel, had been built on the resort side of the island by the same architects as the house. It looked modern with classical religious features: Imported stain glass windows, and dark wooden beams richly carved with symbols of Catholicism. A crowd had gathered outside the church, people who worked for the Lombardi family, who were waiting to glimpse Bart's bride. As someone helped Raya from the Mercedes, she stopped to say hello to a group of small children who had grown fractious by the wait.

'I'm nervous too,' she said to a pre-schooler peeking out from behind her mother's skirt. 'Please will you hold my hand and take me to Bart?' The child said nothing, but another about six years old piped up, he would. Raya did a quick tally, there were about eight children. 'Thank you, we can all go in together' she opened her hands and children quickly grasped them and each other. Joe waited at the open doorway and grinned as he saw the happy gaggle.

'I'm here to escort you down the isle but I see I'm redundant,' he said. She had grown on him, and he on her. Hearing the noise of children's chatter and seeing the surprised look on Father O'Malley's face, Bart who stood tall, facing the altar, turned not quite believing the sight. Raya had attracted at least a dozen small children whom she herded like a mother hen with chicks under her wings, smiling and chatting to them the short distance from chapel entrance to altar.

'Thank you all,' she beamed. 'Bart will look after me now, but stay, sit on the altar step if you'd like.' Most stayed, some went back outside. A bemused expression furrowed Bart's brows together. He stood speechless.

The priest droned on about, 'the covenant by which a man and a woman establish themselves in a partnership for the whole of life and which is ordered by its nature to be for the good of the spouses and the procreation and education of offspring.' The service began and Mass started. Father O'Malley mindful of Enzo's ill health and the short attention span of the hoard of young children, kept everything as brief as the service allowed. Raya took off her ring and gave it to

Bart. He shook his head putting it back on her other hand. Confused she left it where he had put it. When they came to the ring swapping part of the service, he produced a large baguet cut diamond. it must have been six or more carats. Did he own a diamond mine?

When Father O'Malley gave permission to kiss the bride, it felt nothing like the first time. Instead, he delivered a chaste and short little kiss but what did she expect?

The wedding breakfast looked more like a huge family lunch under a pergola attached to a reception room belonging to the resort. It had been Enzo's desire for the Church wedding in the traditional sense which prevented the whole affair from taking place outdoors where there would have been room for everyone. Raya seemed to be continually surrounded by a host of children, whom she encouraged. Watching her with interest, Bart didn't want to dwell on the deeper implications of her situation. He was unaware Mia his sister sat watching the watcher.

'You will make a great father one day,' Mia watched her own little dears playing on the grass as she spoke. 'Soraya looks like she's ready to be a mother now,' Mia said quietly, still watching her brother who by now sat scowling and chewing his lip. Raya, like an errant child picked candy flowers from their wedding cake giving one each to a group of eager little hands and laughing and chatting as she worked.

Halfway along the table Carl, Mia's husband as well as Bart's right hand, sat deep in conversation with Bob Costa. Joe and Maria joined them. Maria commented on how frail Enzo looked and everyone noted he didn't stay for the breakfast. Bart had half an ear on both conversations, noting Sammy regaling Father O'Malley with some story. Looking at his watch Bart decided the time for him and Soraya to leave the feast had arrived. Ignoring his sister, he strode across the grass grabbing his bride by the hand. 'I think we should say our goodbyes and leave,' he said, half under his breath, Raya stood firm.

'Why? Are we going somewhere?' the mischief in her face warmed him and fully aware all eyes were on them he scooped her up in his arms and kissed her thoroughly. She could hear male laughter, so she responded hungrily, the spectators be damned. Bart pulled back breathless and frustrated. She plays dirty but I'll play her game.

'You'll keep princess, we've got a plane to catch.' Seeing he had everyone's attention and it had gone three in the afternoon he said, 'my wife and I thank you for today. We'll be home next week for the board meeting. Arrivederci.' The Mercedes drove them to Bella Vista on the other side of the island.

Raya found her bags already packed and a new dress, a soft peach-coloured floaty number laid out on the bed. She freaked out.

'What's going on? you never told me we were going away,' she accused. Frustrated he shook his head.

'I made a sudden decision. I thought we could get to know one another and discuss our situation. For the benefit of others, you can call it a honeymoon. We leave in half an hour we're going to Melbourne.' A honeymoon put a completely different complexion on the situation, she didn't dwell on it.

'I haven't been to Melbourne in years,' she said excitedly, pulling her hair up into a loose bun.

'Don't,' he covered her hand with his. 'I liked it the way you wore it earlier. Please leave it.'

'I need it tidy at least for travelling. This isn't part of our agreement,' Raya complained.

'You can add it to the list of things to be discussed.' She looked up at him through her thick lashes. Oh, mercy there's a list? The man is so bossy.

As they boarded Bart's jet she saw Carl Moretti, Bob Costa and Joe Kelly were joining them'.

'Looking forward to your honeymoon Mrs Lombardi?' Carl smirked.

'Some honeymoon, I didn't realise the three musketeers were coming too,' she countered.

'At least we're not the three stooges,' Joe laughed, and Raya smiled.

'Yet,' she said, and Joe realised Raya would be no walkover.

Chapter Nine:

The trip to Melbourne took four hours and a half hours flying time plus a fuel stop. The men talked business in hushed tones while Raya slept most of the way, bored out of her brain. At one point she watched a movie.

A limo picked them up at the airport and drove them and the three musketeers to the Grand Hyatt in downtown Melbourne. By nine pm they were settled in their suite. After sleeping most of the trip Raya felt ready to go out on the town.

'I've got an early meeting tomorrow; in fact, I'm tied up most of the day.' Bart told her plainly as he removed his shoes and socks. 'I've ordered us room service; we'll get an early night.' He heard her sigh loudly.

'Is this how it's going to be from now on? Well let me tell you something Mister. If I was your real wife, I wouldn't put up with this crap.' Grabbing a pillow from the king size bed she threw it at him.

'Well listen up Mrs Lombardi, you are my real wife, and I won't be sleeping on the floor tonight.' He stood barefoot; arms folded across his bare chest. Horrified she stood watching him watching her. It appeared to be a Mexican standoff.

'But in our agreement, you said you wouldn't touch me,' she said stunned. He didn't blink.

'What agreement? Where is it written I wouldn't touch my wife?' This sounded unbelievable.

'You said you wouldn't force me...'

'I have never forced any woman and I won't start now. When I make love to you, you'll be begging for it.'

'Dream on you arrogant shit,' she sniffed, and he laughed.

'What happened to I'll make the conscious choice to love him every day?' he said, feigning a sing song female voice.

'You said we'd be able to get an annulment no problems, then I'll find somebody who cares,' her voice cracked, like she didn't quite believe it anymore.

'Yeah, and in the meantime suck it up princess. I've got a business to run.' she harrumphed at his words and slammed the bathroom door. When she finally came out, room service had delivered their meal; a huge antipasto platter, two gourmet pizzas tea and coffee.

'Whose army are we feeding?' she asked sardonically, pulling her wrap around her, wishing she knew where this trousseau came from, because there could be no possible way, she would have chosen any of it. While all the labels were known designers, the clothes were a little too provocative for her taste.

'No army, but I thought I might ask the boys ...' his head connected with another pillow, and he smirked, grabbing the pillow. 'I thought you'd appreciate company,' he said still smirking. 'You need to eat; you hardly ate a thing at brunch, and you had no breakfast.'

'If you fatten me up, I won't fit any of these clothes you've bought me. To be frank I don't care, they're not my choice,' she sniffed, the hauteur back in her voice.

'I didn't choose them for you. I chose them for me,' he cut her off.

'When did you get the chance to shop. You've been on the island with me this last week?' she asked.

'My personal shopper, he's very good. Knows my taste to the last detail.' A supercilious expression crossed his face. She wanted to slap it, but the thought of it halted her. Some strange man had purchased this trousseau down to the lacy intimate undergarments. She felt sick as she sat at the small table picking at the antipasto platter then without warning, she stood up and went to bed turning out the light on her way. Lying with her eyes shut she began to have serious doubts at the wisdom of this marriage. Somehow the civil service didn't seem real not like the full catholic nuptials. Everybody knew they were indissoluble. It had been a huge mistake to trust this ruthless man. The only difference between Bart Lombardi and Tony Romano so far seemed to be he hadn't drugged her or touched her. Yet, his Doctor Jekyll and Mr Hide personality had done a compete three sixty and she could pinpoint the time. It occurred on board his jet while he conducted a business meeting with his people. His people, suddenly in her mind they had gone from being the three musketeers to the three stooges. Only, two of them behaved like they had the call of duty in black ops and with their backgrounds it could possibly be closer to the truth than she wanted to think about. Too furious to think straight she decided she would deal with him tomorrow. The stress of it all made her tired.

When she woke next morning, she grabbed her phone from the nightstand where it stood in the charger, eight am and he had gone. From the look of the bed, he hadn't been there all night. She didn't care. Sitting up, she checked her messages, a text message from Mel.

'Give me a call and tell me who the dickens this Bart Lombardi bloke is? What are you not telling me girlfriend? I'm flying to Melbourne for the weekend. My brother's engagement party or have you forgotten? Weekend Wendy is now weekday Wendy as it's university holidays. She's running the gallery in my absence. Mel'

After showering and dressing in a turquoise wrap around soft silk dress highlighting every curve, she called Mel on WhatsApp. They hadn't spoken since the day before she married Bart on Nicodemus in the Catholic nuptials.

'Mel, where are you? I'm at the Grand Hyatt I flew in last night.'

'What are you doing in Melbourne? I mean I know you were invited to the party but with everything you've been through I just didn't think you'd make it. Love the dress by the way, I'd love to borrow it, only I'll need to do a month of no carbs. I swear I developed love handles from stress eating since you've been away, you know how I love pastries,' Mel said, flicking her wild red mane.

'All your talk of food is making me ravenous. I haven't had breakfast. Fancy getting brunch with me? We need to talk,' Raya pleaded, pulling a silly face.

'Sure, I'm fifteen minutes away. Give me another fifteen to change and put on some lippy. See you in the foyer in thirty,' She waved as Raya killed the call. What the holy Mary am I going to tell her

she wondered as she tonged her wavy hair into curls and applied a little makeup.

Raya had not seen the note from Bart saying he would join her for brunch at eleven. He thought she would sleep later. As soon as she had left their room Bart received a call from one of his people.

'Mrs Lombardi has left your suite, Sir.'

'Follow her and don't let her out of your sight, keep me posted Leo.' He killed the call cursing under his breath. 'I should have realised she wouldn't stay put,' He snarled at Joe.

'I told you to be honest with her. You can't expect her to hide in your hotel room on her honeymoon without you if she has no idea why its necessary.' Joe ran his fingers through his dark greying hair, frustrated because Bart could be so high handed.

'Until we hear from Chad Murphy and the Police again all we know is someone broke into her apartment and trashed it,' Bob Costa said evenly.

'And left a death threat in lipstick on her mirror. Actually, it had been her father's apartment and she inherited it.' Joe added, 'the threat is definitely directed at her regardless of anything else.'

'Except her brother is contesting the will and all her old man's estate planning has turned to shit. Plus, it would be a whole lot easier for Vince if Soraya wasn't around,' Bart countered in lawyer mode. 'From what I've learned from Chad Murphy, Soraya trusted him.'

'Trusts who? Chad? What exactly are you insinuating?' Bob asked.

'Regardless of Vince Ferrantino's challenge to the will, Chad and Soraya will know where the bodies are buried. Mark Farrington is from the same mould as Enzo. They didn't trust anyone he probably hid things, clues, even another will, a later will.' Bart's dark expression softened a little. 'It's what I would have done in his shoes.' Bart's phone rang, he answered it.

'I'm sorry Sir, I lost her.' Leo sighed breathless, into his phone.

'Gees Leo, she couldn't have gotten far in those heels she wears,' Bart sounded ticked off.

'Yes, true Sir, I saw her talking to someone and then she disappeared. I've been up and down the street but...' he tried to mitigate the situation.

'Keep looking.' Furious, Bart killed the call.

'Bob's busy checking the hotel security footage. I've spoken to the concierge and sent him a photo of Soraya; he'll notify us if she shows up on any cameras. Let's check the hotel ourselves.' Joe put on his suit jacket; his weapon now concealed in a shoulder holster.

Raya flew out of her suite and literally ran down the hall to the lift. Filled with an unnerving feeling someone watched her, she kept her finger on the door close button. She did it so the bulldog with a bald head wearing a dark suit, who eyed her up and down and stood with the familiar gate of a trained combatant, couldn't get in the lift if he followed her. It felt like sheer paranoia she knew, but someone did bang on the lift door as she sailed down to the foyer.

Alighting from the lift she ran to the entry where Mel stood through the open doors. The pair hugged and Mel pointed to her youngest brother Harry who had known Raya since their school days. He sat in his Porsche 911 sports car under the hotel portico. Seeing the guy with the bald head talking to someone at the desk Raya suggested Harry park the car in the hotel's underground carpark. She hopped in beside him and bent to attend to her sandal and hide from Mr. Potato head.

'What's going on,' Harry asked. 'Are you avoiding him?'

'He just gave me the evil eye,' she told him, and Mel laughed.

'You probably flirted with him,' Harry teased, then Mel quickly defended her.

'No Raya's had a couple of bad experiences lately,' she shook her head as Harry parked his car. Harry realised there had to be more to this but let it go for the time being.

The three of them took the elevator to the ground floor and from there they went to brunch.

'I'm shouting, the Brunch-Addict menu in the *Snooty Chef's Kitchen* is legendary,' Raya enthused, looping her hand through Harry's arm. 'You look smart Harry, where were you off to before I hijacked you to join us?' She grinned, it felt so good to have her friends around her. They were ushered to a table and left to peruse the menu.

'I had a meeting to attend, it doesn't start till one though, in dad's constituency office.' Harry O'Connor, a sun-streaked strawberry blonde with captivating baby blue eyes and a wicked sense of humour, smiled. He worked with his father with the intention of standing for the senate in his father's seat or another safe seat in the next five years. Mel literally itched to ask Raya about Bart but politely waited while Harry regaled them with his latest antics on the political circuit. After all, to Harry, Raya is almost a sister and a good friend but now she and Melissa lived in Brisbane he didn't get to see much of them.

Bart stood impatiently in the lift on the way to the ground floor having checked all the public spaces on the first floor when his phone pinged a text. Leo sent a photo of Raya and Harry walking arm in arm into the Snooty Chef's.

'What the hell is my wife playing at?' Bart asked anyone who would listen as he proceeded to the restaurant. Seeing Raya and two others he strode up to her and before she saw him, he bent down and kissed her proprietorially.

'I see we have guests for brunch,' he said smiling at Melissa and Harry. The server pulled out a chair for Bart and handed him a menu. 'I'm Bart Lombardi, Soraya's husband.' He offered his outstretched hand to a stunned Harry, who recovered himself quickly.

'Harry O'Connor and this is my sister Melissa.' Harry who stood almost six feet tall still looked a few inches shorter than Bart whose comportment assured he would never be overlooked.

'Ah, Melissa we spoke on the phone earlier in the week. Nice to put a face to the name,' he said remembering her from Tony Romano's restaurant. 'Soraya has spoken of you often.' Melissa eyed Bart with incredulity.

'When did you marry?' she asked watching Bart run his tongue over his teeth thinking how he might answer.

'Yesterday, we married yesterday, we had no time...' Raya didn't want to lie to her best friend.

'Because my father is dying, he wanted to see us married before he died. He has terminal cancer and hasn't got long, you understand.' Bart sounded sympathetic. Raya could see from Mel's expression she had a million questions.

'It is what our families wanted,' Raya tried to explain but Mel didn't quite buy it.

'What about you? Is it what you wanted and what about Paul?' Mel agitated now. Bart put a protective arm around Raya and pulled her closer to him.

'We wanted it didn't we?' he looked to Raya who smiled weakly. 'Don't worry the priest put us both through the third degree before he would perform the sacrament. As for Paul, really Melissa you know Paul is not for Raya. Our families go back a long time, and they had our best interests at heart and Paul's type is not what we're about.' Melissa felt unsure of what to make of this confident man. His handsome features were getting under her skin with his warm smile and rugged good looks. Harry seemed taken with him, but then Harry could be a social climbing names dropper brother or not.

'Are you telling us you had an arranged marriage?' Harry, who also graduated with a law degree, put it out there. Raya nodded, wondering how Bart would cover this one off.

'Yes, our parents arranged it and I planned to go about it the usual Australian way. But Mark Farrington died at the same time as my father was diagnosed with terminal pancreatic cancer. Soraya's father told her on his deathbed what he had planned, and she had a choice. As you know there were...let's say added complications. Security deemed it safer for Soraya to be under my family's protection.' Listening, Melissa did not feel totally convinced Raya had a real choice in the matter.

'Who deemed it safer? You?' she said harshly.

'Among others, including the Australian Federal Police.' Melissa sat stunned and her brother took up her position.

'Still, it all seems very sudden from what Mel has told me,' Harry tried to be the voice of reason.

'Yes, sudden but...' Bart turned to Raya 'look I didn't want to spoil our day but yesterday afternoon I received word from Chad Murphy and the Police, your apartment has been broken into and trashed.' When Raya gasped, he squeezed her shoulder, 'We believe they were looking for something and from a message they left I doubled the security on the Island. I think you gave one of my guys the slip earlier.' Dropping another kiss on her forehead he added. 'So, I didn't want you on your taking off on your own, Sorry I should have told you. It's serious.' Bart looked to Harry for support. 'There are people who envy my family's success, there is always someone wanting to take you down. I promised her father I would take care of her and wait until she had finished her masters before I pressed her to marry me.' She frowned at his choice of words. His promise had been something she had not known about. The brunch food arrived, and Raya insisted they change the subject and dwell on happier things.

Harry, who had knowledge of some underworld families, wondered what kind of business the Lombardis were involved in. Bart almost read his mind, saying his father Enzo Lombardi and Seamus O'Connor, Harry's father, had worked on several projects together over the years. Harry made a mental note to ask his father about it.

When Melissa returned from the powder room she announced,

'Mum is expecting you both to attend Liam and Sarah's engagement party. My God,' she faltered, staring at Raya's hand.

'What a huge rock does your finger ache?' She grabbed Raya's hand, 'how did I miss it earlier. Wow, it matches your wedding ring. Now matching jewellery took time and planning,' she gushed.

Raya pulled her hand back a tad embarrassed. He probably had his personal shopper choose it, or he really did own a diamond mine. For the rest of their brunch the topics were neutral and soon Harry and Melissa had to leave. Bart insisted they were his guests and put it on his tab, then politely asked what time for the engagement party the next evening.

'It said seven thirty for eight pm on the invite,' Raya told him. Before long they were on their way back up stairs. Bart had hold of her hand. In the lift he turned to face her, and she froze. Is she afraid of me? He felt mortified.

'Thank you I enjoyed breakfast with your friends.' he watched her frown. 'Thank you for making an effort to please me today.'

Was he taking the micky out of her? He certainly stood too close now invading her personal space.

'The dress, it suits you well, and your hair,' his voice sounded a little rough. 'It's beautiful, you're beautiful,' he whispered.

Hardly had they arrived at their suite when Mel sent a text. *Wow, he's a hunk he couldn't arrange a marriage for me, could he? Does he have brothers? friends? All I can say is how hard can it be making love to him? He can protect me any time he wants.*

'*Too bad he's taken,*' Raya replied and then wondered why she had said it.

' I suggest you get in touch with Chad and have a talk with him. He believed the burglars knew exactly what they were looking for.' Bart said. 'Then get changed into your swimsuit we're going to have a swim in the heated indoor pool. There's a comedy on at the cinema in town. We could catch it then find somewhere casual for a meal. What do you say?' he frowned and apologised, 'I know I behaved badly last night. No excuses, I'm trying to do what I promised my father.'

Raya didn't understand what seemed to be going on including in her own head. She had begun to have feelings for this man but sometimes she didn't like him at all.

'Chad, it's Raya is my home really trashed, how did they get past the security?' she asked, anxiously biting her lip.

'You mean the concierge? He's an old man in a uniform who couldn't knock the froth off a latte. They didn't hurt him, just bound and gagged him and left him in the broom closet, replacing him with one of their own.' Chad sounded annoyed, as though it had been Raya's responsibility to secure her building.

'Well, what does trashed mean? Is it habitable and what about my art collection?'

'Gone, the walls are stripped and trashed means wrecked. Whoever did this is making a statement loud and clear. They are not happy about something.' Chad was concerned, but not enough to alarm Raya or mention the death threat. '*You are dead.*' The words were written in lipstick on her mirror. The hot water tap had been left on, filling the room with enough steam to make the lipstick run a little. The red skull and cross bones under the words sent an eerie chill through his memory.

'Soraya did your father have a secret hiding place in the apartment? His safe has been cracked open and left empty but did he have another place he might hide something like important papers?' Now Chad's voice sounded kindly. Her father set a lot of store by this man, and she trusted him. Still, she had no idea what seemed to be happening or why.

'Yes, he did but the trouble is sometimes even he forgot what he hid where. I haven't really had a decent cleanout since his death, what with getting the gallery ready and all. I couldn't even get rid of all his things. I gave his clothes to the Charity shop, but I did nothing else. Please, will the police let you in to the apartment? If so, take photos of each room in detail and email them to me to jog my memory.'

In truth Raya didn't want to think too deeply about anything. The man standing next to her, far too close unsettled her, confusing her emotions. Agreeing to send her the email Chad ended the call.

It felt like the end of her world as she knew it. She vowed never to go back to her apartment. The small apartment building overlooked the Brisbane river. Her father owned the building and rented out three floors with two apartments on each floor. The basement floor housed parking space and storage. The top floor had been home to the late Mark Farrington and his daughter.

The Grand Hyatt swimming pool was situated on the ground floor, but access came through the guests' hallway only. Bart had booked it for one hour, for them alone. He used his key card to access the pool.

'I love the water and swimming,' Raya told him her eyes wide, her expression childlike, 'but when you didn't want to swim on the island I could understand. I hope you will tell me about your mother one day and how she died.' Raya remembered the woman had drowned but she knew nothing else.

'One day, but not now,' he said as he took off his robe and stood before her like a bronzed Adonis.

An assault on her senses. Tall, muscular and beautiful his male pheromones competed with his fragrance, sandalwood and citrus. Blinking back thoughts of how he might taste, she undid her fluffy hotel robe and taking a hair tie from around her wrist she pulled up her thick mane of honey brown hair and twisted it tightly to keep it dry.

Aware he groaned as she tied her hair back, she turned to face him. A distressed look covered his features, a mixture of pain and sadness. Her two-piece bathing suit an itsy-bitsy bikini, left little to the imagination but then he remembered she did not choose it. A rush of blood pooled in his groin, and he dived into the water to cool off.

Standing tentatively at the pool edge she watched him cover the width of the pool underwater, before surfacing.

'Jump in, it's good.' Watching her hesitation, he swam towards her and held out his hand. 'Come in I'll give you a dolphin ride.'

'What's a dolphin ride?' she asked leaning over. He grabbed her hand pulling her into the pool.

'This, put your arms around my neck and I'll swim with you on my back.'

'Ooh you lied, it's freezing,' she protested.

'Rubbish, you have to adjust.' He started swimming along with her floating above his back. After swimming a length of the pool, he rolled over in the deep end and she could not hold on. After a dunking, she let out peals of laughter.

'I should have known I couldn't trust you,' she laughed, pushing him in his hard chest. He too laughed, grabbed her around her waist and pulled her towards him.

'You're wrong Soraya, I want you to know you can always trust me.' Then he splashed her. This time, they both laughed as she grabbed and pulled him down with her, catching him off balance. When they resurfaced, she announced, 'except when you're playing games, you don't like to lose.'

This silly horse play went on for a few minutes before he became serious.

'Show me you can swim now, swim two lengths of this pool,' he directed. she knew she must do as he said. Determined to prove to him she could do it she set off at a good speed but by the time she turned to do the second length, she began to slow. Realising she shouldn't have set off at pace to begin with, only sheer determination allowed her to complete the task, breathless and tired. Standing at the finish line to meet her, he clapped. When her breathing returned to normal, he said, 'very good but I would feel happier if you could swim at least four lengths. This pool is only eleven point four metres, and an Olympic swimming pool is fifty metres long. Fifty metres is the minimum schools expect before they say a student can swim.' Although he sounded caring, she became annoyed.

'You can go to hell. you're always moving the goalposts,' she splashed him. 'Go cake yourself, nothing's any fun with you.' Turning, she swam to the edge planning to get out. He grabbed her, with one arm around her waist and pulled her hard up against him. Angry, she thrashed her arms around, trying to push him. A pointless effort he held her firm. Feeling the swell of her firm breasts against him his free hand then brushed her bottom. Breathing deeply, he felt like a bully a frustrated bully.

'I'm sorry I'm no fun, but I promised to keep you safe. You need to have at least basic competencies in the water.' Knowing his mother drowned but refusing to acknowledge her inadequacies, she harrumphed still wriggling. He finally let go of her. Raya towelled off quickly, drying herself before putting on her robe and moving to leave the pool area. In seconds he had caught her up and in a few more seconds they reached their room. She pulled off the hair tie as he opened the door.

Immediately she picked up her phone and checked her emails. One appeared with multiple images and a video clip from Chad. Opening the video, she gasped. As it played out slowly, Chad scanned the rooms of her apartment holding his phone still on occasions for her to see the devastation and take it in. Couches had been slashed and stuffing bulged out from them. Many pieces of art were missing but interestingly there were still some quite valuable pieces left. Plates and glassware were smashed, and furniture strewn about. Pot plants had been emptied and floor tiles shattered. The camera panned the hallway, and the reflection of the bathroom mirror could be seen. The message in lipstick appeared in reverse, a mirror image. She rushed into the bathroom and cried out as she held it up against her mirror to read the written words.

Like a child who had been finally worn down, she sobbed uncontrollably in a crumpled heap, on the bathroom floor. Bart realised what had happened, stood her up from the floor and carried her through to the bedroom where he laid her down on the bed. Sitting beside her as she sobbed, he smoothed the wet matted ringlets of hair away from her face.

'I'm sorry, I didn't want you to see that message,' gently he ran his knuckles down her tear-stained cheek.

Slowly she stopped sobbing and lay still. Bart now lay beside her on the bed, both of . still in the wet swim gear and fluffy robes. He put his arm over her, she faced away from him but snuggled into his arm. He moved closer to her. Both worn out and drowsy they drifted off to sleep.

Chapter Ten

When dusk came, he noticed the night lights peeking in through the open curtains and then realised she had turned and had snuggled into him, her warm cheek on his bare chest, her fingers gently kneading his downy skin covering. The robe, she wore like a blanket. He could smell her skin and feel her soft thighs against him, their wet swimming gear now almost dry. Bending his head, he kissed her forehead as she turned her face up to him. He covered her mouth with his and she responded, wrapping her arms around him. Gently his lips played on hers softly his tongue teased hers into giving and taking. He felt the sudden hardening of her nipples which he could no longer ignore. He kissed the creamy swell at the top of her bikini bra while his warm hands undid the itsy-bitsy thing, softly caressing her, neither spoke. Both were now wide awake. Sometimes Bart groaned he never hurried, simply moving slowly and gently. At one point he watched her face, noting her fully dilated pupils now practically obscuring her unique eye colour. Those dilated pupils told him he had aroused her, confirmed by the way she moved closer to him, pushing her body against him. his large gentle hands eased off her bikini bottoms as he kissed his way down her stomach. Lovingly he pulled back to admire her and run his hands over her now engorged breasts.

Raya refused to beg for him to do more as he had suggested she would. Instead, in a move that surprised him, she copied his actions. Slowly she mouthed his nipples he groaned and arched his back then quickly shed his swimming trunks. Alarmed at the sight of him, her eyes widened but still she said nothing. Instead, she reached out and touched him, running her hand up and down the velvety length of him.

Watching her totally absorbed expression he said in shocked surprise,

'you have never done this before have you?' her eyes grew to saucers. 'I won't hurt you my love, I promise you.' Raya wanted this man, but she felt totally conflicted. There could be no annulment regardless of what they did. Putting her arms around his neck she kissed him, worrying his lips with hers, nibbling his earlobes and down his neck. Running his hands over her bottom he pulled her close and gently massaged her feminine core until she let out a moan against all her best plans. Filled with desire Bart smiled and continued until, breathless and shuddering her traitorous body convulsed in pleasure, then while she moved into the emotional stratosphere, he positioned himself over her, and slowly and gently he entered her. Together they moved, gently at first as her heightened senses inhaled the smell of him. Her tongue tasted his salty neck and her eyes closed in a new pleasure the feel of him inside her. Rhythmically they moved against each other like yin and yang. Complementary forces of pleasure grew with an intensity she never would have believed possible until it erupted inside her. He climaxed filling her with his seed. She shattered in tremors of pure pleasure.

When Bart roused from his slumber, the room appeared dark except for the city's light polluting the sky. The sharp realisation he lay alone in their bed made him sit bolt upright. He relaxed when he heard the familiar voice of the national news' weatherman coming from the adjoining lounge room. Pulling his robe around him he went to investigate. Raya sat dressed in a soft skirt and cashmere top, her feet bare, her wet hair wrapped in a towel.

'Great you're awake. Now I can dry my hair properly, I shampooed it and towelled it dry but...' she shrugged. Nodding, he told her he'd be five minutes. True to his word, he returned showered, dressed in black jeans, and fine merino jersey wearing tan suede boots. The familiar cologne of citrus and sandalwood preceded him into the lounge. Taking her hair dryer from her, he sat down beside her and started drying her hair, as if he did this job regularly.

'Are you hungry?' she asked, 'because we haven't eaten since ten this morning.' She passed him her hairbrush.

'Sometimes other appetites need sating,' he croaked. Instantly she swung around to look at him wet hair flying in the effort. Before he could elaborate, they heard a knock on the door of their suite. Bart stood and opened the door, letting in Joe Kelly who acknowledged her with a smile.

'I've spent the day doing due diligence on the South Pacific resorts. You were right they have a huge cash flow problem, mainly due to under capitalisation and the fact they overreached themselves when they purchased an island off Fiji. The parent company is registered in the Cook Islands which technically are administered by New Zealand but used as a tax haven by offshore companies.' Joe perched on the end of the settee, watching as Bart carefully dried and brushed Raya's huge mane. She sat on the carpet at his feet. The incongruity of the situation was not lost on Joe who passed no comment on the domestic scene playing out in front of him.

'So, they can't be laundering money then?' Bart asked casually.

'They could be and stopped because the Criminal Investigation Commission and the Feds have been blowing smoke up their arse trying to flush out irregularities. Carl's had forensic accountants trawling through their books for 'one of his clients.' Joe made punctuation marks in the air, 'something's off but what, he's not sure yet,' he said putting one leg over his knee as though to inspect the sole of his shoe.

'How long before they go under do you think?' Bart turned off the hair dryer and continued brushing her hair as though he were grooming a pet. 'I'm of a mind we should wait till they're seriously haemorrhaging money, then go in for the kill and offer them a silly cash deal,' Bart said.

Raya took the brush from him then sat on the settee next to him her beautiful long hair soft and shining.

'I'm not sure, Bob should have a better feel for it. He used to be the Feds fraud man after all. Look boss we're about to go down and get a meal, have you eaten?' Joe asked.

'Soraya and I thought we would go out somewhere,' Bart said, and Raya lifted her head. This had been the first she knew of it. He had decided for her.

'Leo can cover you. The Feds will give us a couple of their security blokes for tonight, but only for the hotel, they told me.' Joe stood and made his way to the door.

'To be honest, I don't feel liked going out tonight but tomorrow I must go shopping for an engagement present for Liam O'Connor and his fiancée Sarah.' Raya picked up her hairbrush and dryer, 'also I'm not sure what I have to wear as the party is black tie.' she said honestly.

'That can be arranged.' Bart showed his Jekyll and Hyde personality. Then he turned to Joe who stood with his hand on the door handle. 'Do you think you could get into the Regent where Senator O'Connor and his wife are hosting this party tomorrow?' Bart grabbed Raya's hand almost as though sensing her disapproval.

'Yes, I have a few contacts in the senate security team. But don't worry about it there will be plenty of security there. Bob and I will be in the a la carte restaurant if you need us,' Joe said nodding acknowledgement to Raya before he left them.

'What's the big deal? My apartment is in Brisbane. Burglars are not going to travel interstate to make good on a threat meant to scare me,' that it had worked, she would never admit to him. 'Please can we just go downstairs and get some food, I'm ravenous.' The last thing Raya wanted right now was to be left alone with Bart. She couldn't deal with what happened between them, this could not be happening. She now had feelings for this man.

Bart seemed amused. 'Get some shoes on and we'll be off downstairs,' he said waving her away with his hand just as his phone rang. As she left the room, she heard him say in a surprised happy voice. 'Rachel, I didn't expect...' he closed the door and dropped his voice. Raya felt as though she had been gut punched as she put on her strappy sandals. Rachel, the love of Bart's life? Joe said they were finished. He had even suffered a broken heart if Joe Kelly could be believed. Raya spritzed herself with fragrance and swiped on some lip gloss as she desperately tried to make sense of her relationship with Bart. Why had he lovingly dried, brushed her unruly hair, and made a good job of it she wondered, looking in the mirror.

Did he do it because Joe watched him? No, he started before then. Why did he close the door? So, she couldn't hear his conversation with Rachel? The bedroom door open and Bart stood appraising her.

'Are you ready now?' he asked as though he waited for her.

'Ready.' Why the hell am I being so damned compliant she asked herself, knowing full well the reason, because she had skin in the game. How did this happen? She never meant to feel anything for him, it had simply been bravado for spectators. Sadly, she didn't even believe it herself.

At the restaurant, the Maître de ushered them to a private corner with views of the city. Studying her carefully as she walked ahead of him, Bart could smell her fragrance and noted its similarity to her shampoo. Remembering the feel of her long soft hair between his fingers he wanted to reach out and touch it again. It looked quite different now from when they made love. It had been a wild wispy mess then, but he didn't care, he didn't even care her mascara had run from crying because she wanted him. Her body had sent him the signals. Why would he ignore them. Only a fool would have ignored them, and he could never be called a fool. Sitting opposite her he admired the apple green cashmere top with its figure hugging lines and sleeve to the elbow. The scooped neck showed no obvious cleavage, she would never wear anything like that. A little pale flesh at the top of each bosom teasing his senses was different, just enough to remind him of the feel of her. With an effort he looked into her eyes he announced in his practiced arrogant tone. 'Shall we talk about it, or just let it crop up?' Heat flushed her cheeks and she hesitated, searching for a smart answer. Fortunately, the server came to take their order. Without missing a beat, she asked about the fish of the day. Bart smiled; he recognised her stalling techniques.

'Thank you, we'll both have the pan-fried barramundi and panzanella and a bottle of prosecco' he said in an effort to deal with everything at once, so they could have some privacy.

'Why are we in Melbourne?' she asked, not wanting to address the elephant in the room. 'Is it because you have business here?' He nodded narrowing his eyes wondering what she might be planning. She had heard Joe talking so it should be obvious what they were doing here.

'Burglars didn't need to touch the doorman at my apartment,' she told him completely out of left field.

'Why not?' he asked, surprised at her jumping around with the topics.

'Because we have a helipad on the roof. You have to get to it through a secret staircase behind what looks like a bookcase in my room and another from Papa's room.'

'What are you saying?' he asked in a low tone.

'All the services are on one side of the building, like the air conditioning vents and so on. These services are fenced off and a garden appears to be on the other side of it. But it's main use is as a helipad.'

'Why the hell would your old man need a helipad?' he asked, his voice barely above a whisper.

'Why do you need a private jet?' she re-joined. Fair call, he thought but instead, he asked dismayed.

'What sort of businesses did your father own?'

'Property developments mainly, medium and high-density housing and apartments.' she told him before getting a little smart saying, 'didn't you do your due diligence on me or my father? I'm sure had I been penniless your family would have forgotten the so-called promise,' she smiled. Immediately his lips quirked, he loved her feisty nature.

'Well, we'll never know the answer to that,' he said, as the server poured them each a sparkling prosecco. 'Would you prefer it if I didn't mix business with pleasure?' he asked, reverting to their earlier conversation.

'I thought with you everything is business,' she said, sipping her drink.

'You thought? We've gone a little further than pure business now don't you think?' He held up his glass as if saluting her. It irritated her, how dare he? What game did he play? Especially, after he said he would never touch her. Their marriage had been strictly business, but too late now, she knew they were bound. If he decided, he no longer needed her for his charade, she would be heart broken. Remembering Mel's words, 'how hard can it be to make love to a man like him?' she looked away from him. Not before he saw a look of vulnerability in her face.

'Don't look at me as though you were defenceless Soraya, you wanted it as much as me,' his deep voice almost a whisper. The look of vulnerability, now more evident as he spoke to her.

'I'm a big girl,' she said with total resignation in her voice. It made him feel like a heel who had seduced her, still he wanted to do it again, over and over. But he wanted her to feel it the way he did. At the time, he felt sure she had.

Their food arrived and as their server set down the dishes a thought crossed her mind.

'I think I should go back to Brisbane and check out the apartment for myself. At first, I thought I could never live there again. Someone had violated my home. Now I want to go and check it out for myself to see if I can find what the burglars could not. My father completely refurbished the building from scratch.

It's a small sandstone ex-government building and architecturally unique. He bought it the year before I left home to go to the Germaine Boscardi Academy, seventeen years ago.' Sitting back, she gave a big sigh.

'I felt confident you would come to that decision on your own. I will take you of course,' he said, with his authoritarian arrogance.

'Of course, you will.' she said, imitating his tone. 'Will I ever be able to go anywhere by myself again? Without you or them,' she pointed across the room with an open hand in the direction of Joe Kelly and Bob Costa. His face changed losing some of its superiority.

'Not in the short term at least, until it's safe,' he assured her, and she harrumphed. Leaning over the table Bart took her hand. 'Did I tell you about the first time I met your father?' he asked, his tone a tad patronising. 'Enzo had been in touch with your father who asked to meet me. The three of us had lunch at the Brisbane Club.' Something curious appeared in his expression, 'do you know what he said to me?' She shook her head.

'When did this meeting take place?' She interrupted.

'When you were in Florence doing your master's about halfway through your first year.' He quickly explained, your father said, my Soraya is a good girl, but she won't do for you, then he smiled at me. She's not compliant like her mother, he said. No, she is headstrong and strategic.' Those words made her laugh.

'You can't say you were not warned. Papa would have been too polite to tell you, regardless of my heritage I'm Australian and won't put up with your machismo bullshit,' she laughed. Seeing her laugh warmed his heart and his face broke out in a beautiful smile. Flashing his straight white teeth enhanced by his olive skin, he enjoyed her gutsy attitude. 'What did Enzo say about this?' she asked, regaining her equilibrium.

'Enzo said you were headstrong because you did not have a mother's influence. Your father insisted you be allowed to complete your studies.'

'Really, like it had been your decision to make?' she hissed annoyance.

'Well, they both wanted us to meet when you finished your undergraduate studies. Only it didn't suit me at the time.' His honest admission surprised her, but she said nothing, knowing he had a long-time girlfriend, one Enzo didn't know about. Raya remembered her father insisting she travel with his sister, her Aunt Carmella. Thinking about it now she felt sure her father wanted her out of Australia for some unknown reason. Carmella, a fun aunty, had suggested Mel join them one glorious summer in Tuscany. Around the same time Carmella became ill and simply wanted to stay in one place. Raya became upset until she learned of her Aunt's prognosis, her cancer had come back after many years. Everyone seemed shocked, especially Raya, who never even knew her Aunt had been treated for cancer years before. Then Raya decided to complete a Master of Fine Arts in Italy.

'When did you decide you wanted to marry me?' Hearing the question made him close his eyes as though in pain. 'You didn't really want this marriage, did you?' she asked.

'Look we both understand what's required,' he brushed his knuckles softly against her cheek. I believe we could enjoy it.' She pulled away from his touch. 'Be honest with yourself at least,' he said. When the waiter cleared the table Bart suggested he send a selection from the dessert menu to their room with another bottle of prosecco. 'We're both more honest when we're alone,' he told her firmly, then stood up and offered his hand. To not accept it would have been churlish, so she played his game.

When they arrived back at their suite, Bart went off to phone and check on Enzo, who according to his nurse, still remained 'hanging in there'. Every time he had phoned to speak with his father, the old man had been sleeping.

'I think he's hanging on for some reason.' Enzo's nurse sighed before saying, 'we know he's in God's hands, but I swear he's not ready to give up and meet his maker just yet. Last week I would have wagered money he simply wanted you to marry, Mr Lombardi, now I don't know. He's not had any morphine for days, it's like he has a new lease on life.'

'I'm pleased,' Bart said and meant it. 'Why does he sleep so much?' he asked, concerned.

'Because he's old.' Nurse Duncan replied as though it were obvious. 'Tomorrow, I'll call you when he's had breakfast and is ready to talk with you. Good night, sir.' When Bart returned to the living room, he noticed the trolley with a selection of desserts and the open bottle of prosecco in an ice bucket. Picking up the bottle to pour himself one he noticed it looked half empty. Raya winked at him.

'I like this stuff. Normally I can take it or leave it, but this is very moreish,' she announced. Her eyes gleaming with mischief she set down her glass. Her look took the wind out of his sales.

'What about dessert?' he asked, 'Can I get you something?' She shook her head, but he picked a crème pâtissière with raspberries and passionfruit and leaned in towards her to feed it to her. Turning her head to avoid the confection it smeared her cheek. Annoyed she pushed his hand, and the creamy mess went straight into his face and over his mouth. Setting the remainder down on its plate he grabbed her with both hands and began kissing her and licking the cream off her face. Laughing and unable to move she sat until he'd finished.

'Oh, I had a puppy who licked my face like that as a child,' she said in disgusted amusement.

'Well, eat something or I'll feed you like a child.' His tone didn't sound quite so amused.

'You ordered it all you eat it,' she told him.

'You could have objected; said you didn't want any.' He picked up a small chocolate mousse.

'Bossy man, you never listen.' She watched as he took a spoonful of chocolate mousse.

'Try this,' he insisted as she pulled back, complaining he would ruin her beautiful cashmere top. Pleased she liked at least one item of her trousseau he continued to scoop up a hefty spoonful of the mixture and advance towards her. 'Take it off then because I insist you try a spoonful at least.' Seeing he meant business, she yelled 'wait' as she whipped it up trying to get it over her head and splat the chocolate confection hit her bare decolletage and slid down between her breasts, her arms still up in the air wrestling with the garment. As the cold creamy mousse slid down into her bra she groaned, just before he began to clean her up with his tongue.

Chapter Eleven

When the phone rang Raya lay in bed snuggled up to the body next to her. His long arm reached across and grabbed his phone. 'Nurse Duncan?' they both sat bolt upright in bed, 'what time is it, nine thirty? Wow, no-no it's fine, we er had a late night.' His lips quirked and his eyebrows did a dance at Raya who groaned and pulled the sheet over her head only to be greeted by his early morning tumescence under the sheet. She lept out of bed naked straight into their ensuite and left the door ajar so she could hear whether Enzo's status had changed over night.

Two hours later they were brunching downtown before they shopped for an engagement present.

Bart had been volleying numerous phone calls, which in fairness, he kept brief. Enzo, it seems now alert and keen to talk to him earlier, when the nurse phoned. Raya felt sad for Bart. If it had been her father ill with terminal cancer, she would not have wanted to leave him. Bart's relationship with Enzo felt altogether different from the one she shared with her father. She sensed Enzo had a cruel streak, he seemed hard, but she didn't really know him. There seemed so much about this family and hers she didn't know. Her father had kept her in the dark. If only he had been more upfront and open life would be simpler.

Raya felt it an interesting fact Bart that had changed towards her since they had made love. Sometimes he seemed gentle and affectionate, and other times, he became distant and dismissive. This confused her. Did he worry about his father or the death threats? Did he regret this marriage of convenience? He had been right, she wanted him to make love to her as much as he wanted it. They were drawn to each other, but a marriage predicated on a lie is no marriage. When the time came, she would be the one to end it before he broke her heart. Bart had made his position very clear from the start, he simply had to do his duty, doing what his father expected so he would be the sole heir to the Lombardi business empire. His sister Mia had been given half of her share of the family fortune on her marriage to Carl and the remainder was held in a trust until after her father's death. Mia and Carl were both well aware the family needed Bart to run things. Enzo would not anoint him the heir apparent unless he married Soraya, the daughter of his long-lost love, Sophia.

'Soraya, Soraya, earth calling Soraya,' Bart coaxed her back to the present as she sat sipping her coffee, miles away in her thoughts. 'We need to get going my love if you want to get your shopping done. We've been here two hours at least,' he said, standing up from the table and pushing his cell phone into his pocket.

'I've not been the one on a mobile phone for the last hour. Sure, you had different callers, but really, it's Saturday and we're meant to be on honeymoon, even if it's not real,' she complained.

'It is real, it couldn't get anymore real. I've just got a lot on my plate at present with Papa ...' he watched her eyes glaze over. If he didn't have this excuse of his father's illness, there would be some other justification, she knew. Why bother setting ground rules? He would not be in this for the long haul.

Around four in the afternoon they arrived back at their hotel, dropped off their purchases, well, Raya's many parcels. Bart had continued with his cell phone attached to his ear, trailing a few paces behind her as she took every opportunity to shop. Everything from the engagement present, which she had gift wrapped and delivered by courier to the O'Connor residence immediately to a new outfit for the event, shoes to match jeans, she needed a change from dresses, palazzo pants and a silk kaftan for the island. Also, a new handbag and gifts, gifts for so many people. The only time he waited outside a shop had been the pharmacy, she said she needed feminine supplies. He didn't ask and she didn't elaborate he simply carried the shopping bags looking a tad awkward.

Bart insisted they get high tea at five she agreed provided he agreed they should be no cake fight and it could be room service. Raya kicked off her shoes and didn't intend putting any shoes on again until this evening. After soaking in the tub for half an hour, she donned a fluffy hotel bathrobe when the high tea arrived. Noting the food differed from the hotel high tea menu she realised Bart had organized it. Cucumber sandwiches, egg sandwiches, small savouries and a selection of small cakes and pastries.

'You're trying to fatten me up again,' she mused.

'I have a vested interest in those curves and so you can't afford to lose them,' he told her in his supercilious tone. She rolled her eyes but not before getting two club sandwiches and a cup of tea.

'I need forty winks after this just to get in the mood for an O'Connor shindig.' She took her plate of food and tea into their bedroom and sat on the bed. Sitting at the small dining table Bart continued with the daily papers he had picked up in town, while enjoying his late afternoon tea. It had been a productive day for him with the acquisition of a boutique hotel in downtown Melbourne. The heads of agreement had been reached and signed. The contract would be signed on Monday and the deposit paid. The contract, a mere detail could be faxed anywhere. Due diligence had been completed weeks ago and Carl had checked out every last detail. Bart knew the place well and had seen the photos online he didn't need to actually go there. So, when Joe turned up with Carl in his suite, he closed the door to their bedroom and let the men polish off the rest of their afternoon tea as they discussed the refurbishment plans. They were finished by seven. He went in and woke Soraya before he showered and dressed in his dinner suit for the party. When ready Bart turned on the TV news in the living room. Soraya felt nervous, the O'Connor's were like another set of parents and were sure to put her through her paces about her hasty marriage. Harry always had been his daddy's little darling and would have said way too much for Soraya's liking. When she finally emerged, Bart sat stunned.

He thought she had chosen a red gown, but this creation looked dark blue almost navy. The high-necked sleeveless bodice was made of navy lace, edged with a little gold trim where it mattered and sheer navy the rest of the way. The plain skirt nipped in at the waist and followed the curve of her bottom before softly draping to the floor. An elegant gold clasp held her long hair to one side, draping over her shoulder. The star quality of her makeup moved her to the next level. she looked stunning, a real head turner and she had married him.

'Soraya,' he said as he swallowed hard and walked around her noting the gown appeared sheer at the back from the waist up. Then it occurred to him she would attract attention and the press were bound to be waiting outside the venue. Hopefully Joe would distract them long enough for Soraya to get inside the building. Smiling at him she could see how handsome he looked when dressed up and coiffured, his dark designer stubble tickled when he kissed her in interesting places.

'What about the gift?' he asked.

'I sent it by courier. Mrs O'Connor phoned when it arrived. She invited us to Sunday lunch with the family after Mass.' she raised a thick shapely eyebrow at him. 'I said yes on your behalf. It will give you chance to meet the family without tonight's fanfare.' The thought pleased him.

A huge curious crowd had gathered outside the Regent in downtown Melbourne when their taxi arrived. Quickly Bart scanned her closely, noting the creamy curve of her breasts covered only by navy lace trimmed with gold thread, 'you're not wearing a bra,' he accused.

'I don't need it and since when have you become the fashion police? This is a perfectly acceptable evening gown even if it is one your man chose,' she sniffed as the footman opened her door. When Bart got out and did up the button on his dinner jacket, he looked around for Joe Kelly but couldn't find him. Instead, he saw Bob Costa who averted his eyes in the direction of Joe standing behind him. Bart sighed and caught Raya by the arm, claiming her. Inside the Regent stood a long greeting line; Liam and Sarah followed by the Senator and Mrs O'Connor, who insisted Bart call her Margaret, then Sarah's parents. The line moved quickly, there would be time to talk later when everybody was inside. Mel came up to greet them, her wild flaming red hair enhanced by her pale skin. In the emerald, green taffeta gown, designed to show her sexy curves and full bosom she looked like a siren. Little wonder, her parents had kept a firm hand on her, growing up. Still, she lacked Soraya's grace and elegance Bart asserted to himself.

'Oh, there's somebody who wants to meet you, I'll be back,' she moved quickly across the room.

'Tell me what Liam does for a career?' Bart whispered in Raya's ear. He felt they had met somewhere but wasn't sure. Circulating waiters served champagne and servers with canapes did the rounds.

'Liam's another Lawyer he works for the state government in the office of the premier,' she discreetly advised, accepting a glass of bubbly.

Mel returned this time with an interesting couple about their age. The pale woman with ash blond hair pulled up tightly looked familiar. Next to Raya and even next to fair skinned Mel she looked washed out. Her pale blue eyes lit up when Raya recognised her.

'Alice?' the two women embraced, warmly kissing each other on both cheeks. 'How long is it? It must be ten years.' The colour flushed Raya's already radiant face. 'Forgive my manners, Baroness Alice von Wassburg and her brother, Baron Felix von Wassburg, my husband

Bartolomeo Lombardi.' Bart gave a practiced click of his heels and a little bow. Felix put out his hand laughing.

'It's Felix, what a beauty you have grown into Soraya' turning to Bart he shook his head, 'your wife teased me mercilessly about my name, saying it should be a tom cat's name.' He opened his arms, hugged Raya and kissed her forehead fraternally, then said casually to Bart, 'I'm Liam's friend. I visited the O'Connor home regularly. Soraya's been one of the family for years during the school holidays.' Alice tugged at her brother's arm.

'Please excuse us, we'll come back and chat. I need Felix to introduce me to a friend of his.' As soon as they were out of sight Mel who had directed Raya to a small table at the edge of the dance floor whispered,

'poor Alice she's lovely but so bloody vanilla.'

Bart following behind them felt his phone vibrate in his jacket pocket and excused himself to visit the little boys' room.

'Thank God I thought we were going to have to visit the powder room ourselves. Tell me the truth, what's he like?' Raya smiled it felt easy to be truthful about the good bits. The real truth would freak her out.

'He's generous and the sex is sublime.' Raya had no one to compare him with but Mel didn't need to know. 'Bart is very caring, I'm so lucky. I could have ended up with cheating Paul or worse still, Tony Romano,' she thought, but she wouldn't discuss him with Mel. Just then she caught sight of Sean O'Connor, the second son, a general surgeon at the Royal Melbourne. Sean, now the only O'Connor male with no political aspirations. Seeing Soraya, he made his way across the dance floor doing a silly solo as he moved. The O'Connor features had missed Sean, thank God he used to joke. He had dark hair with a sprinkling of grey at his temples giving him a certain gravitas. Six foot and built to match he always had a string of women wanting his attention and why not? He exuded fun, talent, and absolute joy de vivre. At one time the O'Connor family all of them thought Soraya Farrington would become Mrs Sean O'Connor with their love and blessing. The last few yards across the dance floor he practically skated.

'Raya' he and Mel were the only ones who called her Raya. 'How are you?' He hugged her in a firm embrace, 'I swear you grow more beautiful every time I see you.' Mel rolled her eyes and sipped her bubbly.

'You're too late bro, she's married an Italian stallion,' Mel told him sardonically, he ignored her.

'Come and dance with me, so we can talk.' He eyed her gown particularly the sheer bits, 'mmm gorgeous.'

In the men's room Bart stood in front of the hand basins answering his phone 'Joe, what's up?'

'Guess who's been arrested for the break and enter at Soraya's home?' Joe asked triumphantly.

'Who?' Bart answered, playing his cousin's childish game.

'Tom Walker, Tony Romano's fixer, his hair must be falling out because he left no prints, but a few hairs and they got his DNA. I love this job,' Joe chuckled; the irony of the situation was not lost on Bart. 'He's not talking, and he's been arrested. I bet he rues the day I got Soraya out of Tony's apartment. The problem is she might have to give evidence if we want to get a conviction,' Joe elaborated.

'No, it's not happening,' Bart said as though he made those decisions.

'I have discussed it with the Feds, she may need to go into witness protection. I told them I would interview her on a video link with them, and we'd keep her safe,' Joe said.

'We need a few more people we can trust, can you hire them? I better get back to her, keeping an eye on Soraya is like herding a cat, talk later.' Bart killed the call and walked back to where he had left Raya. Neither she nor Mel were anywhere to be seen. Carefully scanning the crowd, he couldn't see her.

Melissa came into view and taking another bubbly from the server he strolled over casually.

'Have you seen my wife?' he asked. Melissa studied him. He had to be six three or four in height he towered over most people. She had googled him of course, he looked like a real catch. Graduated from the Australian Catholic University, Melbourne with a law degree then did a post grad in international studies also at the ACU, but this time at the Rome campus. He was purported to be the sole heir of the Lombardi empire of hotels, resorts, and property developments. Melissa could be jealous of her best friend, if she didn't love her like the sister she never had. Still, she could have some fun with Bart.

'Yes, some long lost love whisked her off on the dance floor,' she smirked and pointed to Sean and Raya. He held her very close, and they were moving far too slow to be dancing to the music. Curiously, he noted the affectionate familiarity with which they related to one another. Mel felt surprised by the look on Bart's face. Instead of the jealous rage she expected from a hot-blooded Italian, Bart's expression looked one of sadness and she felt bad for having led him astray.

'He's not really a long-lost love, he's my middle brother, Sean. He and Raya well let's just say they have always been close. In fact, right up until my parents learned she had married you; they were hopeful Sean would marry her.' Mel said wistfully.

'I don't understand, what about Doctor Paul?' Bart asked, confused and a tad annoyed he didn't know about this friendship.

'She would never have married Paul, she wouldn't move in with him, she wouldn't sleep with him, they really had no future. He's not the sort of man she would marry, merely a distraction. Sure, Paul's family wanted her, whose family wouldn't? Mine did.' she took Bart's glass from him and put it on the tray of a passing server. 'Dance with me Bart, I'll tell you what I know.' Taking her hand, he led her on to the dance floor.

'So, tell me about your brother Sean and my wife.' It sounded like an order.

'Those two always connected on the same level. He has used his career as an excuse not to marry but everyone knows he loves Raya. At one point when we were in Italy with her Aunt Carmella, I stayed with them, and Sean flew over to join us for a month. Raya was twenty-six and Sean thirty-one. We were all sure he came to Tuscany to ask her to marry him, even Raya felt sure, and Aunt Carmella had been quite blatant about it. I don't know what transpired between them, but their relationship changed from then on. Whatever happened she decided to go to Florence and do her masters. They stayed friends. At the time she looked shattered, absolutely heartbroken and when I asked her, she said, 'don't be silly, it would be like marrying my brother, Sean is family.' Mel added, 'Frankly it's bloody ridiculous and we all know it, but he gave the same line when he told our parents. Plus, something along the lines of, her father had someone else in mind, which may have been true, but her Aunt felt sure Raya could persuade her father if she really wanted to. We didn't truly understand until you appeared.' Mel had told him everything she knew. Bart looked stunned. He believed Soraya didn't tell Mel everything but then Mel liked to gossip, and Soraya kept things private.

As soon as Sean had whisked her off on the pretext of dancing with him, Raya knew he wanted to know everything. Everything.

'So, this man, your husband is he good to you? Does he love you? I mean you haven't really known him for long. Although I understand from Harry your father and his father had some connection. Do they still do that?' Sean looked at her lovingly.

'Do what?' she teased, knowing exactly what he meant.

'Arrange marriages,' he re-joined 'Mel told me about that Tony Romano character. Sounds like he used a date rape drug. Tell me what happened,' he asked as he gently moved his hand over her back. All her life she had been able to talk to this man and so she told him everything, except the marriage of convenience.

'He must be a special man for you to trust him and marry him with a nuptial mass after such a short time. I trust you will give this marriage everything and I hope he loves you like a husband should.' Leaning in, he kissed her cheek, then whispered in her ear. 'You know I want you to be happy, I can teach you the facts of life if you would like.' Laughing she pushed him gently in the chest.

'You did, we discussed them often enough, thank you.' This time she whispered it in his ear.

'Lucky man,' Sean laughed as the music stopped and Raya looked around for Bart.

'Come and meet him.' Raya looped her arm through his as she saw Bart.

'Bart, this is Sean, my favourite O'Connor,' she announced as both men smiled at her. Their twenty second appraisal of each other looked like curiosity and Sean said,

'I'm looking forward to getting to know you tomorrow at the family lunch.' The pair shook hands awkwardly and Sean excused himself. 'I need to find Patsy, my date.' The look he shot Raya seemed sad. They both knew this day would come like the end of an era.

The night went on much as before meeting and greeting, dancing, eating, and drinking. After supper Bart suggested one more dance and then they would go back to their hotel. They twirled on the dance floor.

'What did you and your favourite O'Connor talk about when you were dancing? he asked. She nearly dismissed their conversation until he added 'you two were very close and he obviously loves you.' Looking up at him, she could only see curiosity not jealousy, but then this sham marriage could never be more, and she wondered what exactly he seemed so curious about.

'To be honest, I told him everything, except I never said our marriage is bogus. I just couldn't bring myself to tell him the truth.' As she looked away, he noticed her lip tremble.

'I've told you before, it is real Soraya,' he said in a low tone.

'At the moment,' she sniffed.

'And it will still be in half an hour when we make love again.' He paused to look at her as she stifled a smirk in an attempt at hauteur.

Chapter Twelve

The doorman opened the door of their cab. Once settled inside Bart told her who had broken into her apartment in Brisbane and how he had been caught.

'Good, I hope he rots in jail, and I hope someone gives him a date rape drug and the works.' Her venom surprised Bart. 'Sean said I may need to give evidence in court to secure a conviction. He also said he felt pleased you were an honourable man,' she looked up at him through her lashes.

'What else did he say?' Bart said, fascinated.

'He said, you must be a special man for me to trust you and marry you with a nuptial mass after such a short time. Then he said I trust you will give this marriage everything and I hope he loves you like a husband should. He also said he wanted me to be happy and then jokingly said...' She turned away mumbling 'he could teach me the facts of life.' Hearing her mumbled words, he became annoyed.

'That sort of conversation is entirely inappropriate,' he hissed haughtily. 'It's far too intimate for you to be having with another man.' By now they had arrived back at the Grand Hyatt. Raya didn't wait for the doorman to open her door she pushed it open and strode towards the lift before Bart had a chance to pay the driver.

'Why didn't you wait for me?' He asked now furious she hadn't waited for him instead she sat inside their suite taking off her strappy evening sandals.

'Because you annoy the stuffing out of me,' she huffed. 'You wanted to know what we talked about, and I told you. Sean and I are like brother and sister, no not really true we're...' she struggled to explain, 'we tell each other intimate things.' she walked off into the bathroom and he began to remove his shoes and socks then disrobe. When she came out in her nightie with her hair all brushed out, he continued from the bathroom.

'Some conversations are only for husbands and wives,' he growled, and she laughed.

'Yes, well, we're not quite there yet, are we?' her voice sounding low the words were not intended for him to hear. Grabbing her with both hands he spun her around to face him. Heat radiated from his bare chest as it rose and fell with his laboured breathing. He stood in front of her in his sleeping shorts.

'I know we're not quite there yet. There is nothing for it, we'll need to practice.' In a flash her nightie had gone, and they stood skin to skin. 'You won't need him to teach you the facts of life my love,' he said before covering her mouth with his. Fiercely she pushed him back.

'Not tonight, Bart, I have a headache.' The old cliché sliced through him like a blade. He let go of her and she climbed into bed.

Insomnia had never troubled Bart before, however, at three in the morning he still couldn't get to sleep. Events at the engagement party were disconcerting at times and he rehashed them yet again. Sean O'Connor, the charismatic handsome doctor would have been ideal for Soraya, the chemistry between them evident and electric. What the hell had gone wrong? Had Mark Farrington really said he had other plans for his daughter? Perhaps he referred to the promise he had made to his old friend Enzo. More importantly why the hell did he care? Because he did care very much. Bart had been forced to confront his feelings, his marriage to Soraya, had supposedly been a business contract. He saved her from the dreaded Tony Romano who, let's face it is a criminal with convictions for extortion and money laundering. The man clung to the fringes of society and many thought him mafiosi. Bart needed the commitment of marriage from her because his father insisted, he settle down and marry this woman because it had been arranged years before. More importantly, if he didn't comply with his father's wishes then his uncle would run the Lombardi empire. All of this he knew ... but.

The problem being Soraya had not been privy to all of Enzo's wishes in respect of his son. Had she known the full facts she would never have consented to this farce. Enzo wanted a grandchild. This must be the only reason he hung so tenaciously on to life to see a grandchild. This grandchild became of paramount importance to Enzo to know the Lombardi dynasty would continue. The trouble with all of this came in the execution of the scheme, Bart had become emotionally involved, no longer rational. Soraya annoyed the hell out of him. She argued all the time, never the docile little woman. As the charade progressed, she became more feisty and passionate. When they wed in church she had sworn before God to love him. He felt she had been giving it her best shot until now. He too, promised before God to have and to hold, love and cherish her and now she had him under her spell. How the hell did that happen? The more he thought about Sean O'Connor, the more he realised the man would have saved her honour, and married her if honour, were the only thing at stake...he didn't get it they obviously cared about each other.

Bart tossed and turned. Despite a splitting headache and a list of unanswered questions sleep finally overcame him. His tossing and turning had disturbed Raya or possibly the growing fear of the unknown, she found herself wide awake and worried. Looking over at Bart she noted amused he looked out for the count. He emitted a soft continuous breath making her want to cuddle up.

Seeing Sean at the party had brought back a flood of memories, including how much she loved his fun-loving self-deprecating humour, his mischief and inuendo. What would her life have been like if she had married Sean? Mentally she shook herself from those thoughts because she knew deep down why it would never work.

Today when Raya walked down the isle it happened to be Sunday Mass at Our Lady of Mount Carmel. Bart sat beside her scanning the pews to see who else attended. The three musketeers had followed in a separate cab and were taking up strategically separate pews. All the O'Connor family sat together in one pew, except Sean who probably had business at the hospital Bart thought. In any case he would discreetly bring him up when chatting with the senator.

When mass finished and they were finally outside the church Bart noticed two taxis waiting. Joe mooched over to him and whispered,

'The boys are going back to the hotel. Bob will interview some more security people. I'm coming in your cab, but I've arranged to join the Senator's security detail, outside his residence.'

'How many times have I told you not to text in church?' Bart said, amused, wondering how Joe had arranged it. They stopped on the way to the O'Connor residence to enjoy a cup of coffee, allowing the family time to get home ahead of them.

The O'Connor residence was a federation style brick house, trimmed with white fretwork. It stood on a corner site and filled the complete block; the garage being built at the back with access from the street behind the short block. Above the garage, a purpose-built studio apartment had been built for Harry to use, when he came to Melbourne. None of the other O'Connor children lived at home. As they pulled up near the garage entrance Bart noticed the whole rear end of the house featured a modern architecturally designed addition. The addition became two storeyed and more than doubled the original house size.

The quiet street looked empty, apart from the federal security detail which Joe joined, as though he still belonged to them. Bart and Raya walked around to the front of the house and rang the doorbell. Mel greeted them. Before long, Bart stood deep in conversation with Margaret O'Connor about the success of last night's party and what she had prepared for Sunday lunch. Raya noticed Bart tasted her food, suggesting variations to her ingredients and Margaret stood laughing and giggling, mesmerised by his charm. Sarah, Mel, and Raya were being entertained by Harry, who poured bubbly as though it were tea.

The senator spirited Bart away as Sarah and Liam disappeared upstairs to check the room full of gifts.

'Call me Jim. Jim's what friends call me,' he grinned. 'Seamus is too Irish. He lifted up the hood of the BBQ to fire it up. 'The roast is cooking in the Webber over there,' he pointed to the far corner of the small neatly landscaped grounds. 'You can't beat it. How's your father? I told Harry I remember him well.' Bart twisted his mouth indicating his father's condition was not good.

'Let's just say he's prepared and insists he's had his three score years and ten.' Bart stood, with his hands in his pockets, legs apart wearing black jeans and a black tee shirt with a tan linen jacket and tan suede boots.

'But it's hard sir, I mean, I know I have big shoes to fill and a lot of people depending on me.'

'Now you have Soraya by your side,' the senator clamped a hand on Bart's shoulder in fatherly affection.

Bart sighed, 'yes, our fathers knew best there,' his eyes twinkled until both men noticed Sean had arrived and started hugging Raya as though he hadn't seen her in years. Before long the pair were deep in conversation. The senator eyed Bart curiously before saying, 'those two, we all thought they would marry. But he did the right thing for both their sakes,' he said, before going back to the butterflied chicken he had marinating. Bart didn't comment. He simply tilted his head and an 'oh' escaped his lips. The senator then felt forced to clarify.

'Mmm those surgeons put in a lot of hours, worse than a politician for a family man. Soraya needs a husband who will be around for the family,' he confirmed, wiping his hand on his black chef's apron before accepting a drink from Liam. Bart wondered why the man had even bothered to 'mansplain.' They both knew what a pathetic excuse he offered for what might have been.

The table had been set for ten, even though there were only nine of them. Margaret insisted she thought Sean might have brought Patsy his date from last night.

'She's working,' he explained, an excuse Bart felt sure. He probably hadn't even invited her.

Politics dominated the conversation and then the Senate Committee on Organised Crime. To which the senator added nothing not already in the public arena. He allowed his sons to talk before asking Bart his opinion on various events attributed to organised crime recently reported in the papers including the headless torso found floating in the Hinchinbrook Channel. Bart said quite simply, for years his father had been required to pay for 'security he never received.'

'It's the reason I went to the Federal Police who suggested I form my own legitimate security company. So, I headhunted trusted family members, all ex Federal Police to do the job. We formed our own security company. We use them in all our resorts and hotels. I did give evidence before one of those committees on organised crime,' he explained. 'Yes, they asked me about groups starting their own security companies, you know to get legal access to otherwise illegal weapons to cover their illegal operations.' Bart shrugged. 'These days we have managed to stay under their radar because of the way we operate. Having the Island is a huge part of who we are. Buying it nearly broke my father back in the day, but now I can see

its value. But how long we can afford to live there, is anyone's guess.'
They covered all sorts of topics. When they asked Raya how the
gallery business went, she smiled at Mel and both of them laughed
and high fived each other.

'Better than our wildest dreams,' she beamed, and Mel agreed.
'We each have our specialist area. Mel's is the everyman market and
mine is the high end.' Raya sipped her drink.

'They each have a place and we dovetail well,' Mel told her family.
Still, we've only been operating a few weeks.' Lunch had hardly
finished when Sean took a call requiring him back at the hospital.

'I'm coming to visit you two when your honeymoon is over,' he
told Bart who simply nodded, 'welcome.' By four in the afternoon
Bart insisted they go and felt relieved when Joe called telling him
their cab had arrived. Hugs and goodbyes all around and they were
on their way back to the Grand Hyatt by four thirty.

Chapter Thirteen

'I've thought of two possible hiding places for papers in the apartment,' Raya said, aware something bugged Bart. When she started to go into detail about exactly where these spots were he silenced her and called Joe.

'Tell him all the details,' he said as though he couldn't be bothered with trivia.

'Joe, I've remembered two places other than his safe, my father used regularly to hide things. The biggest space is a secret drawer in his scotch chest.' She scrolled through her phone at the pictures of each room Chad Murphy had sent her. When her father's dressing room came up, she pointed to the chest of drawers all the drawers had been removed and strewn about. 'They were empty anyway because I sent the clothes to Vinnies,' she said handing Joe her phone. 'But the bottom draw of the scotch chest has a false bottom in which he kept foolscap papers in manila folders. The only other place is so common they probably checked,' a silly embarrassed look came over her face. 'He kept money in the toilet cistern. In a plastic container of course.' Avoiding looking at Bart who had a bee in his bonnet over something, she turned back to Joe. 'I would be checking every single book in the big bookcase in his office. They look innocent enough, but he never read the classics and some of those might not be books at all. Even then some are hollowed out and they house his collection of ancient Roman coins. I've been meaning to deal with them but really, it's only been a few months.' She gave a shrug. Immediately Joe said he would go to Brisbane and search the apartment himself. The look on Bart's face and his general hard arse demeanour meant trouble. Joe politely asked Raya if he could speak with Bart alone. As soon as she had gone into their bedroom Joe played some music on his phone, so she had no chance of hearing their conversation.

'I don't want either of you there in Brisbane. Take Soraya back to the island or get away on your yacht. You can sail around within a few hours of Nicodemus in case Enzo deteriorates.' Joe watched his cousin's expression harden. 'What the fuck is eating you bro? You've been like a bear with a sore head ever since you got back from the Senator's place earlier today.'

'Nothing you need to concern yourself with.' Bart's high-handed tone hadn't diminished any. 'Okay organise the yacht. At least I can keep my eye on her on board the yacht.' He diverted his eyes to the bedroom door and Joe smiled to himself Bart had a lot to learn where women were concerned. From there the conversation focused on the logistics of the next twenty hours. By the time Bart joined Raya she slept soundly, and he knew better than to wake her.

However, at seven in the morning, he did wake her. Not being a morning person, she complained.

'We're flying to Rockhampton the jet is leaving Melbourne at nine this morning. You have thirty minutes before breakfast arrives,' his tone so arrogant she wanted to scream.

'Why did you even bother with me? Surely you could have arranged for one of your people to forge a marriage certificate and present it to Enzo. No wonder you had never married before, door mats are more difficult to find in the twenty first century.' Raya forced herself to get up and go to the bathroom. 'Are you going to be in a strop all the way to Rockhampton? I knew it would be too much to ask that we try to get to know one another. The honeymoon is a bigger farce than the wedding.' Harrumphing she didn't wait for a reply, she slammed the door. Bart was now both upset and annoyed by this mood. He had decided to give the nuptials his best shot, though given the way he felt right now he wondered why he bothered. He recognised how childish he'd been, but god dammit, he never expected to feel the way he did. As for the green-eyed monster appearing at the same time as Sean O'Connor, there could be no rational explanation but then he didn't feel like being rational. The security guy, Leo, had sent Bart a picture of him and Soraya in the hotel hallway in their fluffy robes, on their way back from the pool. Also, he attached some smart quip about his macho image and never being seen dead in a dressing gown before he circulated around the Lombardi network. Bart wanted to punch out his lights, he did look bad. Texting a reply saying kill those bloody photos or you'll be looking for another job would not be the way to deal with it. But still, he did it. Joe received a copy. He would never let Bart live it down.

Raya emerged from the bathroom just as breakfast arrived. Noting she did look good in her fluffy robe, he wanted to rip it off her as soon as the breakfast server left. However, her look bored through him with the pain of a red-hot poker and his passion shrank away.

'Are the three stooges coming with us to Rockhampton?' she asked imperiously.

'No, they are only going as far as Brisbane; we'll fly on to Yeppoon pick up the yacht and go sailing for a few days.'

'Really?' she asked suddenly enthused by the idea even though she wanted to ask, are you sure you can spare the time?

Soon they were in a taxi on the way to the airport. Both appeared very subdued and stayed so for the whole two and a half hours of the journey to Brisbane. As the three musketeers disembarked, she spoke to Joe, asking him to please bring her wooden art box and told him where to find it in the apartment. He promised to oblige, hoping it would still be intact.

From Rockhampton, they were in a car on their way to Yeppoon and on-board Bart's yacht within the hour.

This time the only crew she saw were Captain Theo Cooper and his wife Kerryn.

'No security this trip? she frowned; a tad anxious.

'I can take care of you Soraya,' he told her firmly in the privacy of the master cabin.

'But who's going to take care of you? What if some evil frogmen sticks a bomb on the hull of the yacht while we anchor to sleep?' Her anxiety level went up a few notches at the thought of it. Instinctively he pulled her towards him burying his face in her neck to hide his smirk. She cares about me, he thought.

'If that happens, then we'll meet our maker. Just as well we went to confession and mass on Sunday.'

Suddenly she pushed him away. 'Oh, I'm so stupid, you wouldn't take this vessel anywhere without security, it's worth millions.' Now she could see the expression in his eyes, mirth. 'You were laughing at me,' she accused. 'Well, I suppose it's better than the grumpy mood you were in earlier, why? What is your problem?' As if a switch had been flicked on, his strop resumed.

'Don't exaggerate Soraya, you're a drama queen,' he accused.

'This is not what I planned for my life. I miss my friends,' she said, in pure frustration, normally not one for a pity party.

'You have spent the entire weekend in the company of your friends,' he said annoyed. He too had a life before his family obligation to marry this annoying spoilt woman who clearly preferred someone else's company.

'I'd say there is one friend in particular you miss, and we both know marriage to him would never have worked.' he said, dropping his pants, and changing into shorts and tee shirt. The internal phone rang on the night stand he picked it up, listened and said, 'thank you.' Then turning to the petulant Raya, he advised 'lunch is served in the main salon.'

Sitting in the shorts she had purchased on the big shopping spree, with her shirt tied in a knot at her midriff and feet bare, Raya felt out of sorts. Fidgety and really hungry, because out of her normal routine she became bored and fractious. Bart watched her fascinated, but heaven only knew why, she ignored him and her ability to get to the nub of things and turn them around so he became responsible for everything annoyed him, how could the woman run hot and cold? It had been a mistake to go to Melbourne. He hadn't done half the business he intended. Ever since she had caught up with Sean, she had changed towards him. Bart failed to recognise he too had changed. It had been a mistake to sleep with her after seeing Sean and Raya together he felt cuckold and more than a little envious of what they shared. Also, there he could see no time frame for this fake marriage. Only now, it had taken another turn no longer fake it had become very real and quite indissoluble. Hardly eating a bite his mind raced desperately wishing things were different. Enzo seemed to have gained a new lease on life since Bart had married Soraya, maybe he would convince her to stay with him until Enzo died. He never wished his father dead, still life is always easier with certainty. Enzo often said the only certainties in life were death and taxes. Work hung over his head like a giant thunderclap. It wouldn't kill him, but he felt its ominous weight. The sale of the tired boutique hotel now completed it badly needed refurbishing. The refurbishment urgently required his attention, time, and money.

Raya's demeanour seemed to improve as her hunger was sated.

'Eat something the food is wonderful. I used to believe food is always wonderful if you don't have to prepare it. I don't think so anymore, I really want to cook my own food again,' she prattled on like a chatty child, until he interrupted.

'You like to cook?' he asked, incredulous.

'Of course, I'm not the spoiled brat you believe I am. Which reminds me I must work this afternoon. There's an online auction in New Zealand at the country's leading art dealer's site. It starts at four in the afternoon New Zealand time. Mel says there are several Russian icons in the catalogue. I could be tied up for some time. The auction is in real time by zoom. I need to prepare. They sent the code when I registered.' She poured herself another cup of tea.

'Use my office if you like, besides I don't want any part of the master cabin filmed online. My office is set up for such meetings,' he said sounding businesslike.

The Pacific ocean and sunshine provided a beautiful afternoon as they sailed into a safe bay at Great Keppel Island where they dropped anchor. The sun glistened on the water and the bunny pad looked inviting, it extended out over the water and provided a great springboard for jumping off into the sea or sunbathing. Bart enjoyed lying on it on a lounger reading a book. It had been a very long time since he spent time reading. Aware Raya had proved not particularly confident in the water he didn't push it.

As Raya sat in front of her laptop at Bart's desk, she felt good, having changed into a chic pink sleeveless shell top of dupion silk. Today she wore her hair twisted softly in a stylish updo enhancing the stunning south sea pearl drop earrings with their magnificent lustre, a present from her father. Her flawless makeup ensured she looked the part, providing she didn't stand up and show off her fraying denim shorts and bare feet. Earlier she had printed off her buyer's number and attached it to a card. The catalogue offered two items of interest, the first a black Madonna, a small icon, from the Russian 'golden circle' of churches. The second, a miniature of Catherine the Great, authenticated at two hundred and fifty years old and painted on vellum and set in a nine-carat gold frame. It looked like a truly unique piece, and she wanted it, if not to sell in the gallery, then for her own private collection.

The auction went on long and tediously, some items were passed in, others sold at eyewatering prices, beyond her budget. As the lots of interest were in the last section of the sale Raya sat patiently waiting, afraid to leave and miss out as there had been the occasional bargains.

At one point Bart put his head around the door to watch her quietly without her knowledge. Surprised at the picture those at the auction would see, a beautiful woman elegant and poised, unless you saw her tanned shapely legs in fraying denim shorts, displaying bright red toenails atop her bare feet. Withdrawing as quietly as he could it occurred to him just how seriously she took her business.

For Raya, the auction ended at four o'clock Queensland Australian time. It became obvious to Bart she wanted to talk about it, and she sounded upset.

'I managed to buy the Black Madonna and pay through the nose for it. I wouldn't care had it been the miniature of Catherine the Great. But the bloody thing got passed in, it didn't make the reserve, there were only two of us bidding. I bet the other bidder gets it, some dealer in the UK. I went to the limit of my budget and by rights they should talk to me first. I'm sure I'm the highest bidder.' Her disappointment palpable.

'This calls for a drink, in commiseration. I'll get a bottle.'

Soraya walked out on to the deck and slowly breathed in the sea air. Thoughts of the auction vanished from her mind as she surveyed the beautiful beach. The palm trees were illuminated by solar powered party lights. They looked incongruous on the deserted island. When Bart returned with the bubbly in an ice bucket and two glasses, he looked so happy and so handsome. Before he had a chance to open the bottle his cell phone rang. As usual he took the call, Raya heard him acknowledge Joe. They spoke for several minutes before he turned towards her.

'Joe has found the secret drawer full of papers. Files, shares and some things Joe doesn't understand.' He looked at her in dismay. 'He will meet us on Nicodemus tomorrow. Oh, and he'll have your paints,' he finished in a quiet voice. 'Also, Enzo's not good. He had a bad day and he's refusing morphine.'

Without thought she reached up and stroked his face.

'I'm so sorry, we can go back sooner,' Raya said, accepting a glass of bubbles from him.

'No need we'll have breakfast with him tomorrow. There is one thing I want from you Soraya,' his eyes were almost pleading. 'Tell him you are happy and try and be convincing. He won't last long, and I want him to think he made the right decision for me.'

'Anything you say, he can't have much time now.' She turned to avoid his eyes. 'I'll stay with you until he goes then... well we'll see.' No one could be more honest, and Bart thanked her. For several minutes they sat in silence each in their own thoughts. Joe had learned things with the power to change Raya's world forever. Bart worried if he didn't tell her she may well find out he kept secrets from her, and she would never trust him again. 'Without trust we have nothing,' were the words she had used to describe her relationship with Paul. Looking out at the beautiful safe harbour of Great Keppel Island he decided that after dinner he would tell her.

Raya's heart went out to Bart, and she wished they had been introduced the way her father wanted. But it didn't happen and now they were bound together for no man to put asunder. Only he didn't love her. He had been kind and thoughtful at times, cold and arrogant at others. Really, she knew nothing about him a wife should know like how his mother died. what he wanted from his life, is he just moody or did she do things to upset him? It mattered not. What Raya wanted from a husband she did not have. Someone to share her life with, build a home, have children with, and enjoy the normal mundane things, like cooking, bathing their babies and watching TV together. Jetting around on super yachts had never been in her plans. Poverty had not been on her horizon either. A comfortable life without extremes is what she imagined when she thought of herself and Sean.

On their Italian holiday, when he came to visit her in Tuscany, he told her he loved her, but he could never marry her because he was gay. He said he would never come out while his parents were alive. They both cried when Sean insisted, he had told her because to him sex had always been a huge part of a real relationship and she deserved a husband who could truly love her as a woman. He could not be that man. They had always been close and would always enjoy a unique friendship. Sean insisted he had denied his sexuality for years. He had met someone who understood that and shared it. Now he wanted her to understand and accept him for the man he had been born. Both understood why other catholic men in his situation became priests or married, simply denying their true feelings. Raya vowed to keep his secret because Sean had always been a truly selfless good man. All the time she railed against a God who made him this way yet forbad him to behave the way he had been made. When Sean left her in Tuscany that summer, she felt bereft. Neither had considered what they would tell their family or friends who were left assuming they had a fight, and it would blow over. Mel pestered her relentlessly until Raya said he's met someone, another doctor. Sean agreed with Raya saying it didn't last. The only person who felt relieved had been Mark Farrington who never warmed to Sean. He told Raya he had other plans for her and expressed his pleasure when she decided to do a master's degree in Florence.

Bart watched Raya who sat daydreaming her mind miles away. He noticed her eyes well up and she blinked back a tear. Mistakenly he thought it may be for Enzo instead she mourned an impossible relationship with Sean.

Chapter Fourteen:

Kerryn Cooper served them dinner in the main salon. She noticed the forlorn expression on Raya's face and looked to Bart who shook his head and gave her a rueful smile. Squeezing Raya's shoulder, he encouraged her back to the present and their food. A fresh seafood platter, along with a Mediterranean salad of feta, olives, cherry tomatoes of various colours, cucumber and red onion in an olive oil dressing with fresh ground pepper and sea salt. Served with fresh crusty bread and various side dishes.

Raya thanked Kerryn saying, 'doing nothing makes me hungry.'

'You enjoy your food,' Bart said, pleased she seemed brighter.

'I'm Italian, therefore I eat,' she replied as though the two were synonymous.

'Ah no longer Australian, how interesting,' he teased. She ignored him, and they ate their meal in silence. She suddenly felt flat. Now dark, they could see the small solar party lights on the shore looking like fireflies in the distance. A few vessels out at sea had lights showing and the moon shone, a small unremarkable crescent.

'Sorry, I'm suddenly quite tired,' she said, standing up from the table. 'I think I'll get an early night.'

'What no dessert or tea?' he asked. She shook her head saying goodnight and went below to the master cabin. She's avoiding me, why? Bart wondered

In the few seconds it took for him to phone to order a tea tray for himself in the master cabin, Raya had removed her makeup, cleaned her teeth and put on a nightie.

'Do we have to stay at Bella Vista?' she asked. 'I don't feel comfortable there.'

'What's wrong with it? You don't like my home? he questioned. What he really wanted to say was, you can redecorate it when Enzo's gone, because he had no idea what would be between them after Enzo died. 'What if we stay there for one night and I'll have Rosa prepare the casetta.'

Whispering a thank you, she slipped into bed and turned away from him.

When she woke Bart had dressed and sat at the small table reading the paper online. Looking out of the window she could see they were coming into the wharf at Nicodemus with its cliffs and white sandy beaches. It took her breath away. Bounding out of bed without acknowledging him, she showered and dressed in the peasant style dress he had laid out. Why does he do this? she wondered. It made her feel smothered and distrusted. She had to admit she liked this dress, with its bright multi coloured floral pattern and soft full skirt nipped in with an elasticated waist and an off the shoulder neckline.

'And good morning to you too my love,' he said sarcastically. 'Your headache all gone; ah no, the headache came the night before.'

Holy Mary, Raya thought, he annoys me with his supercilious attitude.

'And good morning to you too, my darling husband.' Her syrupy voiced caused him to smirk. He enjoyed her sense of humour.

'We're having breakfast at Bella Vista, five minutes till we disembark,' this time his tone was all business. In less than five minutes she did her hair in a loose asymmetrical braid, swiped on her lip gloss, and spritzed her perfume.

The journey to Bella Vista never failed to inspire her with its magical views.

Rosa had breakfast ready in the dining room and advised Enzo's nurse had said they could see him after breakfast.

Bart asked, 'Rosa will you prepare a casetta for us, so we can give Papa some peace. Also ensure the kitchen is stocked. My wife will cook for us,' his autocratic tone brooked no challenges. Raya watched Rosa's expression she did not look happy.

'May I look in the pantry or give you a list of ingredients?' Raya asked.

Bart then said he had a meeting with Joe this morning, and she could discuss kitchen matters with Rosa while they were busy. Raya protested, saying she needed to discuss with Joe what he discovered in Brisbane. She insisted strongly, Bart didn't like it and said no.

'No? What do you mean no?' she complained. 'We are talking about my home here Bart.'

Rosa, who had been serving the morning coffee almost slopped it in his lap. Raya recognising her angst added, 'marriage is about compromise, darling.'

Sighing audibly Bart sounded constrained in his reply.

'Do forgive me – darling,' he exaggerated. 'I simply need a private word with Joe first.' As soon as he finished eating, he left the dining room after excusing himself. Throwing down his serviette, he almost slammed the door in his huff. When he had gone Raya went to seek out Rosa in the kitchen.

'I'm sorry about him, he's in a strop with me. Don't you worry about it,' she said, putting her arm around the woman only a few years younger than her. Raya's little bit of reassurance had Rosa break down, sobbing and distraught.

'What's wrong Rosa? You can tell me I won't say anything.' Rosa took Raya's hand and the pair walked into the huge scullery.

'Promise me,' Rosa sniffed.

'I promise' Raya affirmed.

'My period is late,' Rosa sobbed.

'How late?' Raya asked, suddenly grateful the light spotting she had experienced over the last two days signalled the onset of her very irregular menstruation.

'Seven weeks, usually I'm regular and I have other symptoms too. My breasts are a little swollen,' Rosa gave Raya a pathetic look.

'Don't worry about sore boobs, I have gone eight weeks with no period and my breasts always swell whether I get the curse or not,' Raya tried to placate the young woman who would not have a bar of it.

'But my bosoms are not like yours I'm normally quite flattish,' Rosa said immediately embarrassed to have mentioned Raya's generous bosom. 'I always get my period every twenty-eight days.'

'You and Dion, have you been...?' She looked to Rosa who nodded affirmatively, 'what about contraception?'

'We ran out and it's not like we can get to a pharmacy or supermarket,' Rosa explained. Raya remembered she had purchased a pregnancy kit in Melbourne before her menses signalled its arrival.

'I have a test kit in my luggage.' Their suitcases were still in the hallway waiting to go to the casetta. 'Come on, we'll test you now,' Raya said, indicating the master suite.

Grabbing her smaller bag with her toiletries in it from the pile in the entranceway, Raya and Rosa went through to the master bedroom. Both heard Bart on the phone in his office, with the door shut. Raya locked the bedroom door and producing the pregnancy testing kit she told Rosa how to pee on it and then she said, 'good luck.' Rosa felt so nervous she misread the blue line as a negative test and held it up elated. From over her shoulder Raya told her the news.

'No Rosa re-read the instructions. You are pregnant; the test is positive, so it means *yes* you are pregnant.' Poor Rosa started weeping,

'Oh, mother of mercy no, my family will be mortified. They will disown me. They're catholic and don't believe in sex before marriage.'

'Stop crying,' Raya said sharply, 'you need to be strategic. Don't tell them. Would you marry Dion if he asked you?' Rosa nodded. 'Then go and tell him immediately. Time is of the essence.' Raya insisted.

'He's gone to Rockhampton to see the doctor for his knee. He injured it playing tennis. He won't be back for days.' Just as Rosa nearly burst into tears again, Raya grabbed her hand.

'You have bad toothache and need to see the dentist ASAP. How would you go?' Raya asked, thinking.

'Theo Cooper is taking some guests from the resort back to the mainland, I'd hitch a ride.'

'Then Rosa, you must do it. Organise it. Say you've taken some pain relief, but it might be an abscess and the dentist will see you as soon as you can get there. Text Dion and don't tell him you're pregnant. You need to tell him face to face. Show me where the Casetta is, and I'll get it ready.' Rosa frowned, unsure. 'I'm not incapable, I can fix a little house. Go, first give me your phone I'll punch in my mobile number so you can keep me posted.'

Hearing Bart calling to her Raya let Rosa out of the master suite via the French doors to the veranda. Then she calmly walked into the hallway.

'You called?' she said knowing the whole household would have heard him.

'We'll see Papa first then you can talk, to Joe,' he said almost pulling her towards Enzo's suite.

To their surprise Enzo was sitting in a chair in his dressing gown.

'Come in my son.' He beckoned to Bart who reverently kissed his father on the top of his head.

'Papa, I'm pleased to see you looking better than I expected,' Bart said in greeting. Raya stepped forward and kissed the old man on both cheeks.

'God bless you, Papa; I hope you're comfortable.'

'I am my dear. this is a good time for me. I wish I could see you everyday at this time, so I can really get to know you my new daughter.' His face lit up and for the first time Raya could see the familial likeness to Bart. She wanted to learn more about her mother from this man.

'I'll come and see you everyday at this time and we can talk. I'd like to very much,' she said honestly.

He gripped her hands in his and a warm smile crossed his face, 'Did you have a good time in Melbourne?'

'We did, well I did although I think Bart didn't get as much done as he had planned. He did take me shopping for an engagement present for my friend in Melbourne, Liam O'Connor, Senator O'Connor's eldest son. I think you know him.' Raya said in her normal chatty way.

'I do know him but how do you know his eldest son, Liam.'

'I went to school with the only girl in their family, Melissa. She is my business partner.' Raya told him.

'Ah right, I remember now, Bart mentioned her.' The old man seemed to tire quickly. Before long Bart suggested he help him back into bed. 'Look after her son she's more precious than rubies,' Enzo closed his eyes to rest, and they left the room.

Seeing the pair of them come out of Enzo's room, Joe indicated with his thumb to the kitchen and mimed drinking from a mug. Bart gave him the thumbs up. Raya shook her head. Minutes later he joined them in the office and pushed a mug of coffee towards Bart.

'What did you find?' Raya asked, a tad apprehensively.

'I found these files,' Joe opened his briefcase and pulled out three manila folders. 'Oh, and a bonus,' he handed her an envelope. 'Ten grand in the toilet cistern in your father's ensuite,' he said proudly.

'In a plastic container I hope?' she turned up her nose as though the notes were infectious or smelt.

'Yes, hidden under a tile made to look like the bottom of the tank. Only the ballcock didn't go down far enough. I've fixed a few here on the island so I know what they should look like,' he said grinning.

'Go you,' she grinned back at him before looking into the envelope. 'One hundred, one-hundred-dollar bills. Ten thousand dollars?'

'Yes, the bank confirmed your father made such a withdrawal two years ago. They record the numbers on notes of one-hundred-dollar denomination and especially if in quantity.'

'So legit then?' Bart asked.

'Yes, but not the only substantial withdrawal. He made many others subsequently; however, they were smaller denominations,' Joe said seriously, 'and regular.'

'What do you think it means?' Raya asked, worried.

'Either he was being blackmailed or liked cards and lost, or he's been paying the mob protection money. My bet is the latter.' Joe eyed her as he sipped his coffee. 'I've got the Feds looking into it.'

Raya covered her face with her hands. Once the mob got their hooks into you, they bled you dry or worse.

'What's in the files? Bart asked, although Raya felt sure he already knew.

'One is a document signed by Vince Ferrantino and witnessed by Simon Murphy, Chad's late father.

It effectively states Mark Farrington gave his son Vince Ferrantino half of his assets as his share of the family estate. Because these assets were handed over prior to your father's death, they had some convoluted arrangement to avoid gift tax. But everything is in order. This effectively quashes Vince's claim on the remainder of your father's estate.'

'Well good, because I want him out of my hair,' Raya announced firmly.

'It's not all rosy Soraya,' Bart said seriously. 'The transaction took not only half his assets but most of your father's liquidity in the remaining businesses. With little equity in those properties, he needed to re-mortgage. So along with these mystery withdrawals it means he was in dire financial straits.'

'Do you think it's the reason why he sold the chopper and made economies? He told me he needed to consolidate his assets, looking to his retirement. I never thought to ask. He gave me two hundred thousand dollars to fund the gallery, buy the startup stock and do the shop refit. He must have borrowed to give me the startup money. At least with Enzo having an interest in the building, it meant Papa couldn't borrow against his share of it,' she said confidently. Bart's expression showed little emotion. Joe however, narrowed his eyes and pursed his lips in his very policeman-like way of considering the facts.

'So, what's in the rest of the files, shares in a gold mine?' she said, trying to be funny.

'Close, a dolomite mine in far north Queensland. But it's in the ground, it's hardly like money in the bank. Although it's a useful commodity in agriculture,' Bart said dryly.

'I bet it's worth nothing in the ground,' she shrugged, and Bart smiled at Joe, Raya really is a princess.

'A great deal of Australia's wealth came on the backs of miners,' he said.

'Anything else I need to know about like oil shares?' a real Pollyanna, she simply couldn't get her head around the concept of being broke.

'There's the deeds to a banana plantation but you would need to actually eyeball the land, because my source says there are no banana plants on the place, the house is uninhabitable and there is an issue with water,' Joe said, as though he'd looked into it.

'Sounds like a liability. Can we sell it?' she wanted to know, and Joe shrugged.

'The good news is Chad Murphy says the contents of the apartment were insured,' Bart informed her.

'And the bad news is the apartment building is mortgaged to the hilt,' she said sardonically.

'She's a fast learner,' Joe acknowledged. 'The rest of the stuff is personal papers, letters and the like. You don't need to read them now.'

'Good because I'm mentally drained. What I don't understand is why Chad Murphy didn't know some of this already? He is my father's lawyer after all,' Raya took the manila folders from Joe as she spoke.

'At first, Chad thought some of this might be to do with his own father, who due to his illness, regrettably left his client's affairs in a mess. Chad applied to the courts to have probate delayed while he sorted through this. Also, Vince had his lawyer inform the Murphy's legal practice, a claim would be coming on the estate of Mark Farrington. A great deal happened in the last six months Raya,' Bart told her.

Chapter Fifteen

A knock on the office door distracted them. Bart opened it to Rosa, who explained she had an appointment on the mainland and intended going over on the resort taxi ferry which was leaving in one hour. She needed to speak with Mrs Lombardi before she left. Raya stood enquiring after Rosa's tooth ache, as she excused herself.

'Lunch will be in the garden at one, I'll be busy until then.' Raya gave Joe and Bart a weak smile. The two women walked together down the long hallway towards a large walk-in linen room off the laundry.

Joe stood across from Bart.

'You haven't told her yet, have you?' he sounded frustrated. Bart shook his head, he felt worn down. 'I warn you bro, Soraya is a very proud woman. The longer you leave this, the more likely it is to destroy you both. Bart agreed the fallout would be paralysing. Joe had been right.

'The bedlinen's stored in here,' Rosa ushered her in to the walk-in cupboard pointing towards the shelves of linen. A wooden ironing board had been set up complete with iron. Both looked like they came out of the ark.

'Do we do the ironing in here?' Raya asked curious.

'No, you don't - we do it, but there is another in the laundry room and pigeonholes, one for each family member. 'There are seven bedrooms and three suites with multiple rooms. The house can easily sleep two dozen people, but we rarely have many guests since Mr Enzo got sick.' Rosa picked up a large bundle of carefully sorted bed linen and towels. 'Follow me,' she instructed. The two women stepped outside and walked across the courtyard through a doorway and across another hallway, till once again they were outside. Set into the side of the hill stood the casetta, built of sandstone and perched high above Bella Vista. The two women walked briskly up a zig zag path so steep, they were both puffing and perspiring when they arrived at the casetta.

Raya could see from the depth of the doorways and window ledges it must be double brick, it felt so cool. A generous open living space looked over the bay. Four sets of floor to ceiling doors opened on to a covered outdoor living space, with the same perfect views. Overhead in the open kitchen, dining and lounge areas four huge ceiling fans whirred. At the front of the modern kitchen stood a granite countertop and beyond it, an oblong dining table with six cane chairs. The other half of the room made the living space, with two long sofas covered in white cotton brocade loose covers and topped with lots of textured cushions in earthy tones. The floor looked like real Italian terracotta tiles. Between the sofas sat a long-wrought iron coffee table topped with glass. On top of it sat a brilliant amber Murano glass bowl. Raya didn't need to check for the mark, she recognised the artist Estevan Rossetti circa 1950. By the time she checked the Casetta out completely, Rosa had made the bed.

'Can I drive you to the Marina? Don't panic I can manage from here.' she assured Rosa.

'No, Theo Cooper is expecting me and my car's at Bella Vista. Thank you for helping me Mrs Lombardi.'

'Call me Raya.'

'I can't, but I will call you Miss Soraya if you like.' Rosa seemed happier now she would be on her way to Dion in Rockhampton. Raya accepted her new title, the Lombardi family had its hierarchy.

On the vine covered terrace in the garden Raya set out the lunch things. They would enjoy an antipasto platter with fresh crusty bread and a low alcohol rosé, lightly chilled. The platter, one Raya had made up from her favourite bits she had found in the fridge and pantry. Luigi, Enzo's old black Lab, began sniffing around for scraps of cheese and prosciutto while Raya arranged bocconcini and other cheeses, with prosciutto, salami, pepperoni and artichoke hearts on a large wooden board along with olives, peppers, almonds, and the bread. Bart had seen her carrying things outside and arrived just in time to carry the large wooden board.

'Glad you managed to get someone from housekeeping to fill in for Rosa,' he said looking around.

'We don't need anyone. Is Joe not eating with us?' she asked.

'No, he's gone home. Who prepared lunch?' he asked as if it were brain surgery.

'Me. Bart I'm tired of all...' they spoke at the same time.

'You? Look Raya can't we call a truce...'

'My thoughts exactly. I wanted to move to the casetta. I can see from this morning's visit with Enzo it will only be for a short time. Let's make an effort to get along,' she really felt fed up with all their sniping.

'I'd like to do what I promised my father,' he said, tucking into the lunch.

'I don't want a husband out of some misguided loyalty to his father. I would just like to know you as a man.' He smiled agreeing at least this would be a step in the right direction. After they had eaten Bart said warmly. 'Thank you, I enjoyed your choice of food. I'm really looking forward to dinner at the casetta.'

'I have things to do this afternoon like you, so what say we liaise at six?' she suggested.

After raiding the pantry and the freezer for food Raya realised the casetta was too far to lug her stash of food and their luggage. Not wanting to call housekeeping as Rosa had suggested, she hijacked the jeep parked outside with the keys in the ignition and loaded it up. The complete exercise took an hour, and she still wanted books from the library Enzo had suggested she borrow. There were flowers to be cut from the garden and so on.

When she finally had things the way she wanted in what she referred to as the 'cosy casetta,' she showered to freshen up and changed into a flowing, shapeless caftan to keep cool. Her semi wet hair hanging free, she sat down and proceeded to look through the three files once again. One occupied most of her time. It had been labelled, personal. An envelope with 'my darling husband' on the front, in handwriting she didn't recognise caught her interest. Opening it, she began to read the letter.

My darling husband Marco,

If you are reading this, then I am no more. Parted by death. Thank you, my love, for the life we enjoyed.

So much better than I ever imagined, back when I was forced to marry you. I thought I loved Enzo, he had been very good to me, and in my youth and innocence I believed there could be no other. Then very early on in our marriage I woke up one day, pregnant, unhappy, and frustrated with my life. We both were so annoying and unyielding in those days. I prayed about it to Saint Raphael, the archangel and patron saint, of healing new husbands. In the Bible he heals their love and drives out the demons, who over and over again wear down and exhaust new love, ultimately destroying it. Saint Raphael cleanses the atmosphere between the couple and gives them the grace to accept each other forever. I gave myself over to him and he told me, 'this is your life now. You made this choice; your attitude is a choice you choose everyday. Just accept this and choose to love this man.' I am so grateful for the advice, especially when you rewarded me with your unconditional love. I pray Soraya is as blessed as we are. Perhaps Enzo can share our joy through our children. Imagine sharing your grandchildren with your best friend. Marco my darling, know that I loved you all the days of my life with you.

Sophia

Raya read and reread the letter in a riot of emotions. It seemed all very well for her mother to say those things she had no way out. Raya never would have married Bart if she had no way out. Deep down in the depths of her conscience, she knew the answer but feared it. Because Bart told her in no uncertain terms, he had chosen a different path and as soon as Enzo died, and Bart ran the Lombardi empire, he would be free to choose his own path again. In a compromise to herself she decided, until Enzo had been buried, she would choose to love this man. Of course, she had no lightening bolt saintly advice like her mother, and she expected it would be gruelling at times. But she could be strong, and no one would say she didn't try.

Jolted back to reality by the sound of his voice as he greeted her, she almost jumped.

'Sorry, I ...a million miles away. I've been going through the sad state of my finances. I've decided not to think about it for a few days, I'm sure Chad will pester me whenever he needs me.'

'Yes, make him earn his ginormous fee.' He sat down opposite her in shorts, tee shirt and sandals. He started fidgeting with a small brown paper parcel. 'Fancy a drink, I don't know what we have here, if anything.'

'I raided the wine cellar and filled the fridge. Glasses are in the fridge chilling.' She stood to get them a drink.

'No, don't get up, I'll get it. This is for you when Joe told me your paints had been daubed around your apartment, the tubes squeezed out and ground into the cream carpet. I asked him to get some more. I hope these will work in the short term.' He handed her the laptop-size flat parcel. Then went to the fridge and took out some prosecco and poured two glasses. 'What's for dinner?' he asked amused, he couldn't see any signs of it.

'Dinner? Oh, holy Mary, I've completely forgotten dinner, it can be ready in fifteen minutes, but it won't be what I planned,' she said. scrambling to her feet.

'What had you planned?' he handed her a glass of prosecco, she set it down on the granite countertop.

'Doesn't matter because you're not getting it tonight.' Raya continued unwrapping the parcel. 'Wow, a travelling watercolour kit and paint quality journal book.' The watercolour kit, made up of blocks of artists' quality pigment and two water colour brushes had been set in a beautiful tin box for travelling. 'Thank you.' Throwing her arms around him, she kissed his cheek. Only, he lifted her off her feet and turned his face, so she kissed his mouth. It felt short and chaste each a tad uncomfortable because of their previous behaviour towards one another. 'Do you eat Mexican?' she asked, keen to change the topic.

'If you've prepared it, I'll eat it whatever it is,' he smiled.

'Good sit there while I prepare it.' Pointing to a bar stool she reiterated 'fifteen minutes.'

He watched with fascination as she finely sliced a medium red onion, then chopped yellow capsicum, grated zucchini, grated some tasty cheese over some nacho chips in a large dish and put them under the grill. She put on a frying pan, added oil and a knob of butter, then a lump of mince meat about 500 grams. As the mince quickly cooked on the gas ring she added a tin of chopped tomatoes, and a tin of red, medium heat chilli beans.

'Set the table,' she told him, 'we're five minutes away.' She turned off the grill and mashed an avocado, adding salt, pepper and plain yoghurt and put it in a side dish. After which she forked through some mascarpone till smooth making another side dish.

Tipping the mince mixture over the nacho cheese chips she then added the salsa salad on top of the lot and took the dish to the table. Complaining he felt starved, Bart hoed in after Raya ground pepper and salt on to the dish. This time, she watched him eat and enthuse about the flavours and the heat.

'I haven't had Mexican food in ages. I forgot how much I enjoy it.' Getting himself, another helping he leaned over and fed her some mince and beans on a corn chip. They both laughed. 'Will you come for a walk with me after dinner if I eat the last helping?' he feigned a pathetic expression and she laughed again.

'We should take Luigi; he needs the exercise too,' she said.

'I think he's done enough for one day. He followed me up the path to the casetta from Bella Vista.' Bart felt sorry for the old pooch. After dinner together, they loaded the dishwasher and set out on their walk. Following the road, they walked down to the marina in the half dark. They sat on the wooden boards of the wharf with their legs dangling over the edge. Together they admired the vast Pacific Ocean. Tonight, the moon appeared a little larger and higher in the sky. Bart told her about growing up on the island and playing five aside cricket with Joe Kelly and his cousins, whose families worked and lived on the island.

'We had the best time. Always so much fun. But things will change. Global warming and these big cyclone events will change this island and I need to be prepared for it.' Bart sounded as though he had the weight of the world on his shoulders.

'What are you telling me? You might have to move from this island?' she gasped; this she had not considered before.

'Every time we get a cyclone the cost of our insurance goes up. There are a great many other hotels, holiday resorts and businesses providing a better return. This is an expensive lifestyle and as you can see, it requires constant maintenance.'

'Wow you have a lot to consider.' She frowned wondering why he decided to tell her this now.

'The problem is Enzo doesn't do change, he's old and it's all too hard for him. As a family, we have a lot to loose here. We don't have the capital to do what is needed. I won't borrow it and sometimes I feel like I'm banging my head against a brick wall. I won't borrow to do up the island because in the last ten years I have seen many of these island resorts wiped out by cyclones. They can no longer get insurance. These events will only get worse, you cannot afford to have all your eggs in one basket.' Bart put his arm around her shoulder. 'I'm sorry I didn't mean to burden you, but tomorrow we have the board meeting, and this will come up again. It's not just about money; its family, its security and its our way of life. A very expensive way of life. I do have another plan, if only the current board would see my point of view.' Leaning in towards her he whispered, 'Thanks for listening, today I spent time lobbying three board members whose vote could go either way. Basically, I'm stalling for time until Papa shuffles off this mortal coil. It's the reason I'm always doing deals, buying and selling property to keep ahead of the game until I can call the play.' He stood up and gently pulled Raya to her feet. 'Come on, I need a decent night's sleep.' On the way back to the Casetta Raya asked,

'What would be your best-case scenario?'

He let out a little laugh and taking her hand kissed her knuckles. 'I'd like global warming to be a thing of the past. Then I'd develop the island and risk everything, but I'm not stupid, we have to live with what we have. So, I need to mitigate my liabilities here with equity partners.' He gave a little half laugh, 'Sounds like hard work, doesn't it? Well, it is.' When they reached the casetta he went off to have a shower and she made him some tea. Ten minutes later he emerged in his sleeping shorts with his hair a mess of wet curls.

'Tea's made,' Raya said, wearing her baggy tee shirt nightie. Bart turned off all the lights and set his tea down on the nightstand beside the only bed in the Casetta.

'Goodnight and thank you for today.' she said.

'Soraya,' he called to her as she turned her back away from him, rolling over in bed. She froze, then slowly turned to face him. 'Thank you for listening to me.'

'You're welcome,' she called turning away from him again.

Chapter Sixteen

Raya woke to a beautiful morning. Quickly she showered and dressed before even noticing him. Both had slept later than planned. Hearing a Pavarotti number coming from the shower, La Donna È Mobile from Rigoletto, she smiled to herself. He seemed happy. Wow this was something new.

'You're good, do you know the words?' she asked as he sat at the table, dressed for business in dark trousers and shirt. He smiled, half embarrassed, shrugging. The expression so boyish, she wanted to ruffle his dark curls and kiss him. Instead, she offered coffee.

'What time is the board meeting?' she asked.

'Ten thirty so we can visit Papa at nine thirty. If he's like yesterday, it'll only be for half an hour and only two visitors at a time. Aunt Teresa likes to visit in the afternoon after three.'

'When does your sister visit?' an innocent enough question, so why did Bart flinch?

'It's a long story, let's just say they don't … they're not close…poor Mia, it's not her fault.' Bart fingered the handle of his coffee cup. He wanted to be honest with Raya so taking a deep breath he said quickly, 'When Mia became a mother, she asked me to get a DNA test she suspected Enzo was not her father and she turned out to be right. We are half siblings. All her life she felt he treated her differently, but he registered her as his own. It is not something either of us has discussed with him. But like the elephant in the room, it is there.' Bart looked across at Raya for her reaction.

'Oh,' she said. For several minutes they sat in silence until unable to contain it any longer she asked, 'Is it connected with your mother's death?' Bart nodded sadly and began sipping his coffee. He would tell her in his own good time. They had come a long way in the last couple of days.

Raya made him poached eggs on sourdough bread with hollandaise source for breakfast. The food reminded Bart that lunch for the board members needed to be catered.

'Don't worry, I'll organise it, for how many and what time do you need it?' she asked.

'One o'clock, and you must come, I want you to meet the board. Tell the resort caterer lunch for twelve people.'

'Consider it organised, see you at Bella Vista at nine thirty' she said as he stood thanking her for breakfast, bending, he gave her a quick kiss. It made her smile. It seemed like they had been married for years. Neither spoke save a few perfunctory sentences about the day, no real affection, and definitely no sex. What did she expect for heaven's sake?

Ratting through the trousseau wardrobe of cotton dresses made for island wear she came across a delightful floral with a black background. Sleeveless and with a shaped bodice and flowing skirt boho style it buttoned through. Just as she started to slip into the dress, the phone rang.

'I need my brief case urgently, it's on the chair in the bedroom,' Barts autocratic tone set her back a good twenty-four hours. Closing her eyes and doing a bit of deep breathing she counted to three. Before she had time to even think of a reply he spoke. 'Oh, I'm sorry Soraya, I didn't mean to sound demanding, I'm panicking. I thought I had left it on board the yacht. Please will you help me?' he asked, his voice conciliatory. Telling him not to worry she would be there in a few minutes; she threw on the dress and failed to notice she had skewed the buttons. Slipping into her sandals she ran down the steep winding path towards the sandstone building, Bella Vista. The offending brief case weighed heavy in her hand, and she changed it from hand to hand to ease the burden. The relentless sun beat down on her and before nine in the morning, she could feel beads of moisture on her forehead. Inside, the house felt cool still she ran to the office pushing open the door. Bart looked up from his desk. He smiled amused at the sight of her.

'Did I sound so frantic you needed to run?' he asked, seeing her out of breath, chest heaving. He noticed the dress buttons skewed, 'I love the dress,' he said taking the brief case and setting it down on his desk. 'Thank you,' he bent and kissed her. The heat had intensified her fragrance, he groaned blissfully, and she opened her mouth and welcomed him. What had happened in the last twenty-four hours she wondered? At first it felt like a beautiful kiss, tender and loving. Soon a fire ignited within each of them, and she had her hands in his hair, and he lifted her onto his desk peeling her dress off one shoulder and dotting kisses down her neck. A loud cough and a knock at the half open office door caused him to turn and she jumped down from the desk. Joe stood in the open doorway with a smirk on his face, he checked his watch, just after nine.

'You're early,' Bart croaked out. Raya seeing her skewed buttons tried to fix them, embarrassment flushing her already heated cheeks.

'Yes, I'm sorry I...' Raya pushed passed him and went to the master suite to straighten herself. Bart shook his head, 'it's not what...' he blurted.

'No need to explain to me, this is your home,' Joe jumped in.

'Yes, it is,' Bart relaxed, amused. 'Actually, we moved into the casetta Raya wanted privacy,' he twisted his mouth in thought.

'I'm not surprised, you haven't really had a honeymoon.' Joe fingered some papers on the desk.

'No, we're just getting to know each other,' Bart bit his lip. 'I worried we wouldn't hit it off.'

Joe shook his head. 'I came to see if you wanted a coffee before, we go over the costings for our newest acquisition?' Relieved, Bart said he did.

When Raya checked her appearance in the master ensuite and checked all her buttons were aligned she realised there seemed to be more cleavage showing than she usually found acceptable. There would be no time to go back and change. In the kitchen she whipped up a huge batch of scones and divided the mixture into cheese and date and turned on the oven, making one dozen of each. At twenty-five past nine she put them in the oven and set the timer for twenty-five minutes at 200 degrees centigrade from cold.

Hovering around outside Enzo's room she wondered at the time so knocked on the door, relieved when she recognised his voice saying enter. Just like yesterday he sat in his wingback chair.

'Good morning, Papa, I thought I may be running late.' After kissing him she positioned herself on the small footstool. It felt comfortable and close.

'No Bart this morning?' he asked.

'He's coming, he's been busy preparing himself for the meeting. Bart takes his role very seriously you know,' she defended him. 'I fear he won't make old bones because he does worry about making the right decisions. It is not a frivolous thing for him.' Her voice rose a little, she controlled it because she had genuine concerns.

'You love him, don't you my dear?' Old Enzo seemed pleased. Raya did wonder. She bit her lips between her teeth as if to mute any dissent. A tear rolled down her cheek and the old man noticed; he took it as a good sign. She wanted to tell him she didn't know, and, in any case, she thought it unrequited. Sure, Bart kissed her and if he could have led it on to other things he would have, men do. Brightening up she told him what she had been up to, and of the water colour set Bart had given her. Even admitting she really enjoyed the Casetta, as people came and went at Bella Vista. It felt necessary for them to really get to know one another. Enzo seemed to understand. Remembering the scones in the oven, she excused herself saying she would be back.

Barely had she left the room when Bart knocked, and not waiting to be invited in entered.

'I'm sorry Papa I've been looking for Soraya, she had been here but then Joe arrived, and I got distracted.'

'Don't you worry about Soraya. She had some scones in the oven. Morning tea for the board meeting she said. She'll be back. We've been having a good chat.

'She didn't need to get food for the board I told her to ring house keeping at the resort and organise it. I think she gets a little bored,' Bart confided in his father.

'Well then, get her pregnant, she'll have no time to be bored if she has babies.' Enzo sounded a little frustrated, afraid he would not be there to see it. Bart fell silent, time seemed to be running out for him. Especially when he and Soraya were not actually making love. How did it come to this? He had never had any trouble bedding any woman before. But his wife, well this was par for the course if what he heard other men say was true.

Raya felt pleased with her never-fail scone recipe. Covering them with a clean tea towel she ran back to Enzo's room Bart had left the door open for her.

'Bart did you tell Papa about our lovely walk last night. We were away for almost two hours. We enjoyed ourselves.' She crossed over to where Bart had moved two chairs for them and sat down, stroking his bare arm on her way.

'We sat on the wharf star gazing and talked and talked. I've not talked so much in years.' He admitted.

'You slept well too,' she said, and Enzo looked from one to the other. suddenly Raya blushed because she just caught herself in time or she might have said he slept so well because he had a cold shower. Bart caught the look in her eye and checked his watch. At ten past ten and already Enzo started fading again.

'Let me help you back to bed Papa.'

Chapter Seventeen:

Raya prepared the morning tea, adding a bowl of fresh fruit to the scones, jam and cream offering. She made tea and coffee and served juice. Some of the board members had travelled for several hours and they may be a little hungry she thought, although the heat always made her appetite disappear. The doorbell rang and she opened it, three older men stood there. Are they the three musketeers or the three stooges? The irony of it made her laugh. Bart collected his people in threes.

'You gentlemen must be here for the board meeting. Come in and I'll get Bart. Go into the dining room and get some morning tea. It's set up for your meeting in there.'

'And you are?' asked one pompous man with thinning grey hair, while his cohorts stood beside him. Another looked like a rat peering over the stiff bristles of a yard broom, his moustache straight and thick. The third whose little brown beady eyes darted around the room, shining in the light reminiscent of a mouse, looking for Bart she presumed. These must be the three floating voters. Surely Bart could persuade these three older men of his point of view. Perhaps not, their dark suits and ties testament to their denial of global warming.

'Please forgive me gentlemen, I'm new at this, I'm Soraya Lombardi, Bart's wife.' Offering her hand, they shook it curious to learn about this young woman. Hearing voices, Bart and Joe arrived.

'I see you have met my bride gentlemen,' he said putting a proprietorial arm around her. 'I believe she cooked some good old-fashioned scones for us.' His patronising tone had returned.

Raya excused herself and went to the kitchen to organise some platters for lunch. Fresh fruit and vegetables had been delivered along with the meats she had ordered from the resort. Raya made four platters and put them in the chiller.

While she busied herself Mel telephoned.

'The Russian icon arrived. It's beautiful I need a price. I think we have a buyer here already. A Ukrainian man, flash clothes, bracelet, very short spikey hair, a few tattoos on his arms says he'll pay what you want.'

'Hello to you too girlfriend.' Raya gave her a price double what she paid for it and in Australian dollars.

To her surprise she heard him say he'd take it and could she get any more. 'Mel, Mel tell him quite possibly, I'll get back to my source. Have him leave his details.' Mel said she would catch up later and she killed the call.

Although she prepared the food and appeared to play hostess, Raya wondered why she had been required to attend this board luncheon. They were being served a finger food buffet, easy to eat and easy to prepare. Carl Moretti engaged her in conversation, and this afforded her the opportunity to study him closer. He looked about Bart's age.

'Did you go to university with Bart?' she wondered aloud. He seemed delighted she would think they did. 'No, he had graduated by the time I got there, same University though. We met through Mia,' he said, and Raya felt embarrassed she thought he looked older a lot older.

'You and Mia, do you have a house on the island?' she asked, taking his empty plate.

Carl sipped his coffee.

'We live on the Sunshine Coast and only come over when required, Mia doesn't particularly like the island,' he didn't offer an explanation. Raya felt sure it had to do with Enzo, but he did raise her and treat her like a daughter. 'I've been unwell and needed to be handy to a hospital, I'm on the mend now. The mainland suits us.' They chatted on without too much detail. Raya would get Bart to fill in the blanks.

Raya noted Sammy in deep conversation with two other board members. He kept checking his watch and although he had greeted her in his over-the-top leery way, she no longer trusted him. Imagining him, blocking Bart at every turn. As she studied the two other board members, Raya wondered about them. Both were swarthy men stocky and not particularly tall both in flashy designer suits, with gold watches and rings. One even wore a gold bracelet, Their surnames were Italian, their accents were Australian. They ignored her; she made a mental note to ask Bart about them.

After lunch she cleared away dishes and left tea and coffee things on the sideboard servery for everyone to help themselves then loaded up the dishwasher. She turned around to see Aunt Teresa standing there.

'Don't worry about the cleaning, I've organised for housekeeping to attend to it.' Raya realised Aunt Teresa liked running this house as Enzo's older sister. Having money didn't necessarily equate to having style. The décor at Bella Vista offended Raya's good taste. For the main part it was all reproductions and fad decorating, dating everything.

'Thank you,' she said, 'Are you here to visit Papa?'

'Yes, I see Enzo every day in the afternoon. I just walk up here from Joe's house. I live with him and his family. I love being with the grandchildren. The house has a casetta for me, but we eat together. Maria teaches school and hates to cook, I love to cook, so does my Joe, we share it.'

'Joe cooks? very nice,' Raya offered 'he's very lucky to have you.' A forlorn expression came over Raya's face and Teresa hugged her.

'Yes, and one day you and Bart can do things for your children.'
Teresa rubbed Raya's back in a motherly fashion, she blushed. Had
Joe told his mother about them in Bart's office already?

'Wouldn't it be lovely?' she said not quite knowing how to
handle Aunt Teresa. 'I'm going back to our casetta I want to cook
a special meal tonight.' She winked at Teresa then felt bad because
she felt slightly deceitful, leading Tersa on to think what she wanted
about them. The trouble being, she half believed the charade herself.

After Raya left Bella Vista, Teresa did a quick reconnoitre of the
house to see what house keeping needed to attend to while Rosa was
away. Some nosey curiosity had her check the master suite Bart had
claimed when Enzo went to the sick room. It could do with a vacuum
and dust she noticed. checking the bathroom, what is this rubbish
in the waste bin? A pregnancy test, she recognised it immediately
as she had seen them on TV. Her curiosity piqued, she picked it up
and read the directions. It read positive. Oh Lord Enzo would be
thrilled, but then obviously it's early days and mothers always waited
till about twelve weeks before they told family because there is less
likelihood of a miscarriage after twelve weeks. Teresa sat bursting
to tell Enzo, but this was not her secret to tell. When the nurse
left them to chat, the old man could tell instantly his big sister had
something she wanted to share.

'Teresa, what's the matter with you this afternoon? Has
something upset you?' he asked his reptilian eyes scanning her
fidgety hands.

'No, it's nothing, well no it's not nothing, but I can't tell you. It
is for Bart to tell you but...'

'Good lord woman, I could be dead before you get it out.' He
half closed his eyes the woman tired him out at times. At his words
Teresa burst into tears.

'Good lord no, imagine dying and not knowing your only son is
going to be a father,' she sobbed.

'A father, what are you talking about woman? is Soraya pregnant already?' Enzo started to run out of breath and leaned forward panting. Regaining her composure, she told him about the positive pregnancy test and how they are never wrong, but it must be very early days so the parents to be would tell no one for another six weeks or so if they followed normal protocols.

'Of course, of course. I will feign surprise when they tell me if I live long enough. But thank you Teresa, at least now I can die in peace.' Soon he tired again and drifted off to sleep.

Back at the casetta Raya waited for Mel to call her. After hours had passed with no call, she called Mel, wishing she could have made the sale herself. The black Madonna looked a beautiful icon when she saw it online, but she had never touched it or closely studied the nuances of the piece. She missed the customer contact part of her work.

'Mel, you made a quick sale you must have only received the icon yesterday,' Raya sounded thrilled.

'Yes, at five yesterday afternoon I signed for it, according to the courier's receipt.'

'Brilliant.' Raya echoed, then she noted something in Mel's voice a certain strain. 'Is everything okay? You sound, I dunno, like you're upset.'

'Just a minute,' Raya heard Mel call to their assistant. 'Please will you lock up Wendy, I could be tied up here for some time.' Wendy said something Raya didn't hear.

'What's going on Mel?' Raya said, panicking, thinking someone had called in their mortgage or some other financial disaster her father had left her with.

'After I got off the phone to you earlier, Mum called me.' Mel's laboured breathing could be heard. 'Her catholic world has collapsed after such a wonderful weekend. Frankly I don't give a flying fig but the way she went on I thought he'd been killed.' She sighed, 'and it's all your fault.'

'Whose been killed? What in God's name have I got to do with it.' Raya's voice reached concert pitch.

'I'm sorry, I'm so sorry I understand now. Sean came out to Mum and Dad. He's gay, apparently, he's met someone, a psychologist at the hospital, and he decided he now felt able to tell them. Shit, I need a drink tonight.' Mel groaned; Raya felt the sharp penetration of cold steel go through her heart.

'Oh my God, poor Sean, I wonder why now, I mean when he told me years ago.' Raya tried to explain as Mel shrieked,

'So, he did tell you,' she groaned. 'When did he tell you this? When he came to Tuscany and stayed with us at Carmella's Villa?' This time her groan grew louder. 'Your aunt intimated there must be a reason. she asked me in her funny way, does your brother like men? what with her accent and all I didn't understand. When she finally spelt it out, I denied it of course, but afterwards I began to think about it. James and I even discussed it. I'm sure Liam suspected but never said.' Mel hardly stopped for breath.

'Mel listen to me, Sean said he would never come out while your parents are alive. He made me promise I would never tell another living soul. So why did he do it after this weekend? I mean he took what's her name Doctor Pasty Whatsy, to his brother's engagement party so why now. Something must have happened.' Raya became upset only because she felt scared of how the O'Connor's would treat Sean from now on with him being such a family-oriented man, who loved them all dearly.

'Pasty Whatsy as you call her is just a colleague. Sean rang Mum on Monday and asked if Dad had gone back to Canberra. He hadn't so they arranged Sean would come and see them before Dad flew back.' Mel kept punctuating her story with expletives and Raya knew she felt upset. He said this is the reason he would not marry you.

Even telling them he is a sexual being and could never have stayed faithful to you. Mum cried down the phone saying he thought at first, he may be bisexual but after meeting Clay Christian, yeah poor bloke didn't have a chance with a name like that anyway, he realised he wasn't. Clay's 'the one' and Sean is a mature loving man who knows what he wants. At the party Sean seemed so happy you had married and after meeting Bart, he could see you loved the man.' Mel could be heard blowing her nose and sighing, Raya realised people only saw what they wanted to see. Obviously, Sean had been desperate to come out.

'Do you have Sean's number ? I think I should phone him.' Raya grabbed a pen and started writing the number. 'Mel? Please make sure those brothers of yours accept him. They both have political aspirations and sometimes they are too concerned with their own image and what other people think. We both know with a big chunk of ethnic voters; the 'good Catholic man' image gets votes. Sean needs to know we love him for who he is. I'll call you tomorrow.'

As soon as Raya finished the call, she put the dinner in the oven on a medium heat. At six thirty pm, she decided Bart must be having a drink with the board members. Their plane had been due to fly out at seven. Thinking she had plenty of time to shower and change she started pottering around, setting the table, decorating the salad, and whipping cream for the dessert. Then she moved the paintings of the bay and the garden she had completed earlier. The old black Labrador with its greying muzzle and sleepy posture was almost finished so she took the time to tweak it. For a few brief moments she sat head in hands sighing and sniffing, not crying. You can't cry when someone you love is doing what makes them happy. Her only concern now, being how the religious zealots in his family would treat Sean. The year is two thousand and twelve and yet nothing much in the church had changed since the dark ages.

Raya didn't hear Bart arrive he had been standing within kissing distance when he asked. 'What's wrong?' His large hand rested on her shoulder.

'Nothing's wrong' she answered honestly. Sitting down beside her he became quiet for a few seconds then he said, 'I thought we were getting along.'

'I thought so too,' she countered, cocking her head to one side.

'Then trust me. I trusted you yesterday and I decided no secrets, we shouldn't have secrets from each other. I felt wonderful today, thank you.' He pulled out a chair to be at her eye level, Raya licked her lips as though she felt uncomfortable with the concept.

'All right, I have a phone call to make, and you may listen but don't say anything, anything at all. Promise me?' she bit her lip.

'I promise' he replied quickly. Picking up her mobile phone she turned over her painting journal and phoned the number scrawled on the cover.

'Sean O'Connor, how can I help you?' Raya set down the phone on speaker. Bart twisted his lips in slight annoyance.

'Sean, its Raya. Mel told me you came out to your parents; does this mean I can tell Bart now because I don't want any secrets between us.'

'We have no secrets between us,' he teased.

'I know and I'm very happy for you I want you to live an open, happy and full life. How did your parents take it?' she asked earnestly.

'It wasn't at all surprising, Mum did the whole drama queen thing about my immortal soul and Dad said he relied on my discretion. We all know what that means. I think he knew; mum just had her head in the sand. Things changed for me when I returned from Tuscany two years ago. I decided not to date women. The only woman I ever wanted was you.' Raya had a sudden intake of breath, 'don't panic Princess, many men were ahead of you and so I always knew it wouldn't be right for you. It would have been easier for me, and you know how much I want kids, but I couldn't. It would be wrong on so many levels. Nothing changed since Tuscany until Clay. I suppose hell will freeze over before the likes of my family allow gay marriage in this country,' he sounded stoic.

'I'd love to meet him, Clay I mean,' her voice deliberately upbeat.

'You will. I promise you you'll like him, but not too much I hope, he's more handsome than me.' Sean gave a feeble laugh. 'Raya, have you ever wondered why a society that allows a marriage forced by coercion and calls it 'arranged,' denies two mature adults who love one another to marry? Simply because the same society doesn't fully understand sexuality,' Sean sounded fed up. 'I haven't given up on God because she's a woman. It's just those patriarchal men who deny their own sexuality and insist I deny mine when it goes against the nature of humanity.' Before she had a chance to reply he added, 'look I'm at the hospital and must go, but please keep in touch and by all means tell Bart. If it were me, I would be bloody relieved, you're a beautiful woman and you deserved to be loved.'

'As do you Sean, love to Clay and take care.' As soon as she killed the call, she sat there, resting her head in her hands. Bart stood up donned some oven gloves and took their dinner from the oven.

'Three cheeses Cannelloni, beautiful,' he lifted it from the oven and set it down on the bench to cool a bit. Then he walked around the counter to Raya, 'Let me hug you.' he encircled her in his arms. 'Thank you for sharing such an intimate moment with me. I had guessed you know; something the senator said the Sunday of the BBQ made me think. he said Sean did the right thing under the circumstances. When he didn't elaborate, and I watched you two together I guessed. If it had been me there with you, there would have been sexual inuendo between us.'

'Rubbish, I have never seen suggestive behaviour from you,' she chided.

'Only because you're my wife, and there is a time and place...' he stopped when she laughed.

'You're so bloody typical I thought it's because this is a sham.'

'If it were purely a sham, I would be full of reasons to get you between the sheets.' Going to the fridge he took out some wine, she waved him away.

'Not for me thank you, I don't usually drink much at all. Can we go for a walk after dinner?'

'Only if I can move, this dinner's a favourite of mine,' he told her grinning.

The time read almost nine o'clock when they set out on their walk. The stars were magnificent totally unpolluted by city lights. As they walked hand in hand down to the wharf Bart still sang her praises about how much he enjoyed dinner, 'your lemon tart is to die for,' he enthused.

'I'm glad you enjoyed something about today. It's good Sean has come out too. I'm happy for him, really, I am. But I worry about his family's red neck bigotry. I know it has the power to crush him and you know I love him and would hate to see him hurt. I would have married him if he would have had me.' Bart knew she spoke the truth and applauded the man's courage and total honesty with the woman he loved. A woman, Bart found himself falling for but with whom he had not been totally honest.

'Why did you not tell Sean the truth behind our marriage?' Bart's curiosity now too, much he needed to know.

'Because it was done, and what could Sean do? He would worry for me, and he didn't need another burden. Still, I think he guessed.' Her honest explanation pained him, thinking about it. Like divine intervention they heard the lone whale calling before they even saw the creature move in the moonlight.

'Isn't it special, you know I heard this the night before our church nuptials, and I understood how this creature felt. Calling to a mate who never hears him. A lonely creature wandering through the world, forever alone. I didn't want to be like him, so I thought I'd give you a shot.' Stretching up she touched his face. He grasped her hand looking into her eyes.

'Let's get back it's been a big day. You're not alone now you have me,' he said pulling her to her feet. Hand in hand in silence they wound there way back up the path the darkness illuminated by the growing moon.

Performing her bedtime rituals in a sad reflective silence she climbed into bed saying good night. Bart gave no reply, until he quietly asked 'Raya?' not Soraya, so she immediately turned to face him. 'Love me tonight please.' He kissed her filling her body with a heat so intense she could no longer deny it. 'Love me Bart,' she whispered and took off her nightie as he shed his sleeping shorts before turning out the light.

The familiar sound of a light plane overhead stirred Bart. He touched his mobile on the nightstand. Three thirty am. A strange time for plane to be landing. Grabbing his phone and pulling on his sleeping shorts, he walked out into the living area so as not to disturb Raya. Then he called the night manager at the resort.

'Is there some sort of emergency I should know about?' he asked. The night manager recognised Bart's number and his voice.

'No sir, I thought maybe it could be the doctor for Mr. Enzo,' he answered, surprised. Bart thanked him and disconnected the call, instead, calling Bella Vista. The night nurse immediately answered.

'Mr Bart, I was just about to call you, your father asked for the priest, and I heard his plane come into land. Please can you fetch him? I would have called you earlier, but Mr Enzo said to let you sleep and wake you when I heard Father O'Malley's plane overhead. He said you need to turn on the lights at the landing strip.'

'How is my father?' Bart asked.

'Quite alert really,' the nurse replied.

He thanked her and dressed quickly in shorts and a tee shirt before running down to Bella Vista and the jeep parked with the keys in the ignition. In minutes he arrived at the airstrip to see Bob Costa had arrived ahead of him and had all the lights on illuminating the runway. The two men greeted each other as the plane taxied along.

'Thanks Bob, Father O'Malley called you I take it?'

'Yes, Enzo and the priest had an agreement, he would call the priest while he still had all his marbles.' As Bob spoke Bart realised the priest might not be there for the sole purpose of administering the last rights. Father O'Malley stepped out of the small Cessna, emblazoned with a crucifix along its fuselage.

'Haven't done a night landing in ages. It felt a bit hairy in places, until I saw the lights.' The amused priest had obviously enjoyed his adventure. The Rev. Frank O'Malley, a veteran pilot who visited his flock by air. Bart imagined him on a Harley Davidson motorbike which he apparently owned. Bob waved them goodbye after directing the Cessna to a site away from the landing strip.

Bart drove the priest, who still exhilarated and on a high from his trip to Nicodemus at night, regaled Bart with his adventures before asking him. 'When did you last see your father?'

'About six last night, he asked for me just before I went home to Raya. We're in the casetta she felt it would be better for Enzo, but I think she just likes her privacy,' he smirked at the priest.

'Quite right too. So how did Enzo seem when you saw him?' he asked, curious.

'Odd, well I mean he seemed excited, or would you call it excitable? It's the drugs I expect,' Bart told him as he pulled into a car port space near the house. 'I'll put your overnight bag in the guest room.'

'Bart, can you give me a few moments alone with Enzo? I'll come out and get you when I'm finished.'

Bart agreed and went into the kitchen and put on the coffee maker. He yawned, yesterday had been hard work and he didn't get to sleep until after eleven thirty. A smile curled his lips when he thought of Raya. The last few days with her had been bliss. What had turned her around? Possibly something she found in her father's papers, maybe the file labelled personal letters. Whatever, he felt grateful for it. Still, the longer he put off telling her the truth, the more difficult it became. Pouring himself a coffee he began to dream about a future with this woman. Sure, sometimes she irritated the hell out of him, but the other times were sublime. Worrying about the future had become almost second nature to him, but last night down on the wharf he had told her his fears, and afterwards it felt so cathartic, like he walked on air.

Father O'Malley's footsteps could be heard in the hallway.

'You can go in and see him now; I don't think it will be much longer.' A firm hand pressed onto Bart's shoulder. It gave him a strange feeling, more like the lifting of pressure rather than placing it.

'Papa, its Bart,' he said, watching the crepey reptilian eyes scanning the room for him in the half dark. Bart touched his father's hand, 'I'm here Papa,' he reiterated.

'I'm tired son, I want to go now' Enzo's voice a mere whisper. 'I've done it and you've done it,' he said but Bart didn't understand what he meant. 'Love her Bart, my Sophia, promise me...' Bart realised his father seemed confused now, and once again mistook Raya for her mother. As he sat beside his father's bed and promised him... he remembered Raya's words, 'I don't want a husband out of some misguided sense of loyalty. Just let me know the man.' He sobbed quietly thinking of all the mistakes he had made, and he hoped he would not be too late. Enzo squeezed his son's hand and for a moment they each held tight. The life slowly drained from Enzo's failing grip. For a few moments Bart sobbed and then taking in a deep breath he stood and mentally assumed the role Enzo had equipped him for.

Chapter Eighteen

The nurse prepared Enzo for his final journey as the family began assembling at Bella Vista. When Bart woke Raya with the news she took it stoically, supporting the family and making everyone feel welcome. Mia, Carl, and their children arrived, and Raya went out of her way to make them feel at home, offering them the master suite so they had an adjoining room for the children.

Enzo had planned his own funeral to be held on the island on the third day after his death. The doctor still had to sight the deceased before he issued the death certificate. Until these last two months he had been in his doctor's regular care and there would be no issue. It's a simple legal requirement. Enzo's body needed to be stored in the outdoor chiller room until his doctor had issued the certificate, then he would be embalmed. Someone from the mainland would come to attend to it.

Sammy had not been responding to Bart's calls and Joe made a mission of trying to locate his uncle. Teresa, Joe's mother, felt both upset and furious her youngest brother had always been difficult.

'He knew Enzo had been close to death weeks ago, before you and Raya married,' she agonised.

Both Joe and Bart worried there may be a lot more to the situation than they could tell Teresa. Bob Costa busied himself trying to locate Sammy, with the help of an old friend from the Feds. Sammy's apartment in Noosa had been found empty as though he had literally moved out, leaving only his furniture. Joe thought it suspicious and said as much to Bart.

The resort manager sent Dion Lamb over to Bella Vista to cook, and Rosa, now recovered from her tooth ache, claimed she felt much better. Aunt Teresa noted she wore a pretty little engagement ring. 'Nuptials due in three weeks,' she said, Dion didn't want a long engagement.

There were uncles, aunties and cousins everywhere. They all enjoyed their meals together at Bella Vista. Father O'Malley, a close friend of the family, planned staying until after the Requiem Mass. He had pre-arranged it. Every day he said mass in the formal living room at Bella Vista or under the huge loggia attached to the house as the weather grew hotter by the day.

After lunch on the second day, Raya excused herself quietly and went to lay down in the cooler casetta. She lay on the bed in her bra and knickers directly under the whirring fan on its fastest speed, with her hair pulled up off her neck and feeling worn out. Bart seemed a bit strung out. His autocratic manner appeared on several occasions, prompting Raya to put some distance between them.

This afternoon as soon as she drifted off to sleep something dancing slowly over her midriff woke her with a start, Bart's fingers. When she opened her eyes, he lay peering into hers, the intensity of his scrutiny surprised her.

'I'm sorry, I felt too tired to sit around in the heat making polite conversation. There was barely a breeze down at the house,' she complained.

'Give me a kiss and I'll give you a present,' his childish humour made her curious. She pulled him down towards her and he all but devoured her, their passion rising and his response becoming more ardent until she pushed him back.

'Let me breathe,' she groaned, 'a kiss you said, not a meal,' she joked.

From the nightstand he produced a small parcel gift wrapped. Raya had no idea what it could possibly be. The parcel didn't look much larger than a cigarette packet, but it felt a great deal heavier. Quickly she divested it of the gold wrapping and large black bow.

From the look on his face, this gift mattered. Inside a small black velvet box held another surprise. The beautiful little miniature of Catherine the Great was painted on vellum and set in a nine Carat gold frame. Delighted she threw her arms around him.

'Thank you, thank you, this is wonderful,' she said in a breathy voice. Suddenly she went quiet,

'Are you mad? Were you bidding against me, pushing up the price?' She realised the stupidity of those remarks and hugged him again.

'You went in after the auction and bought it for me, thank you.' This time she kissed him tenderly but quickly, he raised an eyebrow. 'You want me to thank you properly?' she asked as his mobile rang.

'It might be about Sammy,' he said then addressed Joe. 'Joe, what have you got for me?' Raya watched his fed-up expression. 'Right, thanks Joe, 'look I'm at the casetta if you learn anything. I'll be about an hour or so.' She didn't hear what Joe said next, except she heard Bart's parting shot, 'Yeah, yeah you're only jealous.' Raya could see the mischief in his eyes.

Two hours later they lay in a tangle of sheets hot sweaty and exhausted. Once again Bart's mobile rang. He grabbed it annoyed, thinking he had put it on vibrate.

'Joe, hell's teeth, how bad are they? The three of them? Wow.' Jolted to wakefulness, Raya watched as he listened in silence. His expression changed as he spoke, 'I'll be at the house in ten minutes.' Flabbergasted, he turned to Raya. 'Cripes, you wouldn't believe it. Sammy and two others were shot in Brisbane overnight. He's apparently in a stable condition after a bullet hit his lung, which then collapsed. The doctors got it out, he'll be in hospital for a few days. He's so lucky, Tony Romano took a hit according to Joe,' he looked firmly at Raya to gauge her reaction. 'Tony has been shot dead,' he said quietly. The third victim is your half-brother, Vince Ferrantino. He's being held for questioning. He just got a flesh wound in his shoulder; he returned the gunman's fire.' Bart appeared unaffected by the news.

'I can't say I'm sorry for them. It couldn't have happened to a nicer bunch,' he said, sardonically.

'It's karma,' her only words on the matter. She thought this ended her death threats at least.

Throwing a pillow at Bart, she raced him for the shower. It appeared around half the size of the shower on the yacht or in the master suite at Bella Vista. Bart ran in and out in two minutes. Wondering if the details would be on the early news, Raya dried her hair in front of the TV.

The item came in at number two on the news after some political storm about a married party leader sleeping with his young press secretary.

'A man has been found shot dead outside a club in an area of the Fortitude valley known for it's night life and clandestine bars,' the news anchor said. 'Two other men were also shot. One is helping police with their enquiries. The other is in a serious but stable condition in hospital.' he said. From the pictures on the screen Soraya could see the shooting took place in a seedy looking area, not somewhere she would ever go.

'The dead man has been identified as Tony Romano, a convicted criminal, thought to have connections to organised crime groups in Melbourne and Brisbane.'

For several minutes Raya sat stunned, wondering what would have become of her had Bart Lombardi not come along when he did? Once again, she got out the box containing the three manila encased files. This time she studied the file containing the legal documents. It held the contract Vince signed accepting his inheritance ahead of his father's death and his witnessed signature. The other documents related to the mortgages on the apartment building and various other assets belonging to her father. As she read carefully, she could see there were several mortgages. They had been increased numerous times and other assets were added to the list as security. The mortgages appeared to be held by one company and although the documents were signed, the lender had been a private company, not a bank. Her father's debt appeared to be one giant, eyewatering mortgage. Raya had never heard of the company and desperately wanted to know all she could about *Titan Holdings Limited*. Chad Murphy could find out, so she phoned him.

'Soraya,' he said greeting her, 'Joe advised me about your father in law's death, I'm sorry.'

'It's a blessing as they say, Chad. I rang about a personal matter, well, personal to me I mean. When you went with Joe to my apartment,' she hesitated, 'did you actually read the files yourself?' she asked.

'No, I didn't, I didn't go with him, the police did. I have never seen the files. Joe said they were your private papers and if I needed to know anything you would tell me in due course,' his voice earnest.

'Good old Joe, well, now I want to know something. Can you search the companies register and find out all you can about Titan Holdings Limited? I'm asking you Chad because I know it's going to be a convoluted affair and I need a legal Rottweiler like you to get to the bottom of it,' Raya meant it sincerely.

'You would be far better to use Bart's man, Carl Moretti he's a real terrier. Never lets anything go till he's uncovered every bone. Rottweiler's are Mastiffs, Soraya,' he laughed.

'Exactly why I want you, Chad. I don't want any of Bart's people near this. Also, you're pedantic and I need you.' Raya wanted to sort this on her own, after all she may well be on her own if things didn't go well with Enzo's estate. 'Did you know the names of the men involved in the shooting in the valley?' she asked.

'Yes, Joe told me.'

'I should have guessed he's all over everything,' she admitted. Chad agreed and promised to report back to her as soon as he found what she needed.

Elegant in a sleeveless black linen dress, Soraya walked down to Bella Vista with an umbrella in hand, just in case. It felt a little fresher this evening after a late afternoon shower cooled everything down and reduced the humidity. Teresa insisted she sit in a comfortable chair and fussed over her.

'You know about Sammy?' Raya asked her.

'Yes, and he deserves what ever is coming to him. My Frank, Joe's father, he told me a long time ago Sammy could not be trusted.' Teresa leaned in conspiratorially, 'my Frank was a good man, a police officer all his life. I trust what he and Joe say.' The old woman sat down beside Soraya and sighed heavily,

'You must look after yourself my dear, Bart needs you to be strong and healthy.'

'Don't I look strong and healthy?' Raya asked, surprised. 'I know I felt tired earlier but the heat, it always makes me tired,' she protested.

'You look beautiful, doesn't she look beautiful Bart?' Teresa called and Bart turned. Seeing Raya dressed up and radiant. He smiled agreeing with his aunt, all the while remembering Raya under the sheets and under him. He mouthed the word *beautiful* across the room. 'He loves you so much and I'm so happy for you. Enzo felt happy with you too. He loved your mother and wanted you for his first born.' The irony of her remarks struck Raya; doesn't Teresa know Bart is Enzo's only child?

'Enzo's death, Papa's death,' she corrected herself, 'it's a blessing.'

'You know to stay alert he refused the morphine and suffered the pain.' Teresa told her, in the stoic way older people take the inevitability of death. 'He had time to prepare. It's more than some get,' Teresa said her accent not as thick as her late brother's. 'He comes like a thief in the night,' she referred to the Lord in the Bible, repeating her catechism lessons.

The island hosted legions of mourners, with planes and yachts arriving. The mourners all wore black and brought flowers and food, boxes of fresh fruit and vegetables and bottles of wine. The locals made food and the outdoor ovens and BBQ's were in continuous use. It seemed to defy mealtimes now and Raya found the effort of it all wearing.

It became apparent Sammy did have some support in certain quarters. Bart had heard the rumblings. These men had no franchise on Nicodemus and certainly not in the Lombardi empire. Still, Bart felt obliged to justify his position yet again, simply because they were relatives, and family were a law unto themselves. He also reminded them,

'Now is not the time, gentlemen.' This may be Australia, but some traditions of the old world came with its newer citizens. Raya remembered her father's funeral and what people had said to her,

'I am here with you my daughter,' or 'no matter how far we are from each other I am here if you need me. *Cordoglio.*'

At eight in the evening, the mourners recited the Rosary in the living room. The generators allowed the air conditioning to be switched on early to cool the room. Some of the men, including the priest wheeled the casket in from the chiller room to the large living room. and about sixty people joined the immediate family in prayer.

Afterwards, they made tea, before everyone withdrew to their own quarters for an early night. The sombreness of the whole affair felt draining.

Bart said he would set the tone for the requiem, 'Enzo had more than his three score years and ten.'

Father O'Malley agreed, 'he had been ill for some time and his death is a blessed release. Tomorrow we will not mourn his death but celebrate his life. Bart, I have new instructions regarding his final resting place.'

'What do you mean? Are you saying he did not want to be buried on his beloved Nicodemus?' Bart sounded alarmed.

'He changed his mind at the last moment, so he had his nurse call me. Enzo will fly back to the mainland with me and be cremated. His remains will be scattered here on the island. He did not want a burial site on this island to interfere with any future plans,' the priest confirmed.

Stunned after years of listening to his father say, 'you won't get me off this island, it's my spiritual home,' he realised his father had listened. But perhaps he might still have turned it over to Sammy, since Enzo's little brother always wanted it. Bart had always said Nicodemus is a noose around the Lombardi family's collective necks while Sammy had desperately wanted the place.

Just then, Joe entered the room and signalled to Bart. the two men spoke animatedly for a few seconds and then moved over to Teresa and Raya.

'Sammy is on his way. He must have convinced the doctors to discharge him,' Joe repeated to the women.

'Or he discharged himself,' Bart said, not wanting his uncle to taint the proceedings with his unwelcome presence. 'I wonder whether he's avoiding being questioned by the police?' he voiced aloud.

'They know where he's going, someone would have been posted outside his hospital room.' Joe reminded Bart, 'it's procedure.' Then as though in unspoken conversation they nodded at each other. Joe and Teresa left Bella Vista for Joe's home. Maria, his wife, had already left to put the children to bed, although they didn't want to leave their cousins because they were having too much fun.

'Come on Soraya, let's go we have a big day tomorrow,' Bart said acknowledging his brother-in-law Carl Moretti, with a wave.

'Carl before you retire may I have a word with you?' he asked. He held a finger up to Raya as if to suggest she wait a moment. He put his arm around Carl and spoke in a hushed tone walking him down the hall.

'Do you know who has the will? Do you have a copy because I don't?' Carl shook his head, surprised.

'No, I don't, I believe it's Aaron Levy. He's Enzo's personal lawyer.' Thinking for a moment he added, 'you know what the old man could be like about his dam will, always wielding it like the sword of Damocles and changing it all the time. Aaron's flying in early tomorrow morning. The will's probably got fifty codicils by now,' he laughed.

Bart seemed distracted on the walk up the hill to the casetta and the look on his face worried Raya.

'Is everything alright?' she wanted to know.

'I've got a phone call to make before bed,' he frowned. It seemed late but to mention the time would be to state the obvious, so Raya said nothing. When they arrived, Bart dropped his phone on the dining room table and went to the bathroom. Raya did a quick tidy up around the living room. Bart's shoes lay where he kicked them off, and so did several old newspapers; a week's worth came at once on the supply plane. Bart's phone pinged a text and she looked up from what she had been doing to notice a message,

'*Ring me asap, Rachel.*'

Not wanting to be nosy she quickly moved to the bedroom with Bart's shoes intentionally putting space between her and his phone. Raya had seen or heard other messages from the woman, another reason she wanted to distance herself. It would be business she told herself, besides, it may be a different Rachel not Bart's Rachel.

Bart, seeing the message, went outside to make the call. Raya prepared for bed and couldn't help herself thinking about what may or may not happen after Enzo's funeral. When Bart came to bed, she feigned sleep. Regardless she slept only fitfully as did Bart. On rehashing events over, Raya became only too aware she had made her bed and now she must lie on it. Bart's insomnia related to several far more pressing problems.

Chapter Nineteen

At Bella Vista a continental breakfast would be offered at eight in the morning, to allow the communicants to observe the hour's fast before the requiem mass. Watching Raya from a distance, as he spoke to his sister, Bart couldn't help but notice how pale and drawn she looked compared with the previous evening. Making no comment, he put it down to the funeral, barely six months after her own father's funeral. Still, studying her closely, he admired the dress not one his personal shopper had chosen. This one a black A line creation in a soft draping fabric, looked very smart and entirely suitable for the occasion. The brimmed hat she had tossed on a chair looked good too. The diabolically relentless sun demanded a hat. No dark and stormy funeral scenes on the island today.

From time to time, she had stolen glances at him, wondering what conversation had kept him occupied for almost an hour before bed, the previous evening. She wondered what her fate would be.

Sammy Lombardi had arrived on an early flight with other passengers, including Aaron Levy. The shooting incident had taken its toll. Sammy used a walking stick, and he milked it, Bart believed, unsympathetically. Raya had been the only family member who hugged him and asked after his health, although she did have an ulterior motive.

'How do you know my half brother?' she wanted to know.

'I've known him for years; I didn't know he had a sister until last week,' he told her seriously. 'Vince thought you would marry Tony Romano,' he gave her a knowing smirk. Under any other circumstances she would have slapped him.

At a quarter to ten the family piled into the returning vehicles and headed for the church. On arrival, the casket waited in a black Mercedes four-wheel drive van that resort used to transport guests from the airstrip. The family solemnly followed the casket into the small church. Outside, a huge marquee with an audio-visual system had been set up, with extra chairs for those unable to sit inside. Each male family member, apart from Sammy had a function to perform. Joe gave a reading; Bart followed Father O'Malley's eulogy and gave a brief family overview having liaised with the priest to cover different aspects of Enzo's life. Carl led the male grandchildren in the offertory procession. The whole event took an hour fifteen, and refreshments were served in the marquee, after which the family followed the casket to the waiting plane.

The atmosphere back at Bella Vista had changed. Raya definitely did not imagine it. Friends and business associates enjoyed a cold drink before lunch in the loggia. Aaron Levy, a man in his fifties tall thin and greying, made his way around those gathered and subtly gave certain people a nod, advising them they were invited to the reading of the will at three, in the dining room.

Raya had a small envelope pressed into her hand, which she discreetly tucked into her bra and went off to the ladies room to read it. Cautiously she put it into her small clutch purse, while wondering who else had received one.

Enzo had four other brothers, two older than him both now deceased. However, their families were present and although most were cordial Raya sensed a tense atmosphere and she hung back. There appeared to be a definite separation, the men at one end of the loggia and the women the other. Several women introduced themselves to her and were curious about her. Ever circumspect, she said little in case it later embarrassed Bart or the family. Joe Kelly, who missed nothing seemed impressed with the way she handled herself. The previous evening, he had told Maria as much and she agreed saying she had only ever met two other girls from the St. Germaine Boscardi Academy, and they were ladies too.

By the time three o'clock arrived, the wake attendees had become a little louder, apart from the immediate family. Probably, because they were apprehensive about the will, Raya reasoned. Slowly they excused themselves or slunk away and when Raya arrived in the dining room, she felt surprised to see so few people present. Teresa, her son Joe and Sammy. Carl but no Mia, Bart and Raya, only six of them. Aaron Levy began by suggesting they all take a seat around the table.

After putting on his spectacles he read from the typewritten document in front of him. The first section related to a number of small bequests for numerous people and institutions such as the church, the Flying Doctor Service and the Lombardi Research Institute, various staff members; senior people who had been with Enzo for many years including three of the seven board members.

In a surprise move his resort on Kangaroo Island, the first large resort he ever owned, would be divided equally amongst all of his family except Bart. Even the grandchildren were named and nephews and nieces. One share for his son in law, Carl Moretti and another for his daughter Mia on whom an additional lump sum had also been bestowed. Even the grandchildren were named and nephews these latter bequests were to be held in trust until the beneficiaries turned thirty.

Then Aaron said, 'Soraya Sophia Lombardi is to receive,' he pause for moment and rummaged in his briefcase, 'this piece of jewellery to add to her mother's bracelet.' Without fanfare he handed her a black velvet jewellery box. Raya simply nodded her head in simple acknowledgement as she took the box handed to her. Settling back into her chair, with shaking hands she gripped the box tightly but never opened it. She began to wonder at its contents, almost missing the next sentence.

'To my son Bartolomeo I leave the remainder of my estate except for my beloved Nicodemus.' They heard a loud murmur around the table and Bart, sat his face totally unreadable. Sammy's face came alive. Horrified Raya noticed a jubilant arrogance on it.

'There is a codicil which has been added recently and witnessed and signed by Nurse Helen Raynor RN and the Reverend Father Francis O'Malley. My beloved island of Nicodemus is to be sold and the proceeds from the sale are to be administered by my son Bartolomeo under the strict conditions set out in the attached document. The details of the said document can be accessed by those who have an interest in it by virtue of currently living on the island.' Aaron removed his spectacles and set them down on the table saying as he did so, 'all the beneficiaries will receive written confirmation. Probate could take nine months or longer. Bart's expression still completely unreadable, whereas Sammy's face had taken on a florid hue, his lips thinning in a tight line as he looked around the room for support. People seemed to turn away from him so he cornered Teresa, telling her loudly, 'Enzo has been forced to change his will on his deathbed, this is not over.' The poor woman stood, not wanting to be associated with Sammy, finally she turned to her brother,

'What did you expect? You were only an indulged little brother not a son. Enzo's bequest is very generous.' Teresa felt mortified at her younger brother's petulant outburst.

Bart thanked Aaron Levy and suggested they all get afternoon tea. Carl and Joe followed him to the office. Sammy's rantings could still be heard. As soon as Bart closed the door to his office the three men sat down.

'We have work to do gentlemen. As you both know this island and the Kangaroo Island resort are the only two assets Enzo owned in his own right. The other two resorts and six hotels are part of Lombardi Holdings limited, plus our new acquisition in Melbourne. Carl, I need a current list of shareholders. Who holds what among our family members and the nonfamily board members. Today, we saw some of us are not happy. I need to be sure I won't be toppled if Sammy were to buy out the nonfamily members.'

'Bart,' Carl shook his head, 'you're not thinking clearly. Enzo owned fifty one percent of the shares, add your twenty percent and there is no way you could be toppled.'

'Wrong,' Bart said emphatically. 'At the time of his terminal diagnosis he had just borrowed to refurbish the Kangaroo Island resort. I am not privy to the details because as you know he kept those details separate using separate people to advise him and deal with things. How do I know Sammy didn't buy some of Enzo's shares in the remaining businesses? It's only been seven months. He may actually have a greater holding. We're a private company and you know how the old buzzard kept registering new companies with different directors to avoid signing any personal guarantees. Every hotel or resort is a different limited liability company. By keeping them separate, if one fails, they can't drag the rest down. Sometimes the shareholders are companies. There are companies within companies,' Bart's voice held more than a hint of frustration.

'The only thing we know for sure,' Joe told them both, 'is the Australian Tax Office and the Serious Financial Crime Task Force, both trawled through the accounts and found them to be legitimate. Remember tax avoidance is okay, tax evasion is illegal. Enzo had always been cunning but legit. In the end he became too busy bothering God to commit any crime.' They all agreed. Bart set about allocating them each tasks before saying,

'Nothing much will happen overnight so let's go back to our families.'

Nobody seemed interested in the jewellery Soraya had inherited. She felt afraid to open the box, as if it belonged to Pandora. Raya

discreetly hid it along with her clutch purse in the huge linen cupboard under a pile of winter duvets. She would retrieve it when she left for the casetta. When the guests finally thinned out, sailing off into the sunset or flying out in the continuous stream of light planes leaving the island, only a few family remained so Bart decided he and Raya could return to the casetta.

'I asked Aaron if he could act for me as the largest beneficiary of my father's estate it is hardly a conflict of interest,' he told Raya as they walked arm in arm up the winding hill path to their little house.

Miles away, she said nothing. Once inside the casetta he asked about the jewellery.

'What is it exactly a brooch, a chain, earrings what?' he urged her, amused. Coyly she opened the box half afraid, although she loved her mother's bracelet, she feared if Bella Vista is anything to go by Enzo's taste had all been in his mouth. The gift is likely some ugly thing. While Bart looked on Raya opened the box, unable to conceal her expression. The heavy gold necklace with attached pendant of a central ruby surrounded by diamonds could never be called dainty, or elegant. She closed the box quickly.

'I'm sorry, I don't want to offend you, but I would never wear it. I'm spoiled. I have some truly talented friends who are masters in the art of goldsmithing. They qualified in Florence at the same time as me. Here please give it to someone else.' Suddenly, she felt embarrassed about speaking the truth.

Watching the almost alarmed expression on Bart's face she added insult to injury.

'Life is far too short to wear art you don't like.'

Bart pursed his lips and raised his hand as if to say *whatever.*

'I have a call to make before bed. Wait for me tonight please?' he said in an autocratic tone. He pulled her to him nuzzling her neck before going outside to make his call. Raya didn't wait to hear who he called. she could tell by the chirpy voice he always used when he made those calls. The problem had become obvious, she loved him and now she was in too deep to do anything other than accept her fate. Her riot of wavy curls always had a mind of their own in the humidity. Tonight, they had gone wild. By the time she tamed her mane and just before she ignored Bart's request, he returned with a face like a thunderclap. something had upset him tonight. As he watched her finish her nightly routine, he smiled at her from his side of the bed and even though she had promised herself it wouldn't happen again she felt herself melting under his ardent gaze.

'Thank you for supporting me today. You made it so much easier,' he said before kissing her fervently and enveloping her in his arms. All her fears disappeared in the heat of the moment.

The last of the guests gathered at Bella Vista to join Bart and Soraya for breakfast before departing the island, including Enzo's two younger brothers Tony and Leon and their wives Anne and Sienna from Melbourne, all in their late sixties, along with Carl, Mia, and their children. Teresa and Joe had joined them, offering their apologies for Maria and their three children because they had school today and the children had already missed a couple of days.

Rosa served the breakfast and Raya found an excuse to follow her into the kitchen to speak to her.

'How are you really?' she asked Rosa when they were alone in the kitchen.

'We are both happy, we should have married earlier but you know how it is with families,' Rosa offered.

'I do know, only too well.' Relieved the two women chatted about getting things back to normal on the island.

'Where does Bart usually work from? Here or the mainland? Raya asked. Rosa, feeling emboldened by their new friendship closed the kitchen door and anxiously looked around.

'You don't know?' she asked surprised. 'So, tell me is it true then, what they say? You and Mr Bart were an arranged marriage?' the young woman seemed incredulous. Raya confirmed they were, with a nod of her head.

'Who told you?' she asked.

'Island gossip, plus the marriage on Keppel before the proper wedding. There are no secrets here you know, Miss Soraya.' Rosa smiled impishly.

'Good you can tell me about Bart's previous girlfriends.' Raya mimicked Rosa's body language, noticing the woman's expression change immediately. 'Please we are friends are we not?' she insisted.

'He only ever brought one woman to the island, a tall athletic looking woman, attractive but not like you, well I don't think so anyway.' Rosa waved a dish cloth dismissing Raya and turning away.

'What was her name?' Raya asked quietly, as the young woman vigorously wiped the bench.

'I don't remember,' she refused to look at Raya 'anyway, Mr Enzo became furious with Mr Bart, and they had a huge argument,' Rosa declared, now polishing the taps.

'When did this happen?' Raya wanted to know.

'Just before Mr Enzo got sick, about nine or ten months ago.' Rosa looked up relieved she had no more to tell.

'Ah, you mean Rachel?' Raya acted as though she had been told before.

'Yes, then he came back and lived on the island. She went to New Zealand for work apparently. The rumours said Rachel married three months later,' Rosa felt disloyal and embarrassed.

'I know, Joe told me, is there anymore toast?' she asked sounding casual as Rosa relaxed again.

Back in the dining room with more toast Raya suggested that after breakfast she and Mia take the children up to the casetta so the men could work, aware Carl and Mia were due to fly out after lunch. The three children, all pre-schoolers were fascinated by Raya's hair, Mia had told her, amused. They loved the abundant riot of spiral-like waves she sometimes attempted to straighten, but it always proved a useless endeavour. Raya had grown used to people touching it amazed it felt soft and springy not coarse or wiry.

So, there she sat on the couch in the casetta, opposite Mia as two little girls played with her abundant hair, brushing and plaiting with plenty for each of them. Their baby brother lay on a blanket on the floor kicking and gurgling.

'I'm really happy for Bart, Enzo made a good choice in you. Did Bart ever tell you the story of our mother?' Mia asked in front of her children, who were too young to understand and too busy to care.

'He told me she drowned, but I'm sure there's more to it,' Raya admitted pragmatically.

A voice called them from the doorway, Anna Lombardi, Mia's godmother.

'I wanted to catch up with Soraya, without the others,' she confided in Mia.

'Come in Auntie, Soraya and I were talking about my mother's death. Bart only told her she drowned,' Mia said, clearing a space on the couch for her godmother.

'I was only four months old I never knew my mother. I feel blessed to have Auntie Anna,' she gave her a hug. 'Bart had turned eight and he watched on the shore while people tried in vain to find her. He told me family members shut him down, trying to stop him saying what he saw. Eight-year-olds don't lie about those kinds of things,' Mia spoke as though she had talked about it often.

'Poor Bart, he believes his mother had been upset after an argument with Enzo. They argued all the time I remember,' Anna said, feeling she could speak of it now Enzo had gone.

'My Tony and I were staying here on the island. We were newly weds visiting from the mainland, Enzo had been building Bella Vista.

I remember a handsome young Italian architect he had hired to design and oversee the project. Enzo became jealous of the man who had been working here on the island for almost two years by then. My Tony told Enzo not to be so stupid. He told Enzo he left Alice on her own too much and things between them would be better if he spent more time at home with Alice, especially after Mia's difficult birth. Enzo had a hard, almost cruel streak; if he became fixated about something, he would not let it go. We never believed Alice had an affair with the architect, we thought she had post natal depression. In fact, we all pitied Alice because Enzo could be so unyielding.' Anna covered Mia's hand in a comforting gesture. 'I'm sorry my dear, I believe your mother was depressed and took her own life.' The old woman sniffed back a tear.

'Auntie, you knew what Bart said had been the truth, she just walked into the sea and deliberately drowned,' Mia whispered. Her girls couldn't hear they had become bored with Raya's hair and gone outside to play in the garden. 'Why did all the family try and convince him she went swimming, in her clothes?' Now Mia sounded upset, 'he told me again and again, growing up, she did it on purpose. He couldn't understand why. Everyone refuted it saying she drowned while swimming.'

'They called it an accident to spare Bart. He was only a little boy. He called to her over and over,' now Anna wiped away a tear. 'No mother of sound mind intentionally leaves her child and kills herself. What about you poor love you were still at the breast,' she sniffed.

'Auntie, there is more, all my life I had this gut feeling Enzo was not my father. When I became a mother Bart, and I took a DNA test. We have the same mother but different fathers.' Anna hugged her goddaughter, tears streaming down both their faces. Raya blinked back tears of sympathy for Bart and Mia. She wondered what sort of husband and father Enzo had been as a young man.

'Do you know who this architect is because I'd like to meet him?' Mia asked seriously. Anna couldn't remember.

'It would be easy to find out Mia, there will be records everywhere,' Raya reassured her. 'You should both talk to Bart before lunch he desperately needs to know, he carries scars too.'

'You love him very much don't you my dear?' Anna said. 'Ah well, at least one of Enzo's plan's worked out well,' she said watching Raya who sat biting her lip, unable to speak as a tear rolled down her cheek. Now she felt afraid Bart didn't really want her. Soraya felt like a pawn in Enzo's game plan, scared she would be sacrificed at the next checkmate.

Chapter Twenty

The three women relaxed with a cool homemade lemonade, while the children enjoyed an early lunch of sandwiches and fruit Rosa brought up from Bella Vista. Afterwards they bundled up the girls and the baby and walked back to have lunch with their menfolk. Deciding the time was now right Mia took Bart aside and told him what she had learned. Still, he couldn't find it in his heart to speak to Anna because he remembered the day his mother walked into the sea and drowned and the way all the grown ups had dismissed him. Bart believed his mother abandoned him and his pain cut deep. The family claimed it had been an accident, but nothing would ever convince Bart her death had been anything other than suicide.

Waving them off on the plane after lunch Bart seemed distracted and more than a little cool towards Raya. A self-sufficient woman, she put it down to hearing about his mother and went back to the casetta to work and paint.

Joe joined Bart in the office at Bella Vista. After hours spent pouring over the plans for their hotel refurbishment in Melbourne, the phone rang. Rachel rang to talk with Bart, Joe watched and listened as Bart chatted and she flirted with him. He responded flattered by her attention. Sagely Joe appeared to be busy at his desk, taking little notice as Bart put his feet on the desk and responded to the attention this woman gave him. When the call finished Joe absently commented,

'The bride?' knowing full well it was not.

'Nah, Rachel,' he sighed, his stupid grin reminiscent of a schoolboy crush.

'What did she want?' Joe asked knowing her company didn't win the tender for the refurbishment.

'Nothing, we were just shooting the breeze.' Bart replied, still grinning.

'Do you think that's wise Cuz?' Joe asked casually.

'What do you mean?' indignantly Bart removed his feet from the desk.

'Come on Bart, for a start you're both married,' Joe sounded unimpressed with his cousin.

'Actually, Rachel's separated,' he chewed on the end of his pencil.

'I'm sorry Cuz gee separated, that didn't last long.' Joe stood up from his desk and walked across to Bart and took the pencil from of his mouth. 'Her marital status is not your business; you have a wife and responsibilities.' Joe stunned Bart with these remarks. 'You went out with her for years and yet you never married her. Have you ever asked yourself why?'

Bart interjected. 'Enzo,' this time Joe cut him off.

'Enzo? Don't give me the Enzo crap. When did you ever do what Enzo wanted?' Joe raised his voice.

'As I recall you and Rachel had a huge row and she married her boss pretty damn quickly afterwards.' Joe could see he had struck a low blow. Bart had been heartbroken when Rachel married or he claimed to have been, maybe it hurt his pride more. 'Think about Soraya, I heard your conversation on board the yacht. You didn't give her much choice, but she took her own advice, she's making it work, I've seen the way she looks at you. So have the others.'

'Where do you get off telling me what...' Bart started.

'Apart from Soraya, I'm the only person not afraid to tell you how it is. Do you know why? Because I care about you. We're like brothers. If you trusted Rachel why didn't her company, get the refurbishment contract? Exactly, she's duplicitous, after all their tender looked to be the best. I'm going home before I really throw my toys out of the cot.' Turning on his heel, Joe left.

Sitting alone in his office, Bart knew Joe had hit a nerve. Why did he bother with Rachel? Sure a few of the phone calls had been business. The architectural firm she worked for had done several jobs for the Lombardi group. Rachel as one of the company's architects worked on the jobs. She always gave him a report down to the last tap replacement. It hadn't been necessary he knew. Perhaps she and Bill Styles, the senior partner were having it off long before she married him. They married just months after she went to New Zealand to work on a hotel over there for a Chinese consortium. Worse still, she never mentioned it until she returned to Australia.

Over the last week she called to offer condolences, then she rang just to check on him to see how he had been coping with his father's death. Bart had told her he had married, but then she had trivial business matters she rang about. She flirted like crazy, always flattering him. He revelled in it. Really, he had no need to return her calls, but he did. He knew his behaviour had been unfair to Raya because she had been giving this marriage her best shot until... when did she start getting headaches? Going to sleep before he got to bed? Did she know?

Bart had reiterated *this is a marriage of convenience.* He had told her plainly, but now he wished he had never said it. What he felt for this woman he never planned. There were layers to Raya, many layers, whereas Rachel behaved like so many other women he'd been out with, so shallow she had no substance. The sex had been good but then sex for him was always good, the more often the better. He couldn't compare Raya and Rachel there. Raya had been a virgin when they married, What a surprise. Especially, when she gave herself to him so lovingly and trustingly. Thinking about it made him squirm, was she truly that naïve? Bart didn't think he took advantage because Raya is his wife, and these things went a certain way. The woman was learning, he couldn't complain about that, he smiled to himself. Perhaps Joe's right, next time Rachel got in touch he would tell her it was not appropriate, and he would prefer she went through the proper channels.

Having made up his mind he settled back to study the plans in front of him. Making copious notes, he looked through all the profiles, floor plans, plumbing, and electrical.

He looked up from his work when the hall clock chimed eight o'clock and everyone had gone. Raya hadn't called to remind him of the time. What is she up to? he wondered, as he locked up the place and walked up the steep zigzag path to the casetta. Just as the little house came into sight his phone rang. Rachel.

'I've been thinking about you,' he said, wanting to start on a pleasant note.

'I've been thinking about you too big boy, but I can't tell you what I actually thought because it's X-rated,' she giggled. It had never stopped her in the past.

'Exactly, look Rachel I'm newly married and because of our past relationship I don't think it's appropriate that you phone me directly. I believe now is the time when we should be fair to our spouses and do business through the proper channels.' His voice took on a forceful tone.

'I thought you said it was a marriage of convenience,' she almost had a whine in her voice.

'No, I said it's an arranged marriage. We often arrange marriages you know. So, you understand my position?'

'Some little Italian house frau, is she?' Rachel sneered.

'Don't be insulting. Let's say goodbye while we're ahead, shall we? Good night.' By now he had reached the casetta and opening the front door he could see Raya looking more than a little messy, water colour works covering the kitchen counter. No dinner he could smell. For some reason he wondered if his last words to Rachel had been a mistake.

'I'm starving' he sounded irritated.

'So, am I, are you cooking, or am I?' she asked naively.

'You are, I've been working all afternoon,' annoyed now he sat on the couch and took off his shoes and socks then walked to the fridge and took out a beer.

'Right don't get your knickers in a knot, it will only be twenty minutes, pizza or pasta? she asked. When he said 'pizza' she told him to get a shower and change and it would be ready when he came out. It didn't take her long to assemble the three pizza bases she had previously made and add the prepared toppings. After a quick tidy up of the artworks and supplies she cleared away her computer and set the table.

'I'm sorry,' Bart told her as he sat back down on the couch, in his shorts, his dark curls still wet and his feet bare. 'I had a shit afternoon,' he looked up to see sympathy in her expression. 'Yeah, ended up having a blue with Joe,' he looked pathetic.

'What about? not the conversation you had earlier today with Mia?' she asked, genuinely concerned.

'No, some pathetic little thing nothing really' he lied, unable to tell her.

'Oh, dear it's been a harrowing week, you need to put it right, Joe cares about you,' she replied honestly.

'Do you want to eat your pizza there on the couch in front of TV?' He nodded, his expression like a pathetic little boy. 'Are you tired?' she asked because he did look tired. This time his expression appeared more grown up.

'I'm still reeling over the will. I bet I won't need to advertise the island because some stupid family members will have leaked it around the country and soon, I'll be getting silly offers. Fortunately, there is no time frame and there are conditions. Carl will advise me of those and so will Aaron Levy.' Bart stretched out on the couch after getting himself a third beer. As an occasional drinker Raya noticed. While surfing the channels on the TV as he ate several slices of each pizza, he passed judgement. 'This one's the best,' he said pointing to her own creation, topped with just about everything left over from the other toppings. An Australian version of pizza except the base was thin and there was plenty of stretchy mozzarella cheese covering it.

'Where will we live?' She asked curious. The fact she had said 'we' pleased him still he had to tease her he just couldn't help himself.

'I don't know about you,' he grinned 'but I'll be going home to the mainland,' he teased still not saying where on the mainland home might be or who would accompany him. As soon as the words were out, he regretted his petty joke at her expense.

Raya quickly busied herself clearing away the dishes, to cover her obvious hurt. Guilt and embarrassment over his phone calls with Rachel stopped him from saying what had been in his heart. However, the view of her bosoms when she bent over, putting his coffee on the little table in front of him, stirred his groin. He wanted to touch her.

'Raya' he croaked patting the couch next to him. 'Come on I didn't mean anything by my remark. Please?' He smiled as she gently sat next to him snuggling in her insecurities apparent. Tilting her chin up towards him he kissed her, their lips parted, and he could feel her fingers under his tee shirt gently stroking his back.

When he woke at dawn finding himself naked on the couch except for a throw, his cold coffee had a skin formed on the top of it.

'Wake up beautiful,' he said, carrying her, 'we have a comfortable bed waiting for us here.' Gently he moved the curtain of her hair covering her face. Being woken up with a cup of tea had never been a favourite thing for Raya. When she did finally wake of her own volition the tea looked cold and still untouched, on her nightstand, she began to remember. Vague memories of Bart kissing her saying 'come down to Bella Vista and have breakfast with me,' lingered deep in the crevices of her subconscious. It had gone eight am so once showered and dressed she started to wander down the steep path to Bella Vista. when she heard a phone ringing back at the house, not hers because that one had a different ringtone. Bart had left his phone behind; he must have been anxious to make things up with Joe. Answering it without thinking, she said, 'Raya.' silence for a few seconds. the caller ID read Rachel.

'Hello Rachel, Soraya Lombardi speaking, Bart left his phone behind. Can I take a message for him?'

'Gosh, you're brave for a new wife especially an arranged one. Hasn't he told you never to touch his phone?' the woman sounded a tad sarcastic. 'Just tell him, I'll catch up with him in Brisbane as agreed.'

'Thank you, I'll pass on your message. You're welcome.' Raya said in her best chirpy voice.

As she walked down to Bella Vista she wondered about Rachel, Joe said she had married. The woman seemed aware of her marriage to Bart, so she wondered what had he told her? Why were they meeting in Brisbane? Obviously, they had business. Or did they?

When she arrived at Bella Vista Rosa seemed busy getting breakfast ready, Raya waved to her and walking down the hallway raised voices coming from the office caused her to stop outside the door and listen.

'You're playing a dangerous game. I told you weeks ago to tell Raya the truth. But no, you haven't done it because you know best.' Joe's voice was unmistakeable. 'If you have done anything dishonourable don't expect me to fall on my sword. I'll be off this island so bloody fast you won't see me or my family for dust. In fact, why wait? I resign. Sure, I'm family so our paths will cross, but don't expect my support.' Hearing this conversation, Raya felt paralyzed with shock.

'You're being a drama queen, Joe. Talk to Carl he knows where the bodies are buried,' Bart sounded furious. 'I never thought of you as a good time girl, only supportive when things were easy.' Raya moved away from the door. Once in the kitchen, she spoke to Rosa.

'Please don't say I've been here, those two are having a barney. I'm not hungry and I have calls to make if Bart wants to know.' She left and climbed the path up the hill. On the way she realised she had Bart's phone. At the casetta her own phone rang, and the ID indicated Chad Murphy.

'Chad, I hope you're not in an argumentative mood, Joe and Bart, I've never heard anything like it,' She told him as he laughed.

'They are both pretty fiery those two. Look I've found the maze of companies lending your late father money. They all have one shareholder. Bartolomeo Lombardi.' He sounded pleased. Raya gasped. 'Two hundred thousand of those dollars were a gift to your father about a month before he died for you to set up your Gallery. I transferred the money into your account about two weeks after your father had his first heart attack. Interestingly enough, since your wedding those mortgages have all been stamped as paid in full.' Chad sounded totally baffled and Raya asked which wedding date?

'The marriage certificate had been signed and lodged by the Reverend Father Francis O'Malley and is the only marriage registered,' Chad told her plainly. Thanking him, Raya said she would be in touch. Now her hands were shaking. She felt nauseous. Bart had bought her. What else had he kept from her?

She sat in the casetta, her fury increased, and she felt quite ill. Desperate to get away from the island to think things through clearly. Utterly confused about the convoluted affair she now thought of as her life, she changed into a smart sun dress something suitable for the mainland. She rang the resort saying she needed a seat on the supply plane so she could visit the doctor. The dentist ruse had been used so she played it down by saying she also needed to buy a special gift for her husband. The supply plane would be due to leave in half an hour. After packing a small tote bag, nothing too conspicuous, she phoned Rosa, asking if she could borrow her car to get to the airstrip.

'I'll take you. I'm finished here. Their breakfast is in the warmer till they're ready,' she advised. Raya quickly scribbled Bart a note. He deserved a note at least. But why wait to be dumped. Strike first she told herself.

Determined not to tell Rosa anything she gave her the doctor story and made her promise not to say a word. 'I'll get an incoming flight to the resort for my return trip. I have shopping I need to do first though,' she confided in Rosa.

Finally able to relax when the plane became airborne and headed away from the island, the seriousness of what she had done dawned on her.

'I've left him,' then she tried to justify her position, 'before he dumped me.' Where would she go? Brisbane is out of the question. Mel would spill the beans. Apart from Mel too many people knew her. Paul? she dismissed him without a second thought. Bastard, a favourite epithet of Mel's it fitted quite a few people over the years. Sean he could be a serious contender, except he had his own issues bogging him down and he had refused to address them until he knew for sure she was happily married. No way would she add to his burden now.

Chapter Twenty-One

Bart breakfasted alone. When he went to phone Raya, he realised he had left his phone on the table at the casetta. The papers had been delivered via the supply plane, so he sat and caught up on the news. He loved his cousin Joe and felt sure he would calm down, but he would have to crawl first. He knew how these family arguments went.

Joe claimed to be ropable with Bart's secretive behaviour. Joe had only just learned from Carl, about Bart's mother's affair with the Italian architect who designed Bella Vista. Apart from his Aunt Teresa and his schoolteachers, Bart had virtually dragged himself up. Enzo had only been interested in the finished product. Little wonder Bart had become a loner, an autocrat who came across as arrogant. Not strictly true, Joe understood it to be a front. He seemed to be driven beyond normal men. Bart had big shoes to fill, and Enzo always expected more from him.

Joe sat talking to his mother, Teresa who advised,

'Let him cool his heels, he's got a lot on his plate.' Teresa loved Bart like one of her own.

'Mamma, do you remember the Italian architect who designed Bella Vista?' Joe asked casually. 'All I can remember is a big argument he had with Uncle Enzo one time. I would have been about nine or ten.'

'Frank Santoro, how could I forget him. He looked so handsome almost beautiful. Enzo became wildly jealous of him. 'Frank used to work without his shirt on, he often worked hands on with the builders.' Teresa joined her hands together as if in prayer, smiling. 'Oh, I remember him all right. We lived on the mainland back then and only came over for the school holidays.' Laughing Teresa said, 'Your father used to joke about making sure I was pregnant before we came here to stay.' Then suddenly she asked, 'why do you want to know?'

'Oh, apparently Aunt Anna spoke about him yesterday. Do you think there might have been something between Aunt Alice and this man?' Joe studied his mother; she raised her hands in horror.

'Mother of mercy no. Enzo would have killed him or Alice.' Immediately she made the sign of the cross. 'God rest her soul, what a terrible thing to say.' The look she shot him was a sharp pain between his shoulder blades. Deciding his mother had no need to know the truth, well not from him, he went into his study and phoned Bob Costa for an update on the Tony Romano murder.

As soon as the supply plane touched down in Rockhampton, using her debit card Raya bought a ticket on the next flight to Brisbane. On arrival in Brisbane, she immediately booked a flight to Sydney. The milk run flight stopped at numerous destinations along the way. It didn't leave for another hour. Even though she had no intention of travelling on it Raya needed to shop in a hurry to give the appearance she intended travelling south. Carefully choosing three different designer stores she selected one classic garment in each store and paid with one-hundred-dollar bills from her father's stash which Joe had given her, remembering the bills could be traced. Once done, she had cash and a business wardrobe. Next, she bought a book using a hundred-dollar bill to give her some untraceable cash. At airports tourists often spend the last of their foreign currency so no one commented. Finally, she visited the foreign exchange dealer and cashed in four thousand dollars, feigning an Italian accent and buying American dollars. Raya handed over her Australian passport as identification, no questions asked. Having got this far she had no plan beyond the need to get away, to be alone and think.

When Bart finally finished his leisurely breakfast, he made his way back to the Casetta. The front door had been left open, so he called to Raya. She gave no reply. Seeing his mobile phone on the dining room table he felt his blood run cold. Raya's wedding rings sat atop his mobile. He picked them up instinctively. Then he saw a note and the file Joe gave her from her apartment plus the jewellery box containing her gift from Enzo still on the table where she left it days before.

Annoyance flashed through him as he picked up the note, why had she left these valuable things lying about? As soon as he read the letter, he felt sick.

My husband,

You will always be my husband, regardless of your actions, I don't believe in divorce. I kept my side of the bargain doing everything you required. Only I never bargained on falling in love with you. You paid for me, but I have never been for sale. The mortgage papers in the enclosed file belong to you along with the businesses. You paid for them; they are yours. I will arrange for the two hundred thousand dollars start up money to be repaid to you. I'm leaving while my dignity is still intact even if my heart is broken. You told me you never lied. But you did, by omission.

Raya

p.s. Rachel phoned. She said she will meet you in Brisbane as arranged.

Bart sat at the table with his head in his hands and his stomach churning. How could he have been so stupid?

Instinctively he knew she had left the island. Money had never been a motivator for Raya, unlike any other woman he had ever wanted. They were all, without exception, impressed by his wealth and lifestyle. Raya wanted to play house at the casetta and spend her evenings whale watching and her days cooking and painting. The first inkling he had she that loved him came the night before their Catholic nuptials when she told Sammy about making a conscious decision to love someone. He knew she spoke about him. Feeling empty and bereft he wanted to breakdown and cry. He couldn't. He had never really cried, sure he shed a few tears when Enzo passed, but nothing like the day he watched his mother walk out into the sea and drown. In his boyish heart he believed Enzo had driven her to it. The man showed no emotion all Bart's life. Not until he found himself staring down at the face of death did, he became emotional. Thinking now, Bart resolved he would not be like Enzo, afraid to love because he had been hurt. His phone rang,

'Bart this is Joe, Sammy and Vince have both been arrested in Brisbane. They've been charged with a raft of things, serious things. Money laundering, extortion, firearms charges...' Joe became aware Bart had said nothing. 'Are you there? Bart?' his voice anxious now.

'Raya's gone,' Bart's voice echoed down the line.

After her shopping spree Raya caught the bus into town and from there, she caught a Greyhound bus to Byron Bay only because two women in the airport ladies room were talking about it and it occurred to Raya she had never been there in her entire life.

Moving along the bus, Raya found a seat next to a bubbly cuddly blonde woman, in about her mid-fifties.

Her effervescent personality radiated from her.

'I did enough shopping to sustain a third world economy, I'm ashamed to say.' The woman grinned not a hint of shame in her warm face. 'It is the first time since my Hal died, I felt like it,' she enthused. Then picking up on the sad vibes coming from Raya she asked, 'Are you all right luv?' Raya smiled warmly and nodded.

'Where are you off to?' she asked trying to divert the conversation away from herself.

'Home, I have a little business in Byron Bay, a gift shop, keeps me out of mischief,' she effervesced. Their driver gave an on-board introduction saying the trip would take two hours today, interrupting their conversation. When he had finished the woman turned to her.

'I'm Trish White by the way,' she smiled at Raya who responded on auto pilot.

'Raya ... Raya Farrington' she said before bursting into tears 'sorry I nearly used my married name, but I've left him and now I'm running away.' Composing herself, she added 'didn't mean to dump on you.'

'I'm sure you had good reason; women today don't run away unless they have to. Children?' Trish asked softly. Raya shook her head. 'Well, that's a blessing at least,' Trish reassured. 'Where are you going? Do you have family or friends?' she asked with genuine concern.

'No one he doesn't know about.' Raya watched Trish's face become serious and she felt the need to offer some excuse. 'I can't simply hide, he has friends, police and others. I need to disappear for a while till it blows over.' Why was I telling this woman, Bart would furious.

'I had a girlfriend in your situation once,' Trish had a glint in her eye again. 'Her husband had been in politics at the time. She went off to a small town got a job and lay low for a while. You need to be off the beaten track. Have you ever been to Byron Bay?' Trish asked offering her a Granny mint.

'No never, do you think I'd be able to find a job?' Raya asked accepting the sweet.

'Yeah, I reckon, what sort of work do you do?' Trish seemed interested.

'I worked in an art gallery in Brisbane,' Raya replied.

The two women chatted and an hour and a half into the trip Raya had a place to stay and a few hours a week work while she got herself sorted. Trish seemed like a character, one of those women who attracted people and they became lifelong friends.

Sensible enough to edit her story to a more rational version, Raya felt this break away would be just what she needed. She never told Trish lies, she simply omitted the more incredible facts. Trish lived in a comfortable yet modest looking federation style house in Burns Street, handy to her gift shop in the township. Unknown to the naïve Raya all the real estate in the area tipped the 'millions' mark years ago and had become sought after as a great place to live.

After settling in and enjoying a cup of tea on the veranda, Raya offered to shout dinner insisting Trish choose her favourite restaurant. After inserting a new sim card into her phone, she booked a table for two at Di Vino. Raya thought she had been quite smart ditching her sim card at Brisbane airport. The two women showed each other the purchases they had made in Brisbane. Trish said her late husband had been a real estate agent with his own franchise. Raya said her ex is involved in property also, as a developer. Immediately a kind of kinship developed between the women. Trish never said but she had guessed her new friend's husband had deep pockets. They were needed if you were a property developer. Raya had been cagey about it and Trish never pushed her.

Joe drove his jeep straight to the casetta to find the front door open. When he entered Bart still sat at the table with his head in his hands.

'What do you mean she's gone?' Joe asked before he really surveyed the scene. Seeing Bart's phone, Raya's rings, and other jewellery he could see she hadn't just gone whale watching. Another sweep of the scene and he noted the files, all three of them in the

Manila folders. Bart sighed and handed Joe the note, who read it twice.

'What does she mean when she wrote, you paid for me but I'm not for sale?' he asked earnestly.

'I owned the mortgages on her father's businesses,' Bart admitted, 'me, not Lombardi Holdings or any of Enzo's companies, just me. I lent her father money and took a mortgage on his assets so Vince couldn't bleed the old man dry. Only I didn't know Vince had been systematically bleeding him dry. It must have been him demanding money from his father or even blackmailing him. Anyway, as soon as I had Soraya safely on the yacht, I had them discharged and stamped as paid in full. Unfortunately, the stamping date coincided with our marriage on Nicodemus.' Bart stared into space.

'Cripes, I can see how it looks. But you usually hide these things in convoluted company structures,' Joe began to feel sorry for Bart.

'I did, but my wife is no dummy.' Bart again covered his face with his hand.

'Well, I did tell you to be honest with her. I thought the two hundred thousand start up money had been the only money you gave her father. You didn't deserve her, arranging to meet Rachel after everything we talked about' he shook his head. 'You know what a conniving bitch Rachel can be. I warned you about her often enough.' Joe stood up, went over to the coffee machine and began to make them each an espresso.

'If this situation only affected you, I'd be tempted to tell you where to go. We have to find her because Tony Romano may be dead but both he and Vince have goons who may want to hurt you. Sammy is bound to have told them she's your wife. What better way to get at you than through Soraya?' Joe poured their coffees. 'Get this down yer, we've got work to do.

Before long Bart bounced back to his fighting strength, only now he had something more important than himself to fight for. Joe set up the dining table at the casetta as mission control. Bob Costa arrived, the two of them called in favours all around the state. They worked out she would have taken the ten thousand dollars cash. One hundred, one-hundred-dollar bills. 'The only problem is we'll have to wait until they're banked before we can get a handle on where she might be, if she has made a run for it,' Bob Costa explained. 'She's educated and well travelled so what would a smart girl like her do?' he mused aloud.

Tracy Lane, a bright young detective, who sat on the other end of the phone line had an idea.

'Well, what I would do is wreak as much havoc in one spot while trying to get smaller bills, Like shopping. Brisbane airport has some pretty flash boutiques,' she added. 'I'll follow it through.'

'Yeah, sure but she knows we'll follow her there. She wouldn't even hide it I bet. I'd change currencies with a four-ex dealer.' Bart told them.

'On to it' Bob Costa said and went outside to get some quiet for his call. Minutes later, he returned.

'Look what I've got' he announced triumphantly. She cashed in four grand converting it to American dollars, see here's the photo of her no disguise or anything.' Then he went quiet, 'It's a pity we couldn't go on TV saying she's missing and ...'

'And she'd be dead before breakfast,' Joe reminded him. 'Tony Romano's dead, so the Feds are taking this seriously, so should we. It's not her domestic situation concerning me, it's the mob connection. Plus, Bart stood up to them years ago,' Joe raised his voice.

'Yeah, back in the day when I had nothing to lose. Things have changed,' Bart said firmly. Another mobile rang.

'No Mamma, I won't be home for dinner. you and Maria feed the kids. No, no Bart and I are tied up.

The truth is,' he paused and looked to Bart.

'Tell her Soraya went to the mainland and didn't tell anyone, and we can't reach her.' Bart instructed him. Teresa said she heard what he said, and she'd pass it on. As soon as Joe hung up Teresa called him back.

'Joe, listen to me very carefully, Soraya's pregnant.' Joe stepped outside so nobody could hear his conversation. Teresa gave him a blow-by-blow description of her finding the positive pregnancy test in Bart's ensuite waste bin. As an experienced husband and father, he knew how unpredictable female hormones could be, especially pregnant ones. Swearing his mother to secrecy would be tantamount to broadcasting it on the island radio station. He groaned, 'Yeah, but it's early days yet Mamma,' all he could think of to say. Standing in the open doorway he watched Bart look up and he beckoned him outside.

'Just a thought mate,' he said in a conciliatory tone, 'Soraya couldn't be pregnant, could she?'

'Why do you ask?' Bart said, wracking his brains for answers. 'How the hell should I know? We didn't use contraception if that's what you're asking.' Bart's phone rang, and he stepped aside to answer it as Joe said, 'just a thought.' Joe decided he wouldn't throw the pregnancy test into the mix just yet. After all they may locate her soon. For all their computers and modern policing methods like facial recognition and cameras everywhere Raya had vanished after getting off a bus in downtown Brisbane.

Chapter Twenty-Two

Joe decided to go back to policing 101 how did she get to the airstrip to catch the supply plane? He found Rosa, being very careful not to alarm her.

'We're worried about Miss Soraya; we know she caught the supply plane back to Rockhampton and she had some personal shopping she wanted to do. Although her husband would have preferred, she took some security with her she didn't and now she's late home. Did she mention where she might be going by any chance?' he asked in a fatherly tone.

'She had a doctor's appointment; I don't think she planned to tell me, but I pressed her,' Rosa sounded concerned about the whole trip. 'I thought Miss Raya intended giving security the slip, she's pretty independent.' Rosa felt better now she had it off her chest. Joe agreed and thanked her. Then he arranged for the Feds to trawl through the street cameras looking to see where she might have disappeared to.

Trish and Raya enjoyed a delicious meal and Trish sat fascinated while Raya ordered in perfect Italian, even chatting to the young female server as though she spoke it everyday.

'My family came from Italy originally. I had an aunt over there I stayed with a few times, she's dead now. But my Italian improved.' All true but a complete understatement.

'Actually, there were some Italian girls at the convent school I went to in Brisbane,' Trish advised conspiratorially, 'the old nuns were absolute tyrants back in the day.' Trish ticked another point of commonality although Raya said very little, simply agreeing and letting Trish regale her with stories helped by the bottle of chianti, she had all but polished off. Raya never fancied it, sticking with ginger beer. They didn't stay out late as Trish had to work the next day and Raya seemed keen to learn what she would need to do at the gift shop.

Joe who loved his food trawled the fridge at the casetta finding a large lasagne. It had been prepared but not cooked. On Joe's suggestion Bart put it in the oven and made a salad for the four of them as Leo had now joined the search party. Leo made the comment Mrs Lombardi didn't really like the security detail and had enjoyed giving him the slip back in Melbourne at the Grand Hyatt.

'And she did it right under my nose.' He laughed now, but it had not been funny at the time. Dinner smelled great and looked almost ready to serve when Joe said, 'Boss' and indicated he wanted to talk to him outside.

'Bart, you need to know this, Soraya told Rosa she planned to see the doctor. But she didn't seem ill. Had she been ill?' he asked noting Bart's solemn expression. Then he told Bart his mother's saga with the pregnancy test kit. Bart let out a roar like a wounded animal. Then he became furious, nostrils flaring, fists clenched.

'Don't over think this, Cuz. There could be a simple explanation. Like she wanted to get it confirmed before she told you. Don't lose sight of the fact you were going to meet Rachel,' Joe scolded, while still trying to placate his cousin.

'I had no bloody intention of meeting Rachel,' Bart said, indignant. 'I told the woman as plainly as I could we were both married, and she needed to go through the proper channels if she had some work thing to tell me. Otherwise, I didn't want to know.'

Then thinking about Raya Bart raised his voice. 'She better not be planning on keeping this from me.' by now he looked furious.

'Don't take that attitude, it never did Enzo any good and besides she is totally vulnerable here, not you.'

Joe had never seen his cousin this wild ever.

'Get hold of the pilot I'm off to Brisbane tonight.' Bart yelled at Bob and Leo. Joe grabbed his arm.

'Calm down, eat this great meal your wife prepared for you and then we'll review the situation.'

'What makes you think she made it? he asked suddenly curious.

'Because she asked Mamma for some triple zero flour, yesterday she said she planned making pizza and pasta. I heard Mamma telling her where to find it in the scullery at Bella Vista,' Joe said, noticing Bart relax a little.

'We had the pizza last night. What is going on in her mind?' He asked sounding worn out.

The four hungry men scraped the lasagne dish clean, and all felt decidedly better. All three of them reassuring Bart his wife had put a lot of effort into the meal, so she could not possibly be planning on leaving him anytime soon. He accepted their words but felt less than convinced.

They planned to depart for the mainland tomorrow morning early and decided to call it a night.

Bart felt absolutely miserable, his thoughts ranged from the totally irrational like she had rushed to a doctor in Brisbane to confirm her pregnancy only to be abducted by one of Tony Romano's goons, through to thinking more logically, on the face value of her note. He hadn't told her the truth about her father's finances and his part in it. Rachel made it look like they had an ongoing relationship. The pregnancy was now an added complication, just how he hadn't yet figured out yet, but her letter didn't sound happy. Dear lord what did he have to do to make her happy? Bart, who threw money at any situation where women were concerned, like the breakup bracelets he used to soften the blow, or the I'm sorry flowers if he ran late. What had Raya said, 'just let me know the man.' He found it difficult, it meant opening old wounds and baring one's soul. Stuff like talking feelings, scared the hell out of him. It might expose weaknesses or inadequacies, not the image he wanted to portray. Until now, now he didn't give a damn what people saw, now he wanted Soraya back come hell or high water.

Trish's Gift Shop stood in a good location for retail. However, her taste differed from Raya's.

Sure, there were a number of things in store she could live with, and her first job of the morning would be dusting and tidying up the shelves. Looking at Raya's pretty dress, smart shoes and elegant hair do, Trish could see she had style and asked her if she would arrange some instore displays. Raya, only too happy to oblige enjoyed the work, being creative and showing her artistic flair. The shop appeared a decent size but obviously overstocked and poorly set out. Tackling the window display first, by lunchtime Raya had found all sorts of treasures as she cleaned and sorted the shelves. The new window display an eclectic mix of styles, hinting at what hid inside, but colour coordinated to give the items a unifying theme.

She started inside the entrance of the store by shifting a large rough hewn dining table and setting it up with a centre arrangement of colourful botanicals. Linen placemats and serviettes, beautiful glassware, and unique crockery settings at each place. Then on a side table she arranged photo frames and ornaments with large art works behind them. Each item had a little round sticker on the back saying how many more of the product were held in stock for ordering and the excess had been neatly stored so when the item sold it would be sold from the storeroom supply, the box opened, and the goods checked. Trish thought it an excellent idea but needed to know why she should do it.

'You don't wear all you're jewellery at once, do you?' Raya laughed. 'It's like necklines, you just hint there's more.' Now Trish roared with laughter. The two women worked well together and Raya a little quieter with the shoppers, was a good foil for the effervescent Trish who could be overpowering for customers who simply wanted to look on their own.

The first day proved a novelty for Raya, however it made her anxious to be at her gallery with Mel. So alone in her bedroom after work she called Mel.

'How are you, Melissa?'

'Hell, girlfriend I didn't recognise your voice or your number. Are you ever coming back?' she asked, irritated.

'Yes sorry, I lost my phone, no, not true I ditched the sim card. So, I could go shopping without one of Bart's people following me.' Still, she couldn't tell Mel the complete truth.

'Bart said the security is for your own protection,' Mel insisted. 'But I guess you're a bit safer now your brother and Sammy Lombardi have been arrested. Is Sammy any relation to Bart?'

'His uncle, what were they arrested for?' Raya wanted to know as she lay stretched out on the bed in Trish's guest room.

'Don't ask me, google the news, I just heard it on the radio. When did you say you're coming back?' Mel's voice had a bit of a whine now. Raya felt guilty leaving her to run their business.

'As soon as I get the all clear from the police, I'll let you know. I miss it you know; one can only take so much of island life.' Raya sighed, wondering what she would tell Mel and when would it happen?

Bart and 'his people;' Joe Kelly, Bob Costa and Leo Savalas left the island on board the Lear jet headed for Brisbane and the corporate office of the Lombardi Empire where Carl Moretti would join them.

Leo, the newest member of the team was completely bald. A Greek, nicknamed Kojak after his similarity to his name sake, Telly Savalas, although at thirty Leo had been born long after the long running TV series ended. Usually full of fun and cheek Bart looked solemn and sat alone thinking, while the other three talked shop.

They looked such a cliché in their dark suits, and Serengeti aviator sunglasses or were they Tom Ford, whatever, they seemed to be standard issue. On their arrival at Brisbane airport Carl drove them to the office, a high rise building in downtown Brisbane only minutes from Gallery Euphemius.

Detective Tracy Lane from the Federal Police Department's Brisbane office phoned Joe Kelly.

'We haven't had any luck so far Sir, but there is still one more lead. Could Mrs Lombardi have been travelling with somebody?' she asked. Joe thought it unlikely but asked her to follow it through.

'Raya wouldn't meet up with a girlfriend, would she? A blond in her fifties,' he asked Bart who shook his head and said 'I'm just going out for a few minutes, alone. I'll keep in touch.' Joe frowning watched Bart head for the elevator, felt tempted to have him followed but something stopped him.

As he walked down the street Bart grabbed an espresso from Starbucks and tried Raya's phone, again. Dead. Dead as a dodo. In seven minutes, he arrived at Gallery Euphemius to find it closed. The sign hanging in the doorway window said, "back in five minutes." Five minutes from when he wondered, his watch said ten thirty. He stood rocking backwards and forwards on his long legs as he drank his coffee and cursed the stupid woman who left the message on the door. Within minutes Melissa arrived with her breakfast and a coffee, struggling to open the door. He made a mental note to get a key. Once open he followed her into her office.

'Melissa, how are you? Has Raya been in touch since she got her new phone. She hasn't given me the number yet.' The lie came easily. Melissa looked up at him. God his smile, she thought as it melted her, then his intense gaze made her uneasy for some unknown reason. You wouldn't want to cross him. He leaned across her desk she felt intimidated. 'Melissa?' From her seated position his towering presence felt too much.

'She did call me yesterday, has she not been in touch since then?' Melissa said as her voice trembled.

'Oh Lord,' she moaned.

'I travelled to the other side of the island most of the day and in meetings no cell coverage.' something flickered in Mel's face she didn't believe him. She remembered Raya said she had swapped sim cards to avoid his security. Bart softened his approach.

'To be honest we had an argument, and she had a doctor's appointment I half thought she may have stayed overnight with you. I'm out of my mind with worry Melissa, what with her brother and my uncle and all the things she's suffered,' now she did believe him.

'The federal police are looking for her. I worry the papers will get hold of it and somebody gets to her before I find her.' Bart looked contrite and sounded so caring, why did Mel think there must more.

'Give me your phone Melissa, I'll have it returned when I find her.'

Bart arrived back in his office in under four minutes out of breath and gripping Mel's phone.

'She phoned Mel yesterday on a new number, no guarantees she's still got it,' he gasped 'but it's the best we have.' Bob Costa grabbed it and within minutes the Feds had the number and before long they had a fix on it.

'Byron Bay is where the two woman were going,' Tracy Lane called out. 'But one of the two women looked middle eastern, she wore sunnies and a headscarf. I saw her nose side on... and thought...' Tracy heard Bart laugh.

'Soraya has a strong roman nose; her features are strong and very symmetrical. The symmetry is what makes her exotic looking, a real beauty, especially with her colouring.' Tracy heard the love in the man's voice. Bart called to Leo.

' Hey Leo, how fast can you drive?

'Are we talking within the law?' Leo called back.

Joe interrupted with a 'Definitely!'

Minutes later the two of them were on their way to Byron Bay.

'Joe, do you realise Soraya Lombardi, or her cell has been at Trish's Gift shop in Byron Bay since we located it at eleven this morning.' Tracy Lane told Bob Costa the pair had worked together years before when she had been a rookie. 'So, either she left it there on purpose or she has a job,' she said.

'She may have simply lost it,' Joe said, knowing Bart wanted the chance to talk with her before the police started asking questions.

By the time Bart and Leo arrived in Byron Bay, Tracy had reported the phone was on the move, on its way to a residential street on foot. Bart dispatched Leo to get himself some lunch and he entered Trish's gift store. He checked his phone. Trish was definitely the cuddly blond woman Raya had travelled with on the Greyhound bus. Did they just meet and hit it off? That would be so typical of Raya he mused.

Chapter Twenty-Three

Bart had never been lost for words before, he looked around the store and before long the bubbly Trish approached him. 'What sort of gift were you looking for?' she asked, cautiously arranging some artificial flowers. Good an open-ended question, she knows her stuff.

'To be honest I'm looking for Trish,' he said firmly. All sorts of easy lies were tripping off his tongue, but this lady looked too nice, too honest, and definitely too shrewd to risk being caught out.

'I'm Trish, how can I help you?' she gave him the once over, she immediately guessed him to be Raya's husband because he looked so right for Raya, but was he? If she had been asked to describe the kind of man Raya might be running away from, he would be it. Tall dark handsome, designer suit, classy shoes, and designer stubble to match his expensive aftershave or cologne that wafted around him. Deciding discretion, would be the better part of valour, she would play it cool.

'I'm Bart Lombardi, I have reason to believe my wife...' he sighed. 'The thing is we are newly married, and my wife Soraya Farrington and I had an argument,' well no we didn't, but you're talking semantics he told himself, 'and she left home, it's been a trying few months, we've had two deaths in the family and now apart from me she has no one.' Trish stood looking at him cynically as he spoke. He read her face. 'Look I'm not a wife beater,' he practically pleaded with her she flinched and moved away from him. Bart stepped back, embarrassed she could think him capable of violence. Trish mustered her inner strength.

'Look here Mr Lombardi, women don't leave their husbands without good cause.' Trish stuck out her chin remembering her friend whose bully of a husband, the politician, had threatened Trish because she had helped his wife get away from him. Now here, she was doing it again helping a friend to escape a bad relationship. Only this time, the husband resembled a mob boss. Thank god she had a friend in the police who happened to be handy.

'You're right they don't leave their husbands without good cause. But sometimes what they believe to be 'good cause' is not correct. I believe Raya has gone to your home; I could have gone straight there.' Bart sat down in a chair part of a café setting on sale. He slouched legs apart Trish realised he did it to diminish his considerable height and size. 'However, I have no intention of upsetting Raya or you. I simply need to talk to her, also I need to know she is safe,' he steepled his fingers together in his confident way.

'What say I organise the community sergeant to accompany you?' Trish said knowing sergeant Grant Wilson and she were really good friends. Since her husband's death they had become close.

'Not necessary,' he told her.

'If you don't want it to be burglary and assault, it is necessary Mr Lombardi.' Trish stood beside him now and she looked taller this time.

'Fine, do you mind if I wait here and get a ride with him?' he asked, confident of her answer.

Bart never bothered to acquaint the Sergeant with all the details he let him believe whatever he wanted to believe. In fact, he even stood two paces behind the officer when he rang Trish's doorbell. When Raya came to the door, she looked mortified to see Bart, head bowed, standing behind the Police Sergeant.

'Ma'am this man claims he's your husband and wants a word. Trish insisted I accompany him.' Sergeant Wilson had attended hundreds of domestics but never anything quite like this.

'Come in the pair of you,' Raya said, with utmost confidence. 'Sergeant, this is my husband, and he would never physically hurt me. Go and make us a brew please so we can talk in private.' After he left them alone in the living room Raya told Bart to sit. 'Why are you here? I thought my note said it all.'

'Yes, my love but you are mistaken. Neither of us is perfect. I should have told you about the two hundred thousand, but then technically I'm not obliged to tell the bride about the bride price or the dowry or whatever they call it these days. Your father never did, so I felt unsure. Joe said I should have told you. In our kind of arranged marriage the groom pays the bride's father a dower, it used to be quite high in days gone by. Not now, because women work. It is really so a woman could leave her husband and have financial security. I thought the start up money for your gallery would be the ideal bride price. Remember your father didn't plan on dying before we married so we would have observed all the modern conventions.' Bart sat clasping his hands. Raya noticed the slight tremble as he remained otherwise calm. 'Perhaps your father didn't tell you because he knew you would react this way. Who knows?' Bart's expression softened and Raya realised he spoke the truth. Never would she have taken the money if she had known its source.

'I don't understand, why did you lend my father those eyewatering amounts, when obviously his businesses were not solvent,' She asked earnestly. 'And hide the fact you were lending the money.'

'Firstly, I believe those businesses are solvent, The cash flow problem was caused by someone blackmailing your father. The serious financial crime taskforce are looking into your half brother Vince's affairs. He claims the deposits were legitimate money from his father, so he didn't bother to hide it. The taskforce believe it had been coerced out of him. It's called extortion. Your father didn't know at first who had been behind the Titan Group, he worried how you would survive if anything happened to him. When all of this business started out, I had never met you. I only had a file on you. I didn't know you and I'm ashamed to say, I didn't love you. As soon as we met, I dared to hope for more from our relationship. After our weekend in Melbourne, I realised I had skin in the game. I love you.' His nostrils flared and his breathing became ragged, he had never ever expressed his love of another human being. The words did not come easily.

'You never said,' she accused.

'Neither did you,' he countered.

'But you had all the power and you told me in no uncertain terms what this marriage of convenience was all about.' Sniffing she called out to the sergeant. 'Is the tea made yet, both white no sugar?' The Sergeant, an older man with a white buzz cut, brought in two mugs of tea, and set them on the coffee table then left the room. Bart dropped to his knees in front of her.

'No, I didn't tell you how I felt, I felt scared too. I've never felt vulnerable like this before. Soraya I've never been loved before either.' Taking her hands, he kissed them.

'What about Rachel? she seemed to be featuring almost daily.' Raya asked because she needed to know.

'To start with if I loved Rachel then I would have married her years ago and Enzo be damned. I needed to get to know you. Our parents had so much in common I had been prepared to accept their choice, because heaven knows I made such a hash of my personal life. Making money became an obsession. If you like we can speak to Rachel together, or Joe can deal with her. The woman is devious and married. She's very good at flattery and as Joe pointed out, I'm vain and arrogant. It started out as work, then Enzo's illness and death and at one time we were good friends, but I had told her not to call me and she ignored it.' As Bart looked into Raya's eyes, she watched a sheen of tears cover his.

'Please my darling I want to love you everyday for the rest of my life. Let's go away somewhere and talk about what's important in our lives.'

Putting her arms around his neck she kissed him and before long she too had a sheen of tears glistening in her aquamarine eyes.

'Do you have something to tell me like we might be expecting the patter of little feet...'

'Ah, I see what this is about, you think I'm pregnant?'

'No, I just kinda hoped.' Bart didn't intend spooking her. After all, if it were true, he'd know soon enough.

'It's just Aunt Teresa found a pregnancy kit in our ensuite at Bella Vista. Must be Mia's' he said knowing she found it before he and Raya moved to the casetta.

'When did this happen, before Enzo's death?' Raya frowned as she asked, and he shrugged.

'You know what Teresa's like she probably got it muddled. She loves a baby in the family' Bart laughed.

'Drink your tea, I've remembered it belonged to Rosa, I gave her a test kit I had because she thought she might be pregnant. She became upset. I got it sorted, sent her to the dentist on the mainland so she could tell Dion. They're getting married next week. But you can't let on you know. Her parents don't know.' Bart grinned as she recounted the story.

'Priceless, are you going to be the family fixer?' he asked.

'No, but it's one good reason for having a bit of privacy at the casetta,' she told him.

Two years on:

'Maria, look out there will you, men they're drawn to a BBQ like a magnet?' Raya laughed. 'It's not like they're cooking, they're just watching the chef, must be an Australian thing.' They both laughed.

'Where's the birthday boy? Trish asked, her arms full of gifts, Grant Wilson standing behind her gave an amused half eyeroll, his buzz cut whiter than ever.

'Trish, what did I tell you about no presents?' Raya chided playfully. 'He's outside giving his godfather a run for his money.' She pointed to Sean O'Connor, who had been down on all fours giving one year old Brando Lombardi a piggyback ride around the grass, amid a small crowd of cousins and friends.

'These are not for him, these are for his handsome father, and lovely mother, my famous chutney plus a few bits. Oh, there may be something for my wee Godson,' Trish grinned at Grant.

'Her chutney's a legend in the Bay,' Grant offered. The man looked totally smitten with Trish, both in their early sixties it looked sweet to watch.

More guests arrived and Raya signalled to Bart to come and be the gracious host.

'Bart's been entertaining us with details of his latest venture. It sounds magnificent.' Clayton Christian told the group, 'I can't help feeling it's Raya influence.'

Melissa came in from outside, followed closely by Leo Savalas. They were an item now and a Greek Orthodox slash Roman Catholic marriage had been planned in eight weeks. Maria and Raya joked about the Greek aunties and bald-headed babies.

'You signalled, my love?' Bart stood behind Raya nuzzling her neck, his arms around her and his hands on her stomach. 'How are you both, the two women in my life?' Raya shook her head.

'No secrets around here, yes we're having a girl,' Raya confirmed.

Melissa, quick to point out to the group 'When we were college girls at Germain Boscardi, I never dreamed my pregnant girlfriend would be in my bridal party. In fact, if someone had told my mother she would have forbidden me to associate with the wanton hussy.' Knowing Margaret O'Connor, Raya laughed.

'Our dear mother had no imagination back in the day, and nothing's changed God bless her, Sean added handing Brando to his father.

Don't let Mamma bath him Sean, she's already had three Proseccos.' Joe said carefully giving his tiny daughter to Maria 'She's hungry.'

'Aunt Teresa is enjoying herself and why not, she's the family Matriarch.' Bart mused.

'And I can't wait to have a Prosecco when I've stopped breastfeeding Elena. I'm only doing it for another eight months till she's one.' Maria raised her eyebrows and took her daughter off down the hall.

Raya sighed; her milk had dried up when she became pregnant again. There would only be sixteen months between her babies, still she felt blessed.

'He's looking good Sis, 'Bart commented to Mia on Carl's health. He had his diabetes under control and felt as good as he looked. Mia had become an expert on his diet.

'We're having lunch with Dad tomorrow. I'm glad you persuaded me to get in touch with him. I felt a little embarrassed asking him to get a DNA test. But actually, as soon as I saw him, I knew he must be my father. We have a definite familial likeness. He's good with the kids and he's such a gentle man compared with Enzo,' Mia had spoken before she realised the words were out.

Bart shrugged and sighed, 'Yeah, we need to make sure we don't screw things up for our kids. Raya's father must have been a gentle loving man because she's not screwed up at all.' The little boy expression Bart gave his younger sister tugged at her heart strings.

'You're not screwed up; you just needed a good woman to lick you into shape occasionally,' Mia reassured him.

'Yeah, I like it when she licks me into shape,' he winked, and Mia pushed him.

'Dinner's served,' Bart announced, and everyone filed outside to the veranda where a huge, refectory style table had been set up. The children intermingled with adults at the table. Today there were two servers, but normally Raya insisted they manage on their own. Bart said grace and gave a toast. Nothing to do with the birthday boy, this party had been as much for Bart as his son. Brando, unable to sit still at the table stood rocking backwards and forwards on his chubby legs much like his father did, although Bart's legs were long and strongly muscled like a sportsman. However, Brando liked cake and with a huge piece in each hand he proceeded to plaster the vivid green icing all over his face.

The food, an eclectic mix of Pacific rim, Mediterranean and the Australian fare they all loved.

Bart had relaxed into the role of husband and father with his strongest desire to be the best. He watched amused as Raya chatted with family and friends. She had taught him so much about life and more importantly what money could not buy; the love she showered on her family and friends, the patience she demonstrated we he tired, and the common sense she exercised when things went wrong, or Brando became fractious. Most importantly the absolute trust and respect she demonstrated when she deferred to his judgement, even in trying times. These conscious decisions to love him were priceless and could never be bought. 'I love you,' he whispered in her ear, and she transfixed him with her mesmerising eyes and mouthed back, 'I love you too.'

At around eleven they finally waved goodbye to the last of the guests. Raya sprawled out on the couch, sipping a last cup of tea when she remembered something Clayton Christian or Clay as they called him had said to her about Bart's latest project, so she asked about it.

'Explain again, Nicodemus, you sold the island, and the Lighthouse Group is buying over half of the island and the Titan group buying the rest.' Bart sat on the floor, his feet bare and his back resting on the sofa edge.

'Enzo's dream has come true. The family can use Bella Vista as a holiday home, it's built like a brick out house and it's on the highest point. I've given up counting how many cyclones it's survived. Actually, the Lighthouse Group were lucky, the last cyclone cleared the way for the new resort.' He sipped his tea, satisfied. 'They plan to build a state-of-the-art cyclone proof building,' He turned to see her expression. 'You can refurbish Bella Vista if you fancy.' He watched as she wrinkled her nose, 'or not, over to you.'

'I like the way we all have our forever homes close to each other here on the mainland, but not so close we're checking the ensuite waste bins.' Raya mused remembering Aunt Teresa, 'I value my privacy thank you'.

'Did I update you on the Sammy and Vince saga?' he asked, 'Frankly neither of them will get out of prison much under ten years and hundreds of thousands in legal bills after their failed appeals,' Bart informed her.

'I'm not much interested in either of them. They can't touch us or the rest of the family. Did I tell you I'm running the Gallery while Mel's on honeymoon? Don't worry, Rosa and her mother will mind Brando at their home, she's expecting again due about the same time as us.'

'Come on my love let's get up the wooden hill to bed.' he helped her up 'I'll close all the baby gates.'

The End